HEADLONG

a novel

Ron MacLean

Last Light Studio • Boston

Cover concept and title typography by Jeffrey Bell
Cover photograph © Katherine Nau
Jacket design by Emily Audley

Published by Last Light Studio
423 Brookline Ave. #324
Boston, MA 02215
www.lastlightstudio.com

Publisher's Cataloging-in-Publication Data

    MacLean, Ron, 1958-
      Headlong : a novel / Ron MacLean.
      p. cm.
      LCCN 2013943411
      ISBN 978-1-938692-98-7
      ISBN 978-1-938692-90-1

      1. Fathers and sons--Fiction. 2. Aging parents--Fiction. 3. Adult children of aging parents--Fiction. 4. Labor and globalization--Fiction. 5. Ecoterrorism--Fiction. 6. Boston (Mass.)--Fiction. 7. Detective and mystery stories. 8. Suspense fiction. I. Title.

PS3613.A27377H43 2013   813'.6
          QBI13-600107

HEADLONG

1

I came home to bury my father, but he wouldn't die.

The stroke had taken big chunks of him, and all I could do that spring was visit him at the rehab facility, where every day he'd pretend to be glad to see me and I'd pretend I wasn't waiting to leave. Before I knew it, six weeks had passed.

Everything I did for fun I did with Bo, the teenager who'd once been my sort-of surrogate son. I'd stopped hanging around with anyone my own age. I had no energy for striking up friendships. I was hiding in the land where I'd last excelled, and sitting daily vigil with the old man while he decided whether or not to recover. On a rainy June Saturday after one such visit, I sat in a Brookline coffee shop drinking dark roast more for warmth than caffeine, while Bo – son of my high school friend Lin – went on about the coming revolution.

"Globalization is a crock. The world economy is controlled by a few massive corporations, and the people who run them don't give a shit about living standards, working conditions, or human rights."

Bo was seventeen going on thirty. He had his mother's strong jaw, sandy hair, and stubborn passion. I had an old-people-smell headache and little patience. Bo kept talking.

"They care about profit. Squeeze as hard as they can for as long as they can, then toss a bone every now and then when liberals like you complain loud enough."

Bo and I met semi-regularly at the Daily Grind, a tattoo-nose-rings-and-skull-caps coffee shop in Washington Square. We sat at a wobbly table with a couple leftover sections of the *Boston Globe*. Music screamed from the house speakers. Visits with my father inevitably left me drained and discouraged. Before his stroke, we'd gone six years perfectly content to not see each other. The occasional obligatory phone call. Once I even got a piece of mail: a newspaper clipping from the hometown weekly. One of those "whatever happened to so-and-so" articles where so-and-so was me. My father was gracious enough to send it. Bo still talking. I wanted to weep.

"They're going to be stopped, Nick. There's a movement, just waiting for a spark." He pushed the Metro section across the table at me. Fingered a headline. It seemed a piece in the morning *Globe* had set him off. A small piece. According to the article, someone had thrown a brick through the plate glass window of a Berkley's coffee shop and left behind a hand-painted placard saying *Death to capitalism.*

"I hate to break it to you, Bo, but a broken window doesn't make a revolution."

He was young. Undaunted. He ran track for Brookline High. He slouched on a scarred wood chair in a Dropkick Murphys t-shirt and torn jeans. Tousled hair.

"There's anger out there – a ton of it. Follow the real news and you'd know this shit. Real people – working people – are pissed. Ready to blow."

A thin fog veiled the floor-to-ceiling window and a persistent draft seeped through the glass. I felt fragile in my alleged hometown. *All that potential*, the local weekly had said. Well I may have fallen but I wasn't dead, and there was a reason I stayed in LA after the marriage tanked: nobody knows anybody out there, and if they do they've got the sense to stay away from words like potential.

"Listen, kid. I was in Seattle in '99. The whole WTO thing. You've read about it in history – that class where you study dead things. It went nowhere. Oh, and you go to high school in a wealthy white suburb. You're not allowed to use the phrase working people."

The music changed. The house sound system cranked out extra bass. I recognized the band – The Kills – as one Bo had turned me on to a few weeks before.

"More and more *working people* –" he hit the phrase extra hard – "recognize they're being hosed. It's gonna blow, and this time there'll be no putting the lid back on."

"And you know this how?"

"How can you *not* know it?" Bo's face wore the smug half-grin that made me want to blow away his arguments even though I agreed with him in principle; that made me forget how much more evolved he was than I was at his age.

There was no Dad in Bo's life. Never had been. Lin a perpetual solo act who'd opted to have a child on her own. Enlisted me as a surrogate father/role model back when I had a life. Fortunately, Bo and I had bonded.

3

Behind the counter, two members of the disaffected youth club served the caffeine-crazed citizens of Brookline: him and her, Goth girl and her sidekick in black t-shirts, both tattooed, she also with a metal stud in the flesh beneath her lower lip. I liked the Daily Grind, even though – or maybe because – I found the staff surly.

"I'm sympathetic to the cause, Bo. Really. I just disagree with the tactics. Roll cars. Trash stores. You set shit like that in motion, you can't know – or control – where it's gonna go."

"Right. Don't smoke pot – you'll end up a heroin addict."

Steam rose from our mugs. At the counter, Goth girl scowled as she handed change to a female senior citizen with silver hair pulled back in a bun.

I wondered how the old lady felt about the Kills. Me, I liked them. Bluesy and bitter. "Violence as a path to social change. I don't buy it. The end doesn't justify the means. Never has."

"Violence against property isn't violence against people. When property becomes an economic weapon, attacking it is the only way to set things right."

"Sounds good in theory. Two guys shooting the shit over coffee. But it's a slippery slope, Bo. Violence is violence."

I watched emotions play on his face. A flash of anger he let pass, pull back for perspective. Find humor. His mischievous grin. "You're cynical. Scared. Burned out."

I caught my reflection in the window. Dark, graying hair. Emerging crow's feet. "Not cynical. Wary. A healthy distrust of zeal in any guise." Bo reminded me a lot of Lin when I'd met her – fiery commitment looking for a place to land. "What's your mother say about all this?"

4

"She's like you. Heart's in the right place, but too comfortable to really do anything."

Comfortable. There were times when what maturity I had was all that kept me from strangling the little fucker. I rubbed the back of my neck.

Bo sipped coffee. "So how's your Dad, anyway?"

Shit. I wrapped both hands around my mug. Savored the warmth. "Train wreck. But thanks for asking."

My father lived for now in an extended care facility. The doctor who'd called in April had said "massive stroke" and "critical care" and urged me to catch a quick flight from LA. I did. My father didn't look like he'd make it more than a day or two. But he was a stubborn fuck. A week on his death bed turned into three, and then – *holy shit* – strength coming back. Six weeks later he had his speech, a walker he could get around with and, in recent days, some shadow of his old orneriness. I had a quandary. How long did I stay to help him stabilize? What if he never did? What if he was slowly slipping, and I became the anchor he held on to? Mom had been gone more than a decade, and I'm an only child. But let's be clear: I did not come back out of nobility, or devotion, or even – god forbid – filial love. I came to stave off the weight of the guilt I'd carry if I stayed away.

Brentwood Home sat on a hill next to a Kingdom Hall and not far from Meadowbrook Country Club, where I'd caddied as a kid. Each day I tried to prepare myself by shedding all expectation before I walked in the door. Most days he was alert; more often than not, we could have something resembling conversation as

5

long as we kept the Red Sox or Celtics close at hand. That Saturday he'd been in classic form.

"Nick, you sonofabitch, how you doing." He stood like he'd been waiting for me, leaning on his metal walker. Red-plaid flannel shirt. Worn khakis. Small, disapproving mouth.

"What's happening, Dad? How they treating you?"

"Like a fucking invalid." Thomas Young was always short but solid. Worked 40-plus years in machine shops. In six weeks he'd become soft. The stroke had leveled his right side. He needed the walker to get around; his cheek and eyelid drooped. Speech came thick like it used to when he drank. He was fragile, forgetful. "What are you doing here?"

"Nothing. Came to see you."

The full head of silver hair he'd always kept neatly slicked back was dry, white, and wild on top.

"Don't know why." He followed his walker to a chair. Dropped into it. He had a large single room sectioned into living area, kitchen, bedroom. A nice place. Generous windows. Green stuffed chairs. Stale, overheated air.

I plopped into the empty chair. "You have lunch?"

"You can call it that."

"Steak and beers?"

He scowled. My father has never been an easy man. Part of a generation that didn't talk about their feelings, he took it a step further and didn't talk at all.

I considered turning to the Red Sox, but it seemed too desperate a move too early. I was trying to learn to let the silence happen. That was what Joan, one of the day nurses, kept telling me. His lucidity came and went – this was a good day.

We listened to the clock tick. I'd put in an hour and go meet Bo for coffee.

His voice came combative. "How we gonna pay for this? It ain't gonna be Medicare. There's hospital bills, too."

"You tell me where the money's stashed, I'll take care of it."

He stared at me. His eyes, his face, such a small part of his head now. I didn't remember it being that way.

"You're shitting me," he said. "What money?" His mouth open, the teeth brown and breaking, archaeological ruins.

A rock landed in my stomach. "Pension. Retirement savings. Whatever."

"I don't have any money." He practically spit the words at me. "Couple grand in a checking account."

Another rock, bigger. "Nothing? How'd you expect to pay for this?"

"I didn't exactly plan on this happening."

"Right." Why would I think he'd have money put away. Maybe because he was a regular guy who'd lived a regular life – I figured somewhere there was a regular pension. I closed my eyes. Thought of a quiet beach somewhere.

The clock kept ticking. Outside, rain.

"Why don't you settle it up," he said. "How much can it be?"

Sometimes it seemed he set up entire conversations to drive me to shame. "I've got nothing more than you do."

He cocked his head at me. "The fuck are kids good for if they can't take care of you when you're old." He brushed down his hair. It bounced back up. "A little help is all. I raised you."

Mom raised me. I bit the words back; I wasn't going to give him the satisfaction. "Never mind." I grabbed a small rubber ball off an end table. "You doing your exercises? You're supposed to squeeze this 20 minutes a day."

He grabbed his crotch. "Squeeze *this*."

The room smelled of disinfectant, and traces of the odors it had washed away.

"You watch the Sox last night?" It wasn't a total cop-out.

He squinted. "Toronto, right?"

"From what I read it sounded ugly."

"It was." He started to say more, then didn't. He watched out the window. I tried not to watch him do it.

"So," he said, without looking at me. I've never been the son he hoped for. It's just not clear what he had hoped for. A guy with a family, maybe. A guy who made smart choices. Not a guy who married an actress and followed her around like an eager pup. Not a guy who walked away from a promising career.

"Go home, Nick." There was something resembling vulnerability in his voice. Or I wanted there to be. "Back to your life. All I got ahead of me is a slow rot."

What was I supposed to do with that. While I was eager to get out of Brookline, it wasn't like I had anywhere to go. California was Teresa, Teresa was done, and it was more than past time to acknowledge that. I had nothing to go back to. Nothing here. And nowhere to hide from the terror of that. Just a highly developed set of avoidance behaviors that kept me in a limbo I'd come to hate and had no clue how to escape.

"You're getting strength," I said emptily. "People come back from this."

"Bullshit." He looked at me. Blue eyes gone milky. "Say I come back. To what? To who?"

The sarcastic part of me wanted to shoot back, "To a stack of bills you can't pay," but the bitterness in his voice sapped my spunk. "Plenty of people older than you lead full, active lives."

He stared at me, then through me. "The fuck you know," he said. "You're in your prime and pissing it away."

We extended the effort a few more minutes before it became too much for either of us.

I touched his shoulder. "I'm gonna go. I'll see you tomorrow."

He watched out the window. He may have nodded.

In the Daily Grind, rain had begun to fog the window again. It was hard not to wonder if summer would ever come. Bo was saying something about his girlfriend Marcela.

"...and she's interning at the Center for True Cost Economics."

I got tired just listening to him. His whole circle, their uncompromising ideals and unambiguous commitments. "What the fuck is true cost economics?"

Bo grinned. "A beautiful idea. Price products based on what it really takes to produce them, including the environmental costs."

"That sounds almost reasonable. It can't possibly be a job worthy of the revolution."

"Right. And where are you working, Nick?"

Ouch. My mug was empty, and that was more than I could deal with. "Time out. End of lightning round. I want a refill. You want anything?"

"I'm set."

I took my mug to Goth girl at the counter. Jet-black hair scissor-cropped at the neck. Purple lipstick. In laconic conversation with her cohort. I had begun a secret campaign to win her over. I was no stranger to youth culture: I'd spent the last dozen years in LA. What was unfamiliar – and unwelcome – was feeling pushed outside it. In Los Angeles, everyone drank from the fountain of youth. There was no such condition as middle age. Fulfillment was always around the next corner. I set my mug down loud enough to draw a reflex glance. She had a way of looking beyond, behind, never directly at me.

"Could I get more coffee?"

She looked over my shoulder. Her face registered *annoying old guy* and a set of associations she had with that. I didn't like the associations and didn't want to be tagged with them. But all I could do was take the refilled mug, leave a dollar on the counter and drag my 42-year-old ass back to my table, where Bo sat ogling the *Globe*'s front page.

The lead story concerned another breakdown in labor negotiations between the local janitors' union and the city's custodial companies. The union had set a deadline: if no agreement was in place by Sunday midnight, the janitors would walk.

Bo hungered for it. "There's gonna be a strike, and it's gonna be big." He huddled over his coffee, all righteous and enthusiastic, like at a high school football game against an archrival.

I had to admit it sounded good to me, too: a welcome distraction from my reluctant homecoming.

On the sound system, the Kills sang "Fuck the People."

"The only question is how the mainstream news will handle it," Bo said. "Given that media conglomerates make up some of the biggest multinationals. But you know that, right Nick? One reason you're not a reporter anymore?"

"Touché." I sipped my coffee. "So when do we march on the Winter Palace?"

"Fuck you. I'm serious."

I drained my coffee. "If you were serious, you'd be out there doing something instead of sitting here talking." My finger traced the lip of the empty mug. It was just a rainy June Saturday and I'd reached my limit. I had no idea my words would come back to bite me.

2

Terry's voice on the phone made me miss her despite myself. My beloved ex-wife had been called in to read for a serial horror flick.

"So they haven't said which part. And there's only two possibilities. The ditsy 20-year-old whose primary task is to shriek, and the clueless 40-something mom who makes a couple token appearances before having her throat cut."

I sat on a stool at Buff's Pub, a tiny joint on Washington. Cell phone to my ear.

"Agent boy is trying to put a good spin on it. This is a hot franchise, after all, but we know it can't be a good sign if we don't know which part I'm up for. Too young for one, too old for the other, too smart for both."

Terry would be drinking tequila in a dark bar in Fairfax, hiding behind sunglasses that said *don't even think about hitting on me*. With wild red hair and green eyes, Teresa Lennox was still a neon presence wherever she went, despite Hollywood senior citizen status. Freckles. A full-body laugh that made you want to go on adventures with her.

"What'cha drinking?"

"Herradura." In the background on the left coast, I could hear music and the buzz of loud conversation. Back east, it was the shank of the evening. Just a few serious types left, the Kinks' "Lola" on a jukebox whose selections hadn't been updated in thirty years. "You?"

"Sauza. They don't sell the fancy stuff here." I held my glass by the rim. Turned it slowly on the bar. Terry and I did well as long as we didn't discuss money – more specifically, the fact I was still more or less living off hers. In the right mood, I could make an argument I'd earned it. "That call got to you. How come?"

"I'm becoming a nostalgia name," she said. "A novelty act."

"You don't know that."

"You don't know I'm wrong."

Nothing I could say to that. I waited a beat. "It's good to hear your voice."

"You too. How're things?"

I sipped the last of my tequila, considered the question. "Bizarre. Can't tell if Dad's getting better or worse. But I tell you." I caught the bartender's eye, held up my empty glass. "There's a part of me that wants him to do a quick exit, and that's a shitty thing to feel."

"It's human, Nick."

I stopped myself from saying that an actress was not a reliable gauge of human feeling. "I'm back in the land of the quietly successful, dying a slow death." My drink arrived. I nodded thanks. "I'm having a second. Join me?"

"Way ahead of you."

"I do like a woman can hold her liquor." The silence across

13

the phones felt companionable, nostalgic. Terry and I have long shared a fondness for tequila. One night at the height of her fame we'd decided to get out of LA. Hopped in the car intending to drive to Galveston, an homage to the Glen Campbell song and as good a destination as any. We got as far as Arizona, where we became enchanted with one of the lonelier border towns. I can't remember which, but I do remember we drank a lot of tequila, stole a string of twinkling Christmas lights from a Family Dollar store, and for several blissful hours in a faded glory hotel that string of lights was all Teresa wore. But nostalgia would only get me in trouble – I'd find myself on my ass on the floor. So I snapped back to my bar stool and the tenuous connection to my ex. "Yesterday he told me to go home. Back to my life."

Teresa laughed. "You have a life?"

That stung. "Thanks, darling." I downed my sipping tequila. "He's got no savings. No pension. Nothing. I don't even *know* how much he owes. And he's got barely enough to bury him."

"Ouch."

"It would be easier if I could clear the decks on the bills he already has."

The bartender wiped glasses with a rag.

Terry's voice changed. "Tell me this conversation's not going where I think it's going."

"*What?*"

"You asking me for money."

"Bite me, Teresa."

"Those days are over, Nicky."

Somewhere on the left coast a samba beat played. Three

thousand miles east, I had a familiar knife in my sternum. "I was not asking you for money."

"*Really*? Be honest with yourself."

Fuck her. "Remind me why I loved you?"

"You *love* me because I tell you the truth. It's time to move on, Nick. *Forward*. Get to work. You remember work."

I *did* remember work. All too clearly, being here. I had started down the right road – J-school, a job with the *Boston Weekly* in the heyday of investigative journalism.

"Yes," I said. "Well." Once a conversation took an ugly turn with Teresa, there was no going back. A job I could almost imagine. But a job was part of a life and that, as my ex-wife so delicately pointed out, flummoxed me. *How? From what?* I sucked the last drop from my empty glass. "Let's do this again sometime. Meanwhile, thanks for curing my nostalgia."

But Terry got the last word. Always. "Don't be so sensitive, Nick. It's not healthy."

I walked toward home under an empty night sky, escorted by memories. My career highlights. It was a short film. We'd done good work at the *Weekly*. Made a difference in the life of the city. It was a heady time, and I was lucky enough to help uncover a state spending scandal. Hundreds of thousands of dollars of state contracts doled out to companies who'd lined the pockets of a certain prominent state rep. It took a year or so, but we managed to ferret it out, which got the state rep a quick boot and got me some local notoriety.

There were job offers – TV, point person for the *Globe*'s Spotlight investigative team, the political beat for a national news magazine

– but the truth was I didn't like the attention and didn't want to stay in the news business. Ferreting out corruption brought me fleeting satisfaction, but it didn't bring the money back. It didn't fix anything. A friend and I had talked in J-school about someday starting a magazine devoted to volunteerism. The articles would celebrate good work people were doing and the advertising revenues would help fund those programs. I decided I'd like to use whatever juice I had to launch the project, and launch myself somewhere else. My pal was happy as city editor at a Milwaukee daily, so I moved to Los Angeles and took a whack at it myself. Might have worked, too, if I hadn't fallen for Teresa. Okay, forget that. Terry was an excuse. I didn't have the stuff to see it through.

The next morning, Teresa's challenge to work rang in my ears, and shame that she wasn't entirely wrong about the money poked at me. What kind of son doesn't help his failing father? The broke kind. The kind that said father treated like a soiled washrag. But guilt is stronger than reason, and I'd reached a point where I needed to fill my days with *something*. Besides, replaying my career highlights had made a cocktail of confidence and self-loathing that made me believe it was a good idea to drop in on my old editor.

AJ was at the office, early afternoon. So was the receptionist who looked at me wary when I said he wasn't expecting me. She left him a voice mail with my name in it and had me cool my heels by the front desk. She was maybe twenty, with a cultivated hipster look. "I'll let you know when he's free." An expression poised between disinterest and disdain. Her olive glass frames matched her shirt. I complimented her on that and sat down before she could show me how little she cared.

BusinessForward, a monthly magazine for entrepreneurs, had the eleventh floor of an old brick building in the financial district. Abraham Joseph Hearne was executive editor. Big, drafty windows looked out on Downtown Crossing. Phones rang in distant rooms. I sat on a velvety red modernist sofa and shuffled magazines on a kidney-shaped glass coffee table.

In the six months I'd been in town, AJ and I had talked on the phone a few times and met for lunch a few more. We knew each other well, and not at all. We'd been pals in high school and kept in touch since. I'd helped him get his first newspaper job with the *Weekly,* and he thus credited me with his career, though he'd long since outshone me.

A couple years before, I'd gotten some mileage out of my entrepreneurial failure by writing a piece for AJ about my days as a magazine publisher. It generated some buzz. That led to a second piece about mid-career change, also well-received. While it was fun working with a great editor and good to be back in print, I had no real knowledge of the business world. So even though there'd been some desire on all sides to have me do more, the right idea hadn't materialized.

I glanced at the hipster. She glanced back. I smiled and felt like a pedophile. The fuck was I doing there? Oh, yeah: bills. I'd feel like less of a failure if I could generate *some* cash. And hell, pursuing an assignment was easier – and less dangerous – than concocting a balance sheet weighing what remained of filial obligation. An hour at the library that morning had yielded an idea I could at least plausibly bring to an old friend. I felt a pulsation in my pants.

My phone. Bo. "Thursday night. TT's." His voice enthusiastic. "Very hot band. You up for it?"

"Hi," I said. "Sure."

The hipster shot me a look like I was being rude, interrupting the surfing she was doing on her computer.

"And guess what," Bo said. "Practice today, I beat the school record." Bo ran the 800-meter, the race that's not quite sprint, not quite distance.

"That's fantastic. Congrats." I grinned like an idiot, proud to share the moment.

"Unofficial," he said, backing away from the emotion, "but still."

The hipster answered her phone, which hadn't rung audibly.

"Screw that," I said. "Revel in it."

"I know, right? Doesn't happen every day." He sounded hurried. Almost always did. "What are you up to?"

"Mild self-abuse," I said. "Nothing much."

"Cool." Voices on his end. "Gotta go. Catch you later."

He was off; I lingered, grateful for how easy it was with him. For the ongoing bond. Until the troubles, Bo had spent a week in LA with me every summer since he was eight. The kid fell in love with chili dogs, the arcade at Santa Monica pier, and the allure of the clubs on Sunset strip. When he was 13 and discovering punk, I'd arranged for him to meet Tim Armstrong from Rancid, whose manager owed Terry's agent a favor.

"Nick." AJ was coming down the hall. His voice like a warm blanket. "Good to see you."

We shook hands and he led me away from hipster chick toward his office.

"Sorry to keep you. Trying to finish a messy piece."

AJ looked like an editor. Thick - not fat - body, thick mustache, brown Brillo pad hair. His own father had died the previous winter, stomach cancer. I had come back for the funeral, which to a loyalist like AJ meant we were a step from brothers.

We turned into an office just big enough for the two of us and his cluttered desk. Dark wood wainscoting under pale yellow walls. "What brings you here, Nick?"

"Tired of pacing the den at my father's house. What's up with you?"

"Still in business, but only until the accountants realize we can't survive without ad pages."

BusinessForward had been a solid performer for more than 15 years before Time Warner bought it out. In the two years since the acquisition the magazine had become irrelevant, and only AJ's loyalty and aversion to risk kept him there.

"How is your Dad?"

I blew out a puff of air. "Today he didn't recognize me at first. Few days ago he told me I should go home."

"Ouch."

"Yeah. Secretly, of course, I agree with him."

"Where would you go? Where *will* you go?"

"Exactly." I hated that question. I had no answer, and it only reminded me of my inability to escape the post-divorce black hole. The lost years. There was no gracious way to introduce the subject, but I needed a serious redirect. "AJ, don't you think it's time I did another piece for you?"

"I'd love it. What do you have in mind?"

"A humor piece – public corporations as ponzi schemes."

He waited. Moved papers around on his desk. Not a good sign.

AJ's desk was evidence he worked too hard. Files strewn across, post-its stuck to his phone. "Two problems with that," he said. "One, we don't do humor. Two, we did a thing on ponzi schemes last year, post-Madoff, like everybody." He flushed a bit. "What else you got?"

An estranged father with serious medical bills. "Need your dry cleaning picked up?"

He watched his hands rest on the desk. Forced a laugh. "You know I'd love for you to do a piece. Really. Get your feet under you, give it some thought. We'll talk again."

As gracious a brush-off as a guy could ask for. It was too soon to go, but all we were left with was the awkwardness of my showing up. We both looked at the framed pictures of his wife Emma and three kids at the edge of his desk.

"They're growing up," I offered.

He nodded. "You remember Chris Tillman? From high school?" he asked. "Friend of Seth's, went to Newton?" Seth Gutman was a high school pal of ours who'd gone on to found two wildly successful Boston businesses.

"The Endicott guy. Yeah. Kinda. Why?" Chris Tillman was second in command of one of Boston's largest companies, a financial services and investment firm with a hand in just about anything that made money in New England.

"Hear about the robbery?"

"What robbery?"

"Tillman's house, in Newton. Twelve thousand bucks cash stolen, the middle of the day."

"Yeah?" It sounded empty. I couldn't help it. I lacked sympathy for the problems of the pampered. Twelve thousand bucks could get my Dad out of the hole. It was pocket change to a guy like Tillman.

"They also beat the crap out of his teenage kid."

"No shit." I felt callous. There were a thousand tragedies every day, most worse than rich people being robbed and their kids' pride beat up.

"Broken ribs. Punctured lung. Fractured skull. Broken arm, maybe just for kicks."

"*Fuck.*"

"Yeah. They did reconstructive surgery immediately. Said it was the only chance Evan would ever be recognizable."

While my mind registered this as horrible, my stomach didn't feel it. Maybe I watched too much TV. Maybe I was too preoccupied with my own shit.

"He's in critical condition at Newton-Wellesley. Kid must have been beaten with something heavy. Repeatedly. Like somebody was enjoying it."

I didn't know what to say. "How you know all this?"

"Talked to Seth earlier." I could feel AJ's sadness. "That could have been his kid," he said. "Or mine. Or yours."

"I don't have a kid. Or twelve grand in cash." I regretted it as soon as I said it.

"*Nick.*"

"Sorry." I felt bad for not feeling anything. "Kid gonna make it?"

"Don't know. Right now, it doesn't look good." We were back to watching his family photos. I wondered how – if – I'd feel if it were his son.

"They have any idea who did it?"

"Not yet. Middle of the day. Quiet street. No one saw anything."

AJ and I made plans to get together the next week for lunch, and I promised to think about some story ideas. I headed out feeling worse than when I'd gone in.

Wisteria crawled up the front of my father's seafoam green stucco house, tucked in a lost neighborhood between Brookline Village and Jamaica Plain. It looked like the kind of house that would be inhabited by a sweet, wizened woman in her 80s. It had looked that way when my parents first rented the place more than 40 years earlier.

The den was both my refuge and living quarters. Dingy even when well-lit. Brown furniture, coffee-and-cream carpet. But I couldn't bear to sleep in my childhood bedroom and I wasn't about to sleep in what had been my parents' room, so I'd taken up residence on the ancient fold-out sofa. A never-fashionable brown tweed, it had been new my last years of high school; I could still remember the fresh textile smell that would invade my nostrils on nights I'd do a face plant, too tanked to make it upstairs. Now it sagged in the middle and the springs groaned anytime I moved.

While not the most physically comfortable location, the den offered two distinct advantages: it allowed me to feel temporary, and it minimized the ghosts I was forced to confront.

That afternoon, I walked into an empty house and a letter from the Brookline High Reunion Committee. Fuck that.

I dug out my father's medical bills and sat with them at the kitchen table. First step, figure out what he owed. I started to separate the mountain of paper into three stacks: most recent copies of all outstanding invoices; duplicate copies which could be thrown away; angry letters from insurance companies or physicians seeking payment. A fine plan. But some bills from different practices seemed to cover the same procedure, and others from the same office listed different amounts on each invoice. Soon I had a fourth stack, as high as the first, of bills I was confused about.

I paced the carpeted den floor, where all the furniture faced the television. I had become adept at wasting away afternoons. Reruns of *Buffy* and *Seinfeld* will take a guy only so far, so when I maxed out on those, I'd started checking out videos from the library. My own afternoon film series. First, the American Western – a genre both tough and sentimental. Recently, I'd started on The 20 Greatest Film Noirs as defined by an LA film critic I followed online. After a movie, I'd take a late afternoon run. After the run I'd shower and go somewhere for dinner until I could respectably visit a pub for a few beers before home and late-night TV.

Paced my way back to the kitchen table and went through the fourth stack of bills again with pencil and paper. Still couldn't reconcile it. Went back through the pile of active bills and became less sure I'd sorted even those properly. *Fuck. It's his mess*, I told myself, *let him get healthy and deal.* Paced over to the counter and picked up a DVD of *Double Indemnity*, but I'd already watched it twice, so I slit open the letter from my alma mater.

The letter announced the upcoming 25th reunion. *An exciting time to see old friends. Renew acquaintances.* Someone named Keith Gitner recruiting committee members "to help make it happen" the following year. The afternoon was sunny and approaching warm, but I kept the curtains drawn to prevent daylight from making too much visible, so I read the letter by whatever light seeped through, thinking *shoot me now.* Only thing worse than attending such an event would be planning it.

Back to bills. I should make calls, come up with a plan, but I couldn't even make myself sit at the table. Best I could muster was to sift through the stacks one last time, toss obvious duplicates into a recycle bag, and resolve to tackle it later.

Serious self-flagellation loomed, so I changed clothes and went for a run. Hundred sit-ups as warm-up. I'd been carrying a dozen extra pounds the last couple years, and I'm not a big enough guy to absorb that. So down Cypress and out Walnut, that first mile the hardest, when the knees complain and the breathing isn't right and I felt every inch of the distance between the guy who used to do this easily and the guy doing it now. But three miles broke up my day and gave me some measure of self-regard. Along the reservoir. A burn in my legs. Short of wind. Fighting it after a mile. That easy groove just not there. Not coming. *Fuck it. Turn around.* Once I started down the hill to Cleveland Circle, I'd have to come back up it. Just the thought of quitting helped me churn my legs until the hill carried me down to Beacon Street, where I could loop the softball field and legitimately head for home. Then I sold myself on two blocks up the hill so I didn't quit in crowded Cleveland Circle. Then three more blocks to the Dean Road light. Then pushed through a flat stretch and caught a hint of second wind that carried me all the way back to the reservoir with a small sense of victory. The sweat through my t-shirt started to feel good. I even pushed my pace to stay focused on the physical and keep thoughts away.

Across to Lee Street, then over to Cypress toward home. Shower, dinner, and pub to look forward to.

I cut off Cypress, down a side street that ran alongside a playground, then what looked like an auto body place, closed. Three kids in a small parking lot in front threw a tennis ball against the garage door. Laughter. Bravado. Idle afternoons, simple camaraderie. I envied them. I concentrated on my feet, my labored breathing. The summer wasn't hot yet, but you could feel how hot would finally come. I heard a crash. Voices. Looked back toward the garage door where the boys had now huddled near a broken window. I imagined that one of the boys' dads ran the auto body and thought about what story they might concoct. I trusted it would be ingenious and hoped it would keep them out of trouble. On the next street I turned right, hugged the long side of the playground.

I made a long block and ran back past the auto body. The kids still gathered at the garage door. I had a stitch in my side, so I stopped. Bent over to suck air, then walked, hands on hips. Garage walls painted different shades of blue. One of the kids had some sort of stick or pole he was trying to jam into the door. There were now two broken windows. Small panes, eight or ten inches square on classic, barn-style doors. The situation seemed obvious. They were trying to get their ball – remove the evidence – and get out. Like they were never there. *What broken windows?* Bad idea. They didn't understand messing with the door was only going to make things worse.

I may have flamed out with adult interaction, but here was a chance for me to do some good – provide a little wisdom *and* satisfy a craving for connection. I crossed the street and stood huffing on the sidewalk. Dappled shade from a maple at the edge of the playground. The kids hadn't noticed me. They were twelve or thirteen, a Hispanic kid and two white boys. The pole turned out to be a section of re-bar and the one kid was trying to wedge it between the pieces of a metal hasp that was padlocked shut. I walked closer until one of them looked over.

"Hey," I said.

"Hey." The Hispanic kid ate from a snack-size bag of chips. A dog – a shepherd mix, sand and black – lay on its side near the boys. Rib cage rising and falling heavily, like it had been running.

"What do you want?" asked the stocky kid with the re-bar. He wore an oversized Boston Bruins jersey.

I moved a few steps closer onto the blacktop driveway. Closer to where the tree's dappled shade ended and they stood in sunlight. Maybe I should have known better. But hey, I related to young people. "So let me guess," I said. "Ball's in there, and if your dad finds it he's gonna know you guys busted the windows."

The kid in the Bruins shirt had got the re-bar through the hasp now. He held it there and looked at me. Brown curly hair.

The third kid, skinny-strong, backward baseball cap and baggy pants, chuckled quietly.

"Man, why don't you go back to running and shit?" The Bruins kid poised on the re-bar.

The Hispanic kid smiled. He kicked a pebble idly, toward the dog. "Yeah. Last time this happened, Dad kicked my ass." He smiled.

By now I'd caught my breath. I could feel sweat drying into my t-shirt. "You pop the door it's only gonna make it worse."

The Hispanic kid just kept smiling.

The Bruins kid, back to me, put all his muscle against the re-bar and twisted. The hasp snapped and the doors popped open.

I shook my head. "Not a good idea."

Baseball cap kid had his hands on his hips. "What's your *problem*, man?"

I moved closer, maybe fifteen feet away. The Bruins kid had turned toward me. He leaned on the re-bar like a cane. "I wouldn't come any closer." He gestured at the dog that lay beside him. "That dog there, he doesn't like strangers. He's got a mean streak. Right, dog?"

Baseball cap kid chuckled quietly. The Bruins kid nudged the dog with his foot. "Show him your teeth," he said, then looking at me with a grin, "*get him*." The dog didn't move. Something that would become knowledge started in my head and moved through my veins. The kid looked back at the dog like he was waiting for it to respond. "I said, *get him*." A little breeze made my back feel cold, and then the kid wound up to swing with the re-bar. My body was slow in reacting. Adrenaline charged my brain and as the kid swung I realized the dog hadn't been running. Impact. A sickening thud as re-bar landed a body blow. The animal convulsed. Blood gushed from the dog's mouth into a puddle on the ground. Without thinking, I went after the kid. The other two scattered like blown dust. The Bruins kid held the re-bar like he was thinking about using it on me, then one of his pals called out, and he dropped the bar. Ran. I chased for a block or two 'til they went through a back yard and I lost them. They knew the neighborhood and I didn't. They were young and I wasn't. I went back to the lot. The dog hadn't moved. I knelt down, touched his side. He wasn't breathing. His fur stiffening. The puddle of blood had grown to where I stood. My own blood was hot. My pulse raced. I grabbed the re-bar and thought about cruising the neighborhood. Instead I took a few deep breaths and went in search of a phone. My stomach tensed. Sick. I felt responsible.

It took a few minutes, but I found a neighbor who was home and would call the police. I waited. Shaky. Filed a report. Described the kids for the officer, a well-scrubbed guy in his early thirties.

We stared at the dog. The randomness of it infuriated me.

"Fucking morons," he said.

This was their idea of idle summer fun. I had no clue what made these kids tick. What their world was made of.

"You'll call the dog's owner?" I felt dizzy. Tasted bile.

"No collar. No tags."

"Fuck." My legs trembled.

"We'll remove the body. Ask around the neighborhood. If we're lucky, we'll find the owner. If there was one."

The day felt hotter. "Then what?"

He shrugged. "If we're luckier, we'll find the kids. I'll try to scare them."

"That's it?"

He shrugged again. "What do you want?"

I wanted him to punish those kids and absolve me of the responsibility – the revulsion – I felt. I wanted to find an angry dog and put those kids one by one in a room with it.

I walked the rest of the way home, sick and shaking – convinced that if I'd been smarter or more alert, it wouldn't have happened.

I had a feeling I wouldn't sleep much that night. I was right. Waking nightmares. Metal re-bar against a dog's body. Oozing blood. And one I didn't expect: a teenage kid with a beaten-in face. Human kindness, overflowing.

3

First thing in the morning I took myself out for an egg sandwich, a big-ass coffee, and a newspaper. Sometimes nothing else will do.

The world was sunny. Warm with the promise of hot. Birds chirped. Even the headlines were cheery – the janitors struck a blow for the little guy and said fuck you to their contract offer. I raised a fist in solidarity with the newly unemployed, sprung for both Boston dailies, and headed home to soak in details.

The *Herald*'s headline was, as always, succinct: *No More Talk, Janitors Walk.*

The *Globe* was prosaic, but informative. *Janitors Vote to Strike.* "With labor talks at an impasse, more than 10,000 janitors in Boston have voted to strike, union officials said."

The egg sandwich was deeply satisfying. It and the big coffee helped offset my lack of sleep. Three Advil would help assuage my sofabed-induced sore back. And the strike helped distract me from waking dreams of dog beatings and thrashed teens.

The *Globe*: "After talks stalled with cleaning companies late last week, the union had established a Sunday midnight deadline for resolution. The two sides remain far apart on key issues. The union wants an increase in full-time positions and an expansion of health-care benefits to more workers. Members of Service Workers Union International clean some of Boston's biggest office towers and universities. Yet only 1,900 of the union's nearly 11,000 members work full-time and are eligible for benefits." Seemed like a reasonable request to me. This had potential to be serious sport. A worthy distraction. It tweaked my leftist sympathies and loomed as a possible rooting interest through what looked to be a long summer.

By that evening, I would find myself in the same room with those striking janitors. But first, I spent the afternoon in surreal conversation with my father.

"Hey, Dad. It's me. Nick." *Wait. Count to ten.* His bed cranked to a sitting position. Eyes open. Kind of on me, kind of not. "Your son." It wasn't unusual for him to be groggy when I arrived, even in the afternoon.

"I know who you are." His speech slurred, but forceful. The right side of his mouth dragged a little when he spoke. No matter what shape he was in, it was always a relief to make it to his room. The hallway featured a regular lineup of the least able-bodied, a half-dozen wheelchairs parked all day by the nurse's station, containing the slumped, the moaning and the drooling: a rogues' gallery of dementia.

"How you feeling?"

"I don't want your pity."

"Fair enough."

Thomas didn't get many visitors. You create enough distance over enough time, people get the idea and leave you alone.

He wanted to sit in the chairs, so I retrieved his walker. Set it beside the bed. "How do we do this?"

He pushed himself up, slid his legs off the side. He rested there, hands on thighs. "A little closer," he said.

I slid the walker over a few inches. I felt deficient.

"There," I said. "How's that?"

"Good." He rocked back and forth a few times, then hoisted himself. Didn't make it. "A hand on my back," he said. "A little boost."

We got him vertical, and he made his way over – a tortoise, a snail. He made a little snort. His breathing labored. I could feel his frustration.

An air conditioner hummed behind us. The season's first hot day had arrived, and it was a scorcher.

"Paul was in yesterday," he said.

I wasn't sure how to play this. Did I meet him where he was, or point out that his brother Paul had been dead a dozen years? "You remember telling me about that game you two made up as kids?" I tried. "That baseball game with the dice?"

"We had a good time with that. Helluva lot of fun. Kept stats on all the players."

"I know you two were close. You still miss him?"

He drifted. My father was missing his bottom front teeth and three of his four bicuspids. Up top, the incisors were rotting and the eye teeth gone. His gums black in the gaps. I couldn't recall ever seeing him brush. Once though, he'd been a boy, inventing games with his kid brother, their whole lives ahead of them.

"What do they say about me?" he asked after a minute, or a day.

I pondered. "How do you mean?"

"That doctor tell you anything? Or Joan, the nurse? She's alright, that one. Nice tits. What do they say?"

I shrugged. "Joan says you're making good progress. She says be patient." Easy for her to say. She didn't face a growing pile of bills. But I had something better than patience. Denial. A long track record of more or less successfully blocking out unpleasant truths. Then there was the fuck-it factor: neither Thomas nor I had money and, I told myself, they couldn't take what we didn't have. I told myself that, and the situation slowly ate a hole in my stomach.

Voices drifted from down the hall. I wondered how much cheaper this would be if Thomas had a roommate, and how those decisions got made.

The air conditioner hummed. Even with my absence of a life, the slow pace of these visits was a challenge.

"They say we can't know what to expect. You have to wait and see."

His eyes looked far away again. "Easier for you if I'd just kicked it, huh?"

"Don't worry about me. You just take care of you."

So it went. I kept hearing the sound of re-bar against that dog's body. Kicking myself for not moving faster. Not seeing it coming. Found myself thinking about the Tillman kid, felt like a prick for how I'd reacted with AJ. It was one thing to feel no regret that a privileged family got nicked. It was another to be cold to life-threatening injury to a friend of a friend.

Six o'clock. Thomas and I each sat in a stuffed green chair and turned on the news, grateful for the relief.

The strike was the lead story. The only labor disputes in recent years were the biennial tug-of-war between the mayor and the city's employees – police, fire, teachers. And those were more ritualized haggling than serious disagreement. But there were other factors that helped announce this strike as something different: just hours after the walkout, the action got nods from two powerful sources.

Long an advocate of affordable housing – and a political wild card – Mayor Norm Reeves played populist and welcomed the strike. "The janitors have a valid case that should be heard, and taken seriously. Many service workers can't afford to live here without second jobs, or cramming extended families into small apartments."

The mayor talked at me from the TV. My father talked at me from his chair.

"This guy I worked for, Charlie Rome over at Burch Precision. He was one sharp customer."

"Dad," I said.

"He saw computers coming before anybody else. He was ready. Knew what it would mean – more short runs, less specialty work."

"Dad." I pointed at the TV. "The news. I want to hear it."

He watched the screen.

"It's time," Mayor Reeves said, "for business to show its commitment to the city through responsible action. Business can do more in providing health benefits for workers. In paying a realistic living wage." He urged Boston's leading corporate citizens (and cleaning company clients) – Endicott, Arch Street,

34

FirstBoston – to lead the way by taking the first step away from a hard-line position to back the idea of a negotiated settlement.

It was quite a sound bite. I found myself interested in a way I hadn't been for a while. "Talk about throwing down the gauntlet."

My father looked at me. He didn't seem sure where he was.

"He made a fortune, Charlie Rome. He was ready to automate. I fought him on it – the custom jobs were the ones I was good at. But Charlie knew the money was in production work."

On TV, Smiling Tom the news anchor told how the strike got a second sign of support that day. Boston Area Faith in Action, an interfaith community organization which counted most of the city's religious leaders among its active members and which had (not coincidentally) been a primary force in pushing Mayor Reeves to declare his support for affordable housing, had also voiced support for the walkout.

BAFA's spokesman was a red-faced young Unitarian in a straw hat and clerical collar. I'd never much liked Unitarians and didn't think they were allowed to wear clerical collars.

"What time is it?" my father asked.

I pulled my phone out of my pocket. "Almost six-thirty."

"She'll be around with dinner," he said. Outside, the sun began to fade. "You never did wear a watch, did you?"

I smiled, surprised at any insight into my habits or character.

On TV, the straw-hatted Unitarian said BAFA would sponsor a rally that night, which would be a combination prayer meeting and information session. I decided right away I'd be there.

"I know," my father said. "You think I don't notice."

That was true. As a child, my impression of my father was of a

35

man whose greatest desire was to be left alone. We could coexist as long as I didn't ask him for anything or disturb his refuge.

"Where's your sister living now?" His skin, parchment white, had begun to sag on his bones. Even his forearms, always strong, showed creases of extra skin.

Again, I thought before answering. "I don't have a sister, Dad. I'm Nick." I itched to get out. There was life – hope, possibility - beyond Brentwood's walls, and I craved the spark. I watched his face to try to discern at what level he was tracking.

He nodded, distant. I couldn't help wondering if he was playing me. Mocking me. My father and I were never close. Nothing I did could spark his interest or earn his favor. So early on I decided to not risk anything. To keep it chatty. That was fine in theory, but harder when you were in a room together.

"*Listen to me*," he said. "I'm trying to tell you about goddamn Charlie Rome. He knew what it was to work. Not like today. Fucking kids expect everything handed to them."

"Who, Dad? Which kids? What kids do you know?" The edge in my voice shrank his pupils, pulled him back.

"Quiet," he said. "I thought you wanted to hear the news."

Fine.

Corporate reaction to the strike was swift – and strong. There was a bland statement from Andrew Sarkis of Pollard, the smaller of the two major cleaning companies. Another, slightly more feisty, from Delfi's Diane Evans. But the real sparks came from Endicott, Delfi's parent company and the city's 800-pound corporate gorilla. Marcus Gregory, CEO: "While we respect the mayor's opinion and appreciate his commitment to the city's businesses, we cannot and will not conduct our affairs in blind accordance with public opinion."

Chris Tillman, Gregory's right hand, friend of my high school pal Seth Gutman and father of the burglary/beating victim, was even more pointed.

"We will not be told how to run our organization, any more than we would expect to tell the mayor how to run his city," Tillman said.

I'd not seen Tillman before. He was swarthy, with thick brows, intense eyes and a cool smile. He looked like a scrapper. He looked accustomed to winning. He didn't look like a guy with a son on the critical list.

"As a second generation active member of Trinity Church, I support BAFA. I trust they'll be smarter than to get involved in what is a private – and honest – labor dispute."

It was shaping up to be a big old Boston brawl. I wanted a seat. I said goodbye to Thomas and high-tailed it downtown.

Old West Church was packed, with all the fervor of a revival meeting. Spotlights and cameras and television trucks – Eyewitness News, Fox 25, WB 56. A sea of mostly Hispanic men and women wearing purple t-shirts emblazoned with the union logo and the words "Justice for Janitors"; clergy types in black clerical shirts or coats; a steady, excited hum of Spanish and English. Light and sound technicians scooted across the floor, checking cables. A host of students and regular working slobs with no discernible reason to be there. It had to be 90 degrees inside. No fans. Big old twelve-pane windows flung open. A dark-haired boy in a Justice for Janitors t-shirt sat in one of the sills, looking wilted. The way I felt.

From my SRO spot in the side aisle, I could see into the balcony opposite; there had to be a hundred people up there. I wondered what Tillman or Marcus Gregory would make of this gathering. The crowd. The coverage.

A hand on my clammy arm. I half expected it to be a church minister re-directing me to a seat in some overflow room. But it was Bo, messenger bag slung across his shoulder.

"You got my message," he said.

"What message?"

"The one asking you to come. Telling you it would be good for you." Bo handed me a flash drive. "Brought you something."

"Lady Gaga at Madison Square Garden?"

He smiled. "Pretty much everything I've played for you the last couple weeks."

"*Excellent*. Thanks." Bo had terrific, wide-ranging taste in music. Bo would not beat a dog to death with re-bar. The aisle got tight as late arrivals squeezed in. "Why are *you* here?"

"It's where the action is." He grinned. "Plus, we're kind of aligning ourselves with the janitors."

"Who's we?"

"My friends – Adam, Marcela, others."

There were times when Bo's almost-grown-ness – Bo out in the world – threw me. Times I'd look in his face and see echoes of earlier moments: the six-year-old's pure joy in summer; the eight-year-old's pride in his first soccer goal. Times I'd flash – grateful – on some of the moments I'd been lucky enough to play a role in his life. At nine, when he needed to commiserate because he sucked at baseball, it was me he talked to. When he needed dating advice the summer he turned 12, he came to me. And while I was better in some situations than others, I was always honest with him about what I knew – and what I didn't.

The meeting-slash-rally-slash-whatever was about to start. Paul, the Unitarian minister from the news, stood on stage with a woman and a middle-aged guy in purple t-shirts, who I took to be the union leaders.

Paul kicked it off with a sort of prayer, though it was so vanilla it was hard to tell. Then he introduced a "special guest." Half the crowd strained to see who was lit up in the TV lights. Turned out it was the mayor. Reeves took the stage to loud applause.

I leaned over to Bo. "Interesting."

Reeves was a four-term incumbent beloved in the neighborhoods. He would have the job as long as he wanted it. He soaked in the applause. All the commotion jacked up the temp another notch.

"Don't churches believe in air conditioning?" I asked Bo.

"Only evangelicals."

The mayor was brief, but pointed. "In recent years, the city has shown its commitment to business. Now it's time for business to show its commitment to the city. I challenge the cleaning companies and the city's major corporations to better corporate citizenship, improving quality of life for thousands of city residents."

Another big round of applause – many standing – while the mayor made a grand exit down the center aisle, glad-handing the crowd. After the mayor came the union lady, Juliana, who encouraged the troops.

"*Mis amigos. Trabajadores para la justicia.*" Spanish then English. "Members of Local 179, and friends. Your presence here and on the picket lines in the coming days is a powerful, courageous act that will benefit not only you and your families, but those who follow after you."

Fierce applause.

"*Seremos victoriosos.* We will prevail, but not without a battle. Your will and resolve will be tested. Pollard, Delfi, Endicott – they will not move unless they have to. They have the resources to wait us out, and they believe they can break us." Juliana was good. She had a voice that made you believe. Made you want to do things. Plus, a cute little nose. "We must show them that we are strong, we are determined, and we are persistent. We will bend toward reasonable compromise, but we will not break."

I had an idea percolating quietly. I let it brew.

There were a couple hymns, then Paul the straw-hatted Unitarian was back with an announcement: BAFA would officially support the janitors' cause. Standing ovation. "Ministers and other faith leaders will join strikers on the picket lines," he announced.

Beside me, Bo whooped and hollered.

I rested my arm on his shoulder. "Who knew the church was so hip?"

"You should get out more. BAFA gets shit done. They mobilize people like crazy, and because it's basically all the religious leaders, they get tons of press coverage."

The Unitarian was on a roll. "We will lead a daily march from the Paulist Center on Park Street through Downtown Crossing to the Congress Street headquarters of the Endicott Corporation, where we will rally each day at noon." More cheering and whoops. He was riding it. He seemed pleasant enough. Earnest. And I guessed he didn't get that kind of response from the pulpit.

Bo was right. The TV cameras were paying attention. Little red lights on. Paul finished up and handed it to the gaunt union guy, who addressed logistics, again in Spanish then English.

"We need you on the picket lines daily as a show of strength. Come when you can. Send a family member if you have to be at your other job." And on. Finally it adjourned. The press and the overheated headed for breathable air, and factions gathered up front for tactical meetings: janitors talking picket logistics on the left, BAFA rallying civilians on the right.

I hung on the outskirts of the BAFA crowd, where a dozen ministers and lay people planned the noon march in the front pew. Behind them, a larger group with Paul the Unitarian evangelizing in its midst. I drifted back there. "The idea is to generate hundreds – thousands – of phone calls to key leaders over the next week." He stood on the pew with maybe fifty people gathered around him; faces ranged from curious to committed. "Marcus Gregory and Chris Tillman at Endicott. Ray Davis at FirstBoston. There's a list of others. Volunteers are handing them around." He asked the volunteers to wave flyers high to identify themselves. They did. One of them was Bo, happy as a kid at camp. "Call the governor's office," Paul said. "City councilors. You'll get voice mail if you get past the switchboard. But we tie up their phone lines. Hinder business. Let them know we're here." I watched Bo lean across pews, thrusting canary-colored flyers into the hands of frat boys, middle-aged women. Whatever his face was selling, you'd buy it.

I drifted to the janitors' side of the aisle, where most of the talk was in Spanish. Sam, the union guy, addressed a big group, while a few clusters of purple shirts huddled in conversation over clipboards. I watched faces of people risking their livelihoods and tried to dial into Sam. Couldn't. Partly the language barrier, partly his stern face and equally stern voice. I wasn't much for feeling scolded. Headed back to find Bo, now engrossed with a pair of equally strident youths, one of whom sported a white-on-red button: Seattle10. *Go, team.* As I approached, I heard Button Boy ask Bo, "You in?" Ever allergic to recruitment, I steered away. Found myself next to Juliana Reyes, the union organizer. Found myself saying hi. "You were great up there."

She smiled. "You with BAFA?"

"Nope. Just a concerned citizen."

"Well." She was one of those people whose eyes took in everything. "We appreciate your support."

I was about to correct her – *I'm just a spectator* – but a male cohort corralled her and she was gone.

Even though the room had cooled some, my t-shirt was sweat through. Between BAFA and the mayor, it had been quite a one-two punch; there was buzz here, and my idea had brewed into something that smelled appetizing. I headed back to Brookline to act on it before the buzz faded.

An old loneliness blindsided me as soon as I walked in the house. Part of it was the quiet. The big empty. There'd always been a ghost of it. My parents had wanted another kid. Mom was never able to. There'd been a late-term miscarriage, a girl, a couple years after

I came along. Or maybe the lonely I felt was the simple contrast between feeling like a part of something for a couple hours and coming home to nothing. Whatever it was, I shoved it aside and called AJ. Got him.

"AJ, I have an idea. You don't have to say yes right away. Just don't say no."

A sigh. "Okay. Shoot."

I told him about the piece I wanted to write. I'd follow the strike from up close. Already it was being cast as a model for future labor relations in Boston, and that model could easily translate regionally, maybe even nationally. The unusual show of public support made this special from the start. I'd look at this and other recent janitors' strikes as a way to talk about the new activism and its implications for labor relations and, more broadly, for business. I finished a little breathless.

Silence on the other end.

Then, "That's not bad, Nick."

I took a breath.

"We'll have to see how it goes. Make sure the strike is going to have the impact you and I think it will before we make it a formal assignment."

"That's fair." I stopped short of begging him.

"Anything you need in the meantime?"

Hadn't occurred to me until he asked. "Maybe smooth an intro to Chris Tillman?"

"Call him up, Nick. He's friends with Seth. He knows Lin."

"He's also dealing with some pretty major shit."

"OK. I'll get you to Seth, he'll get you to Chris." I could hear him stifle a yawn. "I'm going to bed. Double issue for September is kicking my ass. Check in end of the week?"

"Will do."

Hot shit, I thought. *Nick lives.*

4

The signs read "Fair Pay for a Full Day" and "People Before Profit" and *Hacer El Trabajo Pague,* along with the expected "Justice for Janitors." Even more so than the Old West rally the previous night, the noon turnout surprised everyone. Hundreds marched from the Paulist Center down Bromfield Street, past Downtown Crossing, through the edge of the Financial District to Endicott.

BAFA ministers led the march and had recruited heavily from their congregations. It was also a rallying point for other agendas looking to ride a tangential connection to increased publicity. The animal rights contingent joined at Macy's with their own placards – cuddly animals looking out above "your coat cost my life." Janitors turned out in force in front of One Federal Street. I hustled ahead for a good view and camped at the triangle where Federal meets High Street.

There had to be six or seven hundred people and at least four news vans. Marchers filled the plaza and the courtyard to the side. They spilled into traffic, where taxis and delivery vans waited for the Atlantic Avenue light to turn.

BAFA had a big yellow banner with red, green and blue letters that spelled out, "And Justice for All."

Three ministers, including Paul the red-faced Unitarian, made their way to a spot cleared beside the building entrance where they met the union leaders, Juliana and Sam. A handful of smokers stood in the building's shadow on a cigarette break. Car horns honked.

A microphone materialized. A platform. The hum of voices diminished. TV people jockeyed for position, hoisted cameras onto shoulders. It was a perfect summer day. Bright sun, cool breeze.

"*Compañeros sindicalistas.* Union members. Friends." Juliana spoke. Dark hair. Brown eyes. The ubiquitous purple t-shirt. Short enough that even those with a good view would be hard-pressed to see her. From where I stood, on the curb along the triangle's hypotenuse, I caught glimpses. Again, she spoke in Spanish first, then English. "Your presence here today sends an important message. It is time that the janitors of this city – that all the workers of this city – be treated with respect." Applause and cheers. She waited a beat. "*Pago justo por un dia de trabajo.* That means fair pay for a fair day's work. A living wage." More cheers, interrupting her. I wanted to cheer her myself for the way her voice made me feel. "It means creating full-time positions wherever possible, providing health benefits to a greater percentage of employees. Our goal – together – should be full coverage for all. We ask for a sharing of resources that reflects shared labor." She urged the janitors to stay strong. She raised a fist in the air. Drew a huge cheer.

Juliana yielded the microphone to Unitarian Paul. A line of

Boston cops, maybe a dozen, positioned themselves at the edge of the plaza, just into High Street. I watched Juliana melt into the crowd as Paul's voice took command. "We challenge the governor to do as Mayor Reeves has done and stand up for what's right and what's fair." He paused for cheering. Wiped his brow with a handkerchief. A chant began in the crowd, a call and response.

"What do we want?"

"Justice."

"When do we want it?"

"Now."

It quickly built a Spanish echo.

"Se ve! Se siente!"

"Porteros está presente!"

He let it build. You could see how a preacher would love it.

"Se ve! Se siente!"

"Porteros está presente!"

"What do we want?"

"Justice!"

"When do we want it?"

"Now!"

Both languages at the same time. Other chants and calls mixed in. A couple guys in ties wove their way through the maze from street to building, looking apprehensive. Paul stopped to catch his breath, then raised his hands to quiet the crowd, which mostly worked. One exuberant group across Federal Street continued their own chant. A boy held a sign that said "Panarchy." A teenage girl with a blue-and-green crew cut and a shitload of metal adornment had another: "Capitalism Is the Real Enemy."

"Bring it down, overthrow.

Corporate capitalism has got to go."

Their sing-song chant carried as other sounds quieted. I looked for Bo, didn't see him.

Paul brought the mike to his mouth. "We'll meet here again tomorrow. Let's show the janitors we're behind them."

That was it, save for a few logistics. I made my way toward the front and practically bumped into Juliana.

"Just who I was looking for. I'm Nick. We met last night."

"I remember. Hi."

"It looks like I'm going to be doing a magazine piece on the strike." Felt good to say it and have it be likely true. "So I'll be checking in with you from time to time."

"I look forward to it." A hint of a smirk. "Weren't you just a concerned citizen last night?"

I smiled. "Things change."

Things were heating up. If you squinted just right, it was possible to believe justice was around the corner. I spent the afternoon at the library researching the labor movement and avoiding Brentwood Home. It was nice to feel alive, almost part of something.

Thursday night I had plans to do music with Bo. A day of not seeing Thomas had stretched to two, and a third where – I was guilty glad – he slept through my visit. I picked Bo up at home, where his mother – my friend Lin – answered the door.

Belinda Wylie didn't look like a doctor. Except where the fatigue showed around the eyes. "You look terrible," I told her.

"Thanks. Great to see you, too."

We hugged, and it felt good. We'd been friends more than 25 years, and she was someone I had hoped and expected to see a lot of in my Brookline exile. But her schedule at the hospital precluded any regular connection; so far we'd managed only a dinner and a couple tired drinks. She had great dimples, lively eyes and a dancer's body, though she'd been away from it more than a decade.

"So what's got you?" I asked.

"You heard about the robbery at the Tillman house?"

"Yeah."

"Evan Tillman's one of mine."

I let that sink in.

"He's Bo's age." I started to understand the fatigue in her face. I felt something shift in my stomach. "To watch Chris and Maggie go through this, and feel so helpless."

I had nothing to say to that.

"What brings you by?"

I felt myself blush. "I need to grab Bo and run. Music."

"Ah." She raised her eyebrows. "I didn't know he was home." She called upstairs. When she turned back her mouth was smaller. "Who's the band?"

"Helicopter Helicopter. Hot locals."

Lin shook her head. "I don't get it, Nick."

"Keeps me young." I stuffed my hands into jeans pockets.

Sounds of movement upstairs. Footsteps.

"We need to have dinner," she said. "I miss you."

"Agreed," I said. "Call me."

Lin and Bo lived in a big Victorian in the Cottage Farm

49

neighborhood. The houses had an almost apologetic elegance; aging hulks that required loving care.

"How is the Tillman kid?" I asked her.

"No change."

"And the police are clueless."

Lin shrugged. "Middle of the day. Everybody works."

"Still. Cleaning lady. Gardener. Someone." It was starting to piss me off. A kid fighting for his life because some yahoo got mean.

"He'll be okay, right?"

Lin started to not answer, but then Bo appeared, untucked flannel over a t-shirt. Jeans.

"Hey." He rubbed Lin's head.

"Thanks." Lin had her hands on her hips. "How was today?"

"Fine." He looked distracted. Tousled. "I'm going out."

"Don't be late. You've got early track."

"Don't be annoying, mom."

I tried, unsuccessfully, to suppress a grin.

"You look like your mother," I told Bo once we got outside. A car's headlights swept us. "You know, back when I met her, –"

"Stop. I do *not* want to know about the secret life of Mom."

Helicopter Helicopter was a power pop trio: guitars, bass, drums. I got a beer and we staked out a spot by the stage. I'd had a rough afternoon. Close encounters with the world of functional adults left me fragile. I'd called my high school friend Seth Gutman to ask if he'd smooth an intro to Tillman.

"I'd be glad to. Chris and I are friends. We serve on a couple of boards together."

Of course you do.

"It's great to have you back, Nick."

I'm not back.

"We should do a Sox game. It'd be fun."

If by fun you mean terrifying.

Seth left a message for Tillman. So did I. Also left one for Andrew Sarkis at Pollard, and managed to reach Diane Evans at Delfi. Had a perfectly nice conversation. She emerged as a perfectly nice lackey who would forever recite the company line. Good to know. But all that adult activity made me fully aware of the state of my life. Isolated. Idle. My closest friend a senior in high school. I felt like shit. Needed the physical impact of loud music to drive away the bad juju. Helicopter squared delivered. Lucky for me, 'cause Bo was in a teen snit. I let him be. Guitar wailed in my ears, the kick drum pounded my chest, and I happily lost myself in the beat and young bodies. Yearning for contact. Closeness. Hard-eyed blonde. Brunette waif. Pony-tailed prep. Didn't matter. The irresistible appeal of youth – all they have before them, all they haven't screwed up yet. Yes, it was sketchy, but I let the music drive that away, too.

Sometime late in the set, Bo hit my arm. "I need a favor." His voice in my ear.

"Name it."

"I need you to find Marcela."

The happy sound of jangly guitars. Bo and I, side by side, heads huddled. "What do you mean, find her?"

"She's disappeared. Can't reach her. Not on IM. Not on her cell."

"How long?"

"Three days."

Two young women slid past us to dance, their moves completely attuned to one another. I watched, grateful.

I laughed. "You're fucking with me, right?"

Bo shot me the death glare.

"Three days is a mood. A whim."

"*Nick.* I'm serious. No one's heard from her."

I had no stomach for the vicissitudes of teen romance. "She just graduated. Give her a break. Her parents worried?"

"Her parents flaked. She lives with her grandfather."

"He worried?"

A new song. The band kicked into a slower gear.

"No. But he's a grandfather. Clueless." Bo's earnestness was a touching reminder that he was his age. "And she always answers her cell."

"What do you want me to do?"

"Go see her grandfather with me."

"Fine. Done." I wanted to stop talking and lose myself again in the vibe. Watch the grind.

"Tomorrow. After track."

"Okay." And we left it, to the band's slow groove, to the slip and sway of the women dancing in front of us. One of them became Marcela for a minute, and I let her. What Bo didn't know couldn't hurt him.

I had met Marcela Pruett exactly once. She wasn't someone you forgot. Long dark hair, distant green eyes and a half-sleeve tattoo on her right arm. She was smart, sexy, and older than her 18 years. A gaggle of boys followed her silently and at a distance. Teresa had that, too. Still does.

The night I'd met Marcela, Bo and I were headed to TT the Bear's in Cambridge. A friend of his was in the opening band. The band sucked, but Bo's guitarist friend was okay. I spent most of the set listening with closed eyes. Periodically I'd re-orient, make sure I hadn't been carted off to the home or paired for the evening with an earnest Norwegian. On one of my reality re-entries, I opened my eyes to see Bo and three other teens – two male, one female – looking at me. It was surreal, mostly because of the girl. One who changed the energy of a room. Bo leaned in and spoke. I felt his voice in my chest, but caught few words.

"… and this is … and Adam … art project"

Other sounds registered, but nothing I could decipher. The song ended. Bo leaned back toward his friends and I could hear him above the applause and the ringing in my ears.

"This is Nick. He's okay. Likes the Murphys."

Bo and I had first connected musically over the Dropkick Murphys, Boston's Irish punk *wunderkind*.

One of the boys – Adam, I thought – had a buzz cut and a wry grin. The other had a serious flannel-shirt slouch. The girl was Marcela, and these boys moved in the long shadow of her force field, though I didn't sense they knew it, or that she cared. She wore a tank top that showcased a glorious clavicle. Full lips, long neck and what I thought at first was a world-weary set to her face. She met my eyes. I nodded as if I understood.

Marcela scanned the room. Her head moved to the music. She whispered something to buzz-cut boy, who spoke to me.

"I'm Adam." His voice operated in a register that allowed him to be heard underneath the music. That alone, I thought, must give him cachet. "Good to meet you."

He was polite. I liked him. Marcela drifted. I found myself following her with my eyes. Moving easy to the beat. Leaning in to greet a tall boy. A black-haired girl. She caught me looking. I broke away, lost track. At some point she reappeared, Adam and slouch-boy at her side. A vague nod, then Adam's voice.

"We're getting out before the poppy shit starts."

A quick wave in my direction, and they looked a question at Bo – was he coming. I shot him a grin to tell him it was all okay. That the groove was good and I was glad I came, that I appreciated him bringing me and recognized it took guts, every time. He gave me a nod and followed his friends to the door.

Three beers later, my eyes drawn across the room. There was Marcela, talking to a string-bean Asian kid. No sign of the others. I made a point of not watching. Eventually joined a knot of dancers and forgot about it. Next thing I knew, a poke at my arm. Marcela Pruett dancing next to me.

"You're brave," she said.

I let it go, afraid it was sarcastic. "I thought you left."

"I did."

She danced sexy. All the more because she wasn't working it. I tried not to watch her. I decided it wasn't world-weariness on her face, but something dormant behind her eyes, only intermittently engaged. When it was, it would be transcendent.

She looked at me. It was no doubt the look she'd shot all those boys who moved in her wake. It worked. Like adrenaline. "You could have invited me to dance."

"Thought you were with someone."

"Don't think so much." Her voice teasing. She danced away.

That was my first encounter with Marcela Pruett.

Now I was on my way to her grandfather's house with my pal Bo. Picked him up at school and headed to Newton.

"So I'm the enforcer. Beat some answers out of the old guy?"

"Funny," Bo said. His eyes behind sunglasses. "You're old. He won't blow you off."

We had the windows down in the car. The 1972 Dodge Dart with the sleek lines and the chrome and the rare slant-six engine was the one possession of my father's I'd coveted. We each had an arm out the window. A breeze toyed with my hair. I was testy, having just left another fragmented session with Thomas, who didn't know where he was, or how he'd got there. I asked Nurse Joan about these recent lapses. She confirmed my impressions and raised the specter I feared: Alzheimer's. *But,* I protested, *he's been making progress. Yes,* she pointed out, *and the risk of Alzheimer's doubles in people who've had a stroke. So,* I asked through gritted teeth, *if it is that, what do I do? Get him talking. Connect him to reality. His own stories. Current events.* After that, I was not eager for more time with the geriatric set. But even a fool's errand with Bo was better than more time with myself. We went through Newton Centre and into Oak Hill. Bo directed me to a modest brick ranch house on Sheldon Road. We headed up the walk.

"So he's retired. You know from what?"

Bo rang the doorbell. "Police chief."

The man who answered the door didn't look more than sixty, though I would later learn he was seventy-three. He was maybe five-eight, physically unimposing for a former cop. He kept a well-trimmed beard, mostly gray, and about fifteen extra pounds. He wore a large pair of rimless glasses.

"Hi, Bo." He pushed open the screen and stood aside for us. Put his hand out to me. "Lawrence Sparks. Larry."

I'd never met a police chief. I tried not to sound intimidated. "Nick Young. Friend of Bo."

Sparks looked at me over his glasses. He led us into the hall. Behind him on the dining room table was a set of plastic pots, some clear tubing and what looked like a pump.

He noticed my looking. "Hydroponics. A system to grow winter tomatoes."

"Cool. What's the idea?"

He walked me to the table. Bo, a couple paces back, oozed impatience.

"No soil. Mineral nutrient solutions in water. In theory, you can better control the nutrient levels the roots absorb. If you get it right, you can produce a very stable crop." He smiled. "You can also grow indoors in winter. Worth a shot. I get it figured out now, I'll be set."

I nodded a thanks. Sparks turned his attention to Bo.

"Marcela's not back, if that's what you're wondering."

Sparks' bluntness took the wind out of Bo's sails. Took him a few seconds to find words. "I think something's wrong. She's not returning my calls."

Sparks looked at me and then at Bo. He kept a smile off his face. "She's fine, Bo. She's staying with her sister for the summer, and they're off on an adventure."

Bo looked wounded. He didn't like the answer, but it was what it was. Sparks didn't seem like a guy who'd cut much slack to a hand-wringing boyfriend. We didn't have much else to say, and after we'd stood in the hall not saying it, we left.

"Satisfied?"

"No," Bo said. "It's still not like her."

"She needs time away from the boyfriend. Buck up, cowboy."

Bo flushed.

"What?"

"Technically, I may not be her boyfriend."

I unlocked the car. "Come again?"

"She sort of broke up a couple weeks ago, but it was hormones and shit. She didn't mean it."

"*She didn't mean it.*"

"Shut up."

I rolled my eyes. "So I just made an ass of myself for nothing."

He looked stung. I backed off. "Remind me: how long were you two together?"

He shrugged. "Month. Month and a half."

Confession: I wasn't entirely disappointed at the idea she'd dumped Bo. Made me feel less guilty for thinking about her.

I got in a run before dark. Extra-long. Quiet. Reflective. Just me and my demons. Ran through south Brookline, over toward Putterham, getting my legs – and my wind – back. So much of the time here I walked around in a stupor, mesmerized by nice houses nice people nice streets. People mock Los Angeles as one big suburb, and on a superficial level it's true. Strip malls. Sprawl. In a deeper sense, though, it's not. Because Los Angeles is hungry.

The allure of punk fashion and anarchy in the suburbs was obvious – a way to blast past monotony into something that felt vital. Sure, I thought. Like beating a dog to death.

Four miles later, I landed huffing at the Daily Grind. Parked at a window table with a steaming mug served up by my favorite Goth queen. Outside, people hurried along the sidewalk to places they were needed. Wanted. I grabbed the *Globe* and re-read the morning's stale news. The latest sport in town seemed to be tagging SUVs; spray painting the behemoths with environmental messages. The *Globe* reported on a spate of incidents in the area.

Goth girl was looking my way. Okay, maybe looking at the window, but caught my eye, then looked away. I chose to think I intrigued her.

In other news, buried in the Metro section, a brief item: police had unearthed a clue in the Tillman robbery. A black Lexus driving through the neighborhood early that afternoon. That was it. No update on the kid.

Time for some sport. I took my half-full mug to the counter.

Goth girl looked at my ear. "Hey."

"How you doing?"

A sardonic grin. She was perched on a stool. Had a book open. She looked out the window.

"You go to school around here?"

Nothing. I perused the sticker-adorned counter. Mock-graffiti, *The end is extremely fucking nigh*, from that zombie movie. A small corkboard of community postings. Nanny wanted. Futon for sale.

She looked up, vaguely. "You want a refill?"

"Yeah." Human interaction. It counted. "That'd be great."

She glared when she saw coffee in the mug, but dutifully filled it and set it on the counter with a fake grin.

"Thanks." Exaggerated. I stuck my hand out. "By the way," I said. "I'm Evan." It came out. I had no idea why.

Lin and I did have dinner. Went to Revere Beach, to Kelly's, for clam rolls. "All my years in Boston," she said. "I've never been here."

"Me either."

We carried our food, tucked into those cardboard trays, across the street to the sand. Behind us, a run of new housing construction. A blue-collar town's effort to go upscale.

"I'd expected broken-down arcades, abandoned souvenir shops," I said. "Maybe some decrepit carnival rides. Fewer condos. Didn't they used to have an amusement park?"

"That was Paragon. At Nantasket."

We staked out a bench. Sat side by side facing the water. Sun setting behind us and a stretch of beach to ourselves.

Lin picked her clams out of the roll. "Sounds stupid but here it is. I felt like the Mom the other night." She licked her fingers. "I don't want to feel like you're my son's friend and not mine."

"I get that." A twinge of guilt. "I can be both."

"He sees you. I don't." She held up a hand. "I know. Not your fault."

We ate clams. Soft waves of an ebb tide.

"It's hard parenting a teen. Everything you do is wrong. And it's all natural and normal, but still, it sucks sometimes."

"Like lately?"

She chewed and swallowed. "He's in brooding mode," she said. "And mad at me for *abandoning my activist values*."

Good food. Salt breeze. A car passed behind us.

"He's quite a kid." I wiped grease on my shorts. "Reminds me of you." She'd always been committed. Clubs and organizations in high school and college. Peace Corps after. It was no great surprise when she'd told me she wanted to have a child on her own. And Bo was so much her son. Weaned on rallies and demonstrations. Lin's first doctoring was in Central America, a clinic in El Salvador when Bo was little. "But it's different, too," I said. "More grounded."

A group of kids passed behind us, laughing. One of them walked the curb like a balance beam.

"It's a different generation. A different time." She ate fries from a paper cup. "They're less innocent. For better and for worse."

"You worry about him?"

"Of course. He's got a good head, though." She watched the water. "We've talked a lot about the privilege of having choices. In Central America those years, I thought seriously about staying, making that struggle my own."

A breeze carried the briny scent of seaweed.

"But I wanted Bo to have the same opportunities I'd had. I left because I could. Other families couldn't. In a way, I chose comfort and convenience, and have ever since."

"That sounds like Bo talking."

A dimple. "He's not wrong. But it's not simple, either. Long-term thinking is inherently conservative. Teens are attractive – and scary – because they have no concept of ramifications."

I waited for more. It didn't come.

"Enough," she said. "How're you doing?"

"My ex-wife keeps asking that." I sipped coffee. "Not great, I guess."

"Your dad?"

"Partly." I told her about the recent developments, and she echoed concern about Alzheimer's. *Fuck me.*

"So it's only partly your dad."

Bench slats poked at my ass. "It's the whole thing, being back here."

"What's next for you?"

"I hate that question. I wish I knew. I'd like to not just fill time. I'd like to think there's more for me than that."

"Give yourself space." She punched my knee. "I have faith in you."

A band of purple-pink spread on the horizon. I'd had space. Time. Too much of both. I finished my clam roll. Watched the ocean while Lin finished hers.

"You and Teresa still close – all things considered?"

"We're good as friends." The waves barely audible. "It was nuts. I helped create it all, then I couldn't let go of it." After the magazine failed, after I'd met Terry and we'd fallen in love and married, I became her manager. It seemed like a good idea to both of us. I had just come off a tough go on an idealistic gig and was happy to invest myself in someone else's dreams. But then Terry became what we both believed in. Even though we stuck with it for a few pretty good years while her career took off, it eventually killed us: she gained confidence, I lost it. The end.

"I wish for a minute you could see yourself the way others see you," Lin said.

I started a quip, but she cut me off.

61

"No sarcasm," she said. "You'd be surprised."

We dumped our trash in a rusted metal barrel and walked the beach. Arms around each other's shoulders. Felt good. Lin stumbled in the sand, leaned into me. Caught my eye and smiled. I missed her. Missed closeness. I lowered my arm around her waist. My fingers crept up along her side, cupped her rib.

She pulled away. "What are you doing?"

"What?"

I was getting her parental stare, the scolding look she'd used since we were kids.

"We're having a moment."

"We *were*. Until you tried to cop a feel."

I laughed. Forced. "Gimme a break."

She crossed her arms, stopped herself from saying something. A wave broke, trickled toward us. She walked on, a little apart. "I understand lonely, Nick."

I groaned. "Bite me, Lin."

"Translation?"

"Don't be patronizing."

"Didn't think I was." We'd veered toward the packed sand near the water's edge.

I chewed my lip. Old frustrations rising. *Fuck it, why do this.* "So what if it was there. A little. Would that be so terrible?"

"Yes." The vehemence in her voice stung. "*By the way, Bo, I slept with your friend.*"

Our feet followed the tide line. "I was your friend first." I didn't want to sleep with Lin. "Okay," I said. "Maybe a little lonely." I grabbed her shoulder. "A little."

"Knew it."

I shook my head. "You are not, always, a hundred percent right."

"No? Name one time."

Playful, but still.

She turned to face me. "*Kidding*. Geez."

We walked. I let it go. Plenty of beach before us. She grabbed my hand, a sibling move. I went with it.

"I know people here," she said. "Lovely, interesting women."

Beside us, the Atlantic Ocean slowly receded.

"Next topic."

We walked the beach. Goofing around. Connected. Almost intimate.

Still and all, I woke up alone the next morning. Clawed my way out of a sagging sofabed and stretched my sore back. Ate a power breakfast of plain yogurt, bananas and honey. Opened the *Globe* to see who the day's strike coverage favored (sentiment leaned toward the janitors) and whether the governor had squirmed away from a definitive statement (he was traveling, unavailable for comment). Dreamed of a good night's sleep on a real bed.

A headline below the fold caught my eye:

Coffee Shops Vandalized; Employee Injured

In a series of vandalism acts police agree are connected, three Berkley's coffee shops in Boston's Western suburbs were damaged yesterday in late-night attacks.

A 24-year-old Waltham man was in the process of closing the Moody Street shop when a brick came through the store's plate glass window.

I thought of Bo and his elusive distinction: violence against property, not people.

I thought of futons, and how they weren't expensive – especially if you bought one used – and how my father wouldn't be reclaiming his house anytime soon, and how little he would care.

My phone rang. A bit of a shock, but I managed to answer.

"Nick Young? Andrew Sarkis from Pollard returning your call." Cold.

Right. Strike. Cleaning company. Wake up. "Thanks for getting back."

"What did you want?" His voice had the icy professionalism that often threw me.

"Uh, I'm probably doing a piece on the strike for *BusinessForward*..." What *did* I want? Really just to announce myself. Toss a couple softball questions to establish a context. But I was blank.

"Yes..." Waiting for me to get to it.

"So I'll be checking in from time to time. Just wanted to touch base. Let you know."

My stupidity hung in the air between us. "I'm not familiar with your work. Do you cover labor issues?"

Fuck. "Not exactly."

"Are you their Boston guy?"

I shook my head. "No." What was I doing. Yes, he was a dick. But I'd been out of this game forever, and I expected to sail back in on a whim?

"What expertise *do* you bring to this, Mr. Young?"

It was a fair – if bitchy – question. I had no answer.

5

"Dad, we need to get you a roommate."

"No. Fuck that. No."

I'd spent the morning finally tallying bills. Traced the source of each contradictory or confusing number until it made some kind of sense. Whittled the mystery pile down and came up with a total estimate that made me nauseated.

"Dad, –"

"Listen to some geezer whine and complain all day." His face was all lines – under his eyes, around his mouth, across his brow. "No thanks. This place is bad enough as it is."

Assuming I was right about insurance payments and duplicate charges, my father owed $11,780 to various hospitals and physicians. If I wasn't right about the other bills, it could be as much as $16,000. And that didn't count Brentwood. After I finished hyperventilating, I decided it was time to look into the possibility of a roommate for Thomas. Found out from Nurse Joan we could save eight hundred a month if he bunked with someone. *Of course,* Joan reminded me, *he'd have to agree to it.*

"It's not about companionship, Dad. It's about money. You can't afford this."

"*No.*" That small mouth, set.

My back hurt. I wasn't in the mood. "We need to talk. You can't just ignore it. It's this place. It's the hospital. It's adding up. A roommate's a good step."

"No, Paul. I won't do it."

Great. Thomas unmoored. Stark sunlight pierced the blinds. I squinted against it. "How convenient."

"What."

I stared my father down. Shame him into coming clean if he was dodging. I looked into his eyes. The archaeological ruin of his mouth. I could read nothing. And what if he was yanking my chain. Orneriness was something I'd inherited from Thomas, and he was the master. I could push this and fuel his resolve to resist. Or I could regroup and come back at it.

"When did you get here?" His eyes distant. His voice soft. The fucker.

I had no strategy. No financial acumen. No meaningful relationship with the accused. *What expertise* do *you bring to this, Mr. Young?* Whatever.

Somewhere a clock ticked and there were people to whom the minutes mattered.

"You remember your grandfather?"

I didn't want to think about my grandfather. I wanted to think about futons, one in particular. With an eight-inch coil mattress I was eager to meet. I'd turned my self-loathing over

Andrew-fucking-Sarkis into a long-term promise of payback in print and a short-term promise of pain-free sleep. I rode vengeance energy to Craig's List, where I found – and bought – a fancy futon. In a couple hours, Bo and his pal Adam and a friend of theirs were meeting me at the house to ditch the sofabed. But first.

"Hey," my father said. Sharp, not soft. His ears were huge. Had they always been big, or were they the one part of him not shrinking? "Do you remember your grandfather?"

"Not really," I confessed. "Not much." I wanted to sleep and wake up someone else.

"He was a fighter."

I'd known Stan only as an addled fossil his last few years. I knew he'd worked as a railroad blacksmith. I had a dim memory of him in a recliner, plaid blanket on his lap, tea mug beside him, saying he'd once been a boxer.

"I guess I knew that," I said. Time would pass. This would end.

"Bare knuckles," Thomas said.

I looked at him, impressed. "No shit?"

"No shit," he said. "Tough son of a bitch."

"Must have been." Even as an old man, body crumpling into papier maché, you could see the power in Stan's hands. Feel it in the way his feet pounded the floor to the bleat of his beloved bagpipes. A honed hardness at his core. *That* I remembered.

"I saw the old man once a week. He'd come home Saturday morning and be gone Sunday afternoon." I vaguely remembered some story about how Stan had worked out of Western Mass.

"I remember him shaving, seemed like before supper, on

Saturdays. I'd sit in the hall, outside the doorway, and watch. He'd talk to me."

"What would he talk about?"

"The boxing." His x, like his s's, hissed. He told me how Stan had fought, sponsored by the railroad, in a clandestine but not illegal bare knuckles association made up of laborers in groups and clubs across the state. The fights had no limit on rounds. They went until one man or the other went down and didn't come up.

"Twenty rounds was typical," he said. His face pink. "I think twenty-nine was the most. He broke a man's jaw more than once. They fought hard, brutal. He and the humpback porter." That phrase registered. Snippets of old anecdotes, half-heard and dismissed.

"But Dad –"

"I know. You think what you want. They beat each other purple. Knocked out teeth. What both of them wanted most was to end it and get paid. But they were both too stubborn. Too proud."

"Humpback porter, huh?"

"That's what they called him. Club fighter for the gym."

"Which gym?"

"Over by North Station. I don't know."

"Did Stan win? Was he good?"

His voice grew impatient. Urgent. "He was a good fighter." The faster he spoke, the harder he was to understand. "But listen what I'm telling you. He'd be in there, shaving, a straight razor, telling boxing stories, his whatzit, his Adam's apple, bobbing up and down, with the razor and the words. I'd lose half the story thinking he was gonna cut his neck open."

I was hearing my father's voice, seeing my grandfather; the casual bulk of Stan's arm working his razor. I pictured my elderly father, enormous ears and unruly hair, sitting outside the bathroom door of a Watertown flat, me beside him, sausages frying in the kitchen. The old man's face in the bathroom mirror, half-slathered in shaving cream, the menthol smell drifting out to Dad and I in the hallway. The generations together. The casual camaraderie of knowing and being known.

I was dimly aware of my father's voice. "What?"

"No roommates, Nick."

On the way back to the house I played out the responses a tougher Nick would have made. *Where you going to get eleven thousand dollars – a yard sale?* And: *You don't want a roommate. I don't want to be in Boston. Here we are. What now?* Someone else always defining the terms of interaction. The allowable possibilities. Score that round for Thomas.

I walked in to find the den polluted with sunlight. Bo, Adam, and a Hispanic guy about my age stood in the midst of it.

"Who opened the curtains?" We were all reflected on the dusty TV screen.

"I did," Adam said. "Couldn't see shit."

The sofabed had already been relocated to the middle of the room. The three of them stood tentatively around it.

"There were reasons for that," I said.

Bo stepped forward. "Hey, Nick. This is Eduardo."

He nodded hi. A janitor and union rep the boys knew, Eduardo had a pickup truck and a perpetual weariness to his square-jawed face. According to Bo, he had a wife and three kids in Dorchester, and at least as many jobs.

"*Hola.*" I shook his offered hand. "*Gracias* for coming."

The carpet smelled musty. Daylight did nothing for its looks.

Adam said something to Eduardo in Spanish. I didn't catch it. Struck by things I mostly managed to ignore in the enforced dusk. A clock on the mantel, all ornate veneer and filigreed plastic. Dingy threadbare curtains, once white. Age veins in the naugahyde of my father's easy chair. Did I really want to make a claim on this space? Hell, no. I did want a better night's sleep.

Bo rescued me. "Anyway, Nick. We've got it scoped out."

Adam's eyes were on me. Eduardo's were on the couch.

Focus. "Cool. Tell me."

Adam laid out the plan: we'd set the sofa on end to make the turn through the doorway to the hall. Adam had a small, powerful body. Musculature evident through a gray t-shirt.

"Sounds good," I said. "Let's do it."

We flanked the brown-tweed beast, one man to a corner. I lost my grip on our first try.

"*Pesado,*" Eduardo said. He smiled. "Made from brick?"

"Steel and stone," I said. I grinned. Felt dumb for not knowing some Spanish.

We settled ourselves under the frame and eased it through. Bo and Adam led. Eduardo had the heavier back end. I grabbed front and middle, trying to share the burden.

"*Su padre,*" Eduardo said. "*Él es muerto?*"

I shook my head. "He's old. *Viejo?* Sick. Nursing home." *And he has no idea we're redecorating his house.* Fuck that. I was setting

Thomas up, too. If he ever came home, he'd have his chair and a place to sleep without going upstairs.

With the sofa on end, we managed to wiggle it through the hall. The front door was easy, as was the pickup. Eduardo and Adam anchored the behemoth in the truck bed.

Bo and I on the sidewalk. A perfect afternoon. Bright sun, cool breeze. He wore a Los Lobos t-shirt I'd given him.

"Any word from Marcela?"

Bo's eyes narrowed. "No."

Adam wiped at his forehead. "You're not still worried?"

Bo turned away from him. "Adam says she's restless. It's who she is."

I watched Eduardo winch a mover's strap around the sofabed. "That true, Adam? Is Marcela the restless type?"

Adam shrugged. "She's not the win-back type."

"He's got zero credibility," Bo said. "Adam's an ex, too."

"We're a club," Adam said. "Monthly meetings and shit."

I caught a smile on Eduardo's face. I shared it, but I also understood how such a club would exist. There was the obvious, but I'd checked out the true cost economics blog where she had a few posts. Read one – a primer. I hadn't expected much. But it was reasoned and articulate as well as ardent. *The price of products is based on cost, right? Well, take any product you can think of – any product, anywhere. It's underpriced. Why? Because the environmental costs – the energy it takes to produce, distribute, and dispose of it – aren't taken into account. True cost economics simply says we must include those costs. It says the price of every product should reflect the ecological truth.* And on.

Very practical – consume what you want, as long as you truly pay for it.

Eduardo finished securing the sofabed. I had to pop inside to pee. Stopped in the den on my way out. Daylight and open space had exposed its shoddiness. Made me angry to think what I'd been living with. What I'd allowed myself to live with. The physical evidence of how far I'd sunk.

Bo and Eduardo came looking for me.

"Good to go?" Bo asked.

"Humor me," I said. "Five minutes."

"What?"

I ripped up one corner of the carpet. Bo laughed.

"Shut up and rip."

He shook his head. "You wanna think this through?"

"Absolutely not." I pushed aside second thoughts and pulled. The carpet came up easily.

Eduardo smiled and started on the opposite corner.

Bo shot me his skeptical look. "So you bought a bed."

"Futon." I walked the room's length with carpet edge in my hands. The gratifying pop of dislodged tacks. "Eight-inch coils. Ergonomic."

Bo and Eduardo lifted furniture while I scooched rug out from under it.

"I don't think a futon can be ergonomic."

"This one is."

We had the relic folded and stood, haloed in dust, a salvageable wood floor under our feet, by the time Adam came to see what was up.

"We ready?" Adam said. "Eduardo's working this in between other jobs."

"Fuck. I'm sorry," I said.

Eduardo shrugged.

"Where to?" Bo hoisted the carpet.

"Trash."

Eduardo helped, and the two of them wrestled the bundle out the back door.

Adam stood arms folded, silently judging me. *Yeah, I get it. Eduardo's working a fourth job to help make room for my brand new bed.* Nothing to do but go with it.

The room felt almost livable. Almost. I walked to the windows and ripped down the curtains. The tin rods came with them. I thrust the pile at Adam and headed for the door. On my way out, I grabbed the plastic clock. I heard Bo laughing behind me.

"Cheap stuff is bad enough," I called back. "Cheap stuff that pretends elegance is unforgivable." I tucked the clock under my arm and left without another look.

We got the sofabed to a thrift store and I paid my helpers in cash. The boys were easy. Twenty bucks each. I felt bad giving only that to Eduardo. Felt awkward giving him more.

"*Cuando*? How much do you charge?"

"*Viente. Iguales que los otros.*"

We shook hands. I pushed an extra twenty on him. "*Para el...*" I didn't know the word. "For the truck."

Eduardo had to go, but the boys let me buy them dinner. Adam drove, a nice change for me. He had a lack of inhibition that I liked. Over Thai food in Brookline, we got talking about slow-burn sit-ups

– a subject on which Adam was something of an authority – and when I had difficulty envisioning the technique Adam described, he dropped to the restaurant floor and demonstrated. No self-consciousness.

After, I tried to convince them to take in a summer flick – a wholesome sci-fi action tale of extraterrestrials who become refugees in South Africa – but they had plans. They drove me home. I stretched my legs as best I could on the back seat. Bo's backpack on the floor below me, a Seattle10 button pinned to it. The boys played angry music loud up front.

Somewhere deep in a pocket, my phone rang. "Hey. Turn that down a sec." I dug the phone out. "Yeah."

"Nick? Chris Tillman, returning a call." I sat up. Slapped the headrest and gestured for Bo to *really* turn the music down. He did. "I hope it's not too late."

"Not at all, Chris. I appreciate the callback. I'm hoping we can sit down. I'd like to get your take on the strike, and the whole climate right now. For the piece I'm doing. Deeper than sound bites."

He chuckled. "Time's tight. But if you can be flexible..."

"Understood. Anything you can do."

We worked out a time. I stole a pen from Bo's backpack, wrote the info on my hand, and thanked him again for the call.

"What was that?" from Bo.

"That was Chris Tillman."

"*Tillman?*"

"Interview, for the article."

"Why you talking to that prick?"

"Know him, do you?"

"You hear him on the news? *Nobody's going to tell us how to run our company.*" Bo's voice dripped with self-righteousness. "Think he makes more than eight bucks an hour? Think he has health benefits?"

Adam watched the road. His head moved to the music.

"He's a guy trying to do a job," I said. "I feel for him. Kid in the hospital." We sat at a light in Brookline Village.

Bo wasn't done. "Nobody forced him to become the Man."

I tugged at my jeans to keep them from bunching at the crotch.

"You part of this too, Adam?"

"Which this?"

"Young Anarchists' Club. Disaffected Youth League."

I caught a smirk in the rearview.

"So I'm surrounded," I said.

"Guess so," said Adam. He fumbled with his iPod, scrolling for something, then switched the music. "Here you go, Nick. You might even know this one."

I did. Rage Against the Machine's *Battle of Los Angeles*. "Bless you, lad."

Bo drummed on the dashboard. "Anyway, we'll see pretty soon how Tillman handles the heat."

"Meaning?"

"Endicott's been targeted. There's going to be actions."

"What kind of actions?"

"*Actions*," Bo said. "I know it's a difficult concept."

"What?" I said. "Firebombed buildings? A plague of frogs?"

"Ooh," Adam said. "Frogs are a good idea."

"And then," Bo said, "a massive radioactive waste spill, 'cause you know we don't give a shit about the planet."

"Okay, I get the idea." We passed a playground. A woman walking a greyhound. "Just be careful."

"I'm not stupid, Nick. And I'm not ten." Bo put a foot on the dashboard.

I looked at houses and rode the groove of "Calm Like a Bomb," Rage's best single.

Adam's eyes found me in the rearview. "So are you one of those *objective* journalists who hides his viewpoint?"

"I don't trust corporate capitalism. What I don't know is whether unabashed greed is inevitable, or whether we've got some diseased offshoot fed by bad policy."

Adam laughed. "And you write for a *business* magazine?"

"What's unabashed?" Bo asked.

"It means shameless."

"Why didn't you just say shameless?"

"You know there are smart people inside corporations who share a lot of your values."

"Yeah, and they can't change anything," Bo said. "It's rotted from the core, Nick. It's gotta come down."

"You're seventeen. How can you know that?"

"How can you *not* know it?"

It felt past my bedtime. "I don't trust certainty," I said. "Too much ugly shit happens in its name."

My jeans bunched. I felt cramped.

"Extremism isn't the crime, Nick. Standing around while people get shit on, that's the crime."

"Sounds nice, but it's not that simple."

"It *is* simple. You just gotta choose which side you're on."

I was too tired to debate. I thought about my upcoming interview with Tillman. I wanted him for context as much as anything. The strike had already commanded center stage in town. The janitors were not going away. Contrary to what Tillman and other corporate leaders predicted, crowds at the daily rally had only grown. The union decided, based on the strong show of support, to extend picket lines to FirstBoston and Arch Street. BAFA's phone campaign generated more than five thousand calls, and you could tell from the set faces of corporate spokesmen on TV sound bites they knew they were in a fight. Me, I overcame my Andrew Sarkis nightmare and had a short, professional interview with Sam Abigail, who provided me with all the data I could ever want on union membership, contract demands, and the overarching righteousness of the cause.

We bent around the back side of Jamaica Pond. Woods on one side. The water and a line of parked cars on the other. Including a big SUV with its back end sticking into the street.

Adam flashed his high beams like lasers. "Asshole." He eased his foot off the accelerator. He and Bo shared a look.

"Art project?"

"Do it."

Adam pulled over. They hopped out, rummaged in the trunk. I was too groggy to speculate until they emerged with spray paint. The metallic clack as they shook the cans. Laughter.

I hauled myself out of the car. "Guys," I said.

Adam walked around front. Bo in back. The vehicle, a Highlander, shone glossy black under the street lamp.

The hiss of sprayed paint.

"Guys," I said. "What the fuck."

They worked quietly. Quickly. The air was still. No breeze.

I had a sour taste in my mouth. Principle. Squeamishness. A fear of getting caught. I looked for witnesses. Listened for cars. "Bo. Knock it off. This is just mean."

On the hood, "go hybrid" emerged in white. "Downsize" in green on the rear windshield. It was over faster than a ska tune; we were in the car and gone. Silent. I'm sure my displeasure was palpable. Up front, they listened to Rage rage.

Finally, Bo. "Jesus, Nick. Get over yourself."

"What the fuck, Bo? What was that?"

He caught Adam's eye. Smug grins. Adrenaline.

"Homework," Bo said. "Art project."

I felt middle-aged. Tired. "Great," I said. "Funny."

We missed the light at Perkins Street. Bo turned toward the back seat. "Fuck you, Nick. I'm *doing* something. What are you doing?"

A fair question. We sat in the glow of the dash lights.

"How's it any different from the shit you used to pull?" Bo tapped his forehead. "Oh, right. It *is* different. We're changing the world."

I had nothing. Just my displeasure, hanging in the air. Ineffectual. But not wrong.

"No," Chris Tillman was saying to me, "you know what this is. It's a witch hunt. Check that. It's a distortion of reality. An attempt to polarize positions, to reduce a complex situation to two simple sides, define one as evil, and rally the public against it."

We sat in Tillman's corner office on the 32nd floor of the Endicott building. We sat in adjoining leather armchairs turned at ninety-degrees, forming half of a square. We sat in the fading light of late afternoon because I wouldn't cross the picket line. A tape recorder hummed quietly on the table between us. A fancy glass of sparkling water fizzed next to it.

"So you think BAFA's out of line," I prompted.

"I think BAFA's way out of line." Tillman was dressed casually – rust-colored oxford, gray slacks, tassel loafers. Dark curls starting to go gray. I had struggled to find a clean shirt. Unwrinkled khakis. Tillman's dark eyes always sought contact. You felt you had his complete attention. I liked that.

"Don't get me wrong. BAFA has done some great work in the city. Hell, my church is active. I've been active." He leaned toward me. "And will be again. But look at the record. BAFA came in and galvanized support around two issues. Affordable housing and public education. Problems that resonate throughout the city. They've – we've – worked hard to develop practical plans, to approach city and state authorities with specific requests. Hold feet to the fire for real answers. They've gotten commitments that way. They've been able to hold officials accountable and get things done."

Outside, down on Atlantic Avenue, construction crews worked on Big Dig repairs. Earth movers groaned distant, like crickets. Commuters crossed toward South Station in golden light.

"But isn't this just another case of BAFA holding feet to the fire? It's just that this time it's your feet."

"No," Tillman said, leaning forward again. Enthusiastic, not angry. "A couple of important differences. Here they have taken sides in a private dispute between two parties, then magnified that into a cause."

"Okay, wait." Felt good to have my shit together. I could almost believe Tillman and I were peers having a real conversation. "I see your point. But they could argue – and have – that this dispute *is* centered on issues they're committed to. That part of what makes housing affordable is the ability to earn a living wage. That another issue they've had on the back burner is health care, health benefits."

"You want to address wage issues," he said, "great. You want to talk health insurance. Fine. We're at the table with you. On the streets." His teeth were perfect. "But look at the issue as a whole. The city. The metropolitan area. And look for the most effective ways to address it. You don't latch onto one isolated incident and make it the straw man for issues you want to address."

I started to speak, but he held me off with a hand.

"Especially," he said, "*especially* when you haven't fully studied those issues. That," he stabbed the air with his finger, "is what fries my ass." Nothing in his face or his manner showed agitation. "I believe in BAFA. I support them with my time, my money. But this smacks of a cheap publicity grab."

I sat with that. The tape recorder hummed. While I didn't agree with everything Tillman said, I thought he was a reasonable guy. He could be the father of any of Bo's friends. He could be Bo's father.

"Okay," I said. "But you could also argue that Endicott, because of your size, your power in the area economy, that whatever you're involved in becomes a public issue, will have an area-wide impact." Now it was Tillman eager to jump in, but I held him off. "That just

80

by virtue of your position, you bear added responsibility. You set a tone."

He wagged his head back and forth. Nearly out of his seat. "Don't even start with the whole corporate citizenship thing. I'm furious with the mayor." He took a breath. Slowed down. "It's insulting. The Endicott Foundation pours tens of millions of dollars into the community each year." He reinforced each point with his right hand, thumb and forefinger held together. "We are the primary source of funding for a dozen nonprofits. I personally sit on five boards. Marcus Gregory more than half a dozen. Apart from being a major arts patron on his own. So I won't even dignify the corporate citizenship argument."

A stripe of pink and orange banded the sky.

"I understand. I'm not disputing. I'm devil's advocate."

"Go ahead," he said. Still agitated, but a grin.

"Come at it another way. What if I argue that any corporation's first duty – before the foundations, before the nonprofits – is to treat workers fairly. Be responsible to the community it serves. Pay a living wage. Provide health benefits."

He leaned back in his chair, then came forward again. "A corporation's – any corporation's – first responsibility is to be profitable. Period. We don't turn a profit, we don't grow, we don't stay in business. No wages. No benefits. For anyone."

"Hard to see how a dollar an hour more for a few thousand janitors is going to tip Endicott into the red."

"That's simplistic," Tillman said. The tips of his ears red. "Nothing happens in a vacuum. Everything takes place in a context. One factor among many."

A flurry of car horns sounded a hundred miles below. Tillman – and even more so his boss, Marcus Gregory – helped engineer the life of the city, impacting thousands from his corner office. I marveled at anyone who could presume knowledge about what was best for the many. It took confidence and a certain ruthlessness. My turn. "I want to bring this back a little. Let's talk about what's at issue in this strike. How those issues reflect on the state of labor relations. How this might be a paradigm –"

He sliced the air with his hand. "This isn't a paradigm for anything. You know what this is? A labor dispute. Anyone who wants to turn this into anything else, I'll fight them tooth and nail. The union wants something we can't give. In a perfect world, we'd be able to accommodate. But we don't live in a perfect world." He waited a beat. "My job is to do what's best for Endicott. Now there are significant areas of overlap to what is best for Boston and what is best for our employees, but in the end, we're accountable to our shareholders."

"Even if that means replacing the janitors?" Dusk began to settle on the city. I was wearing out my welcome.

He sighed. Rested his chin on folded hands. "Ultimately, yes. That's not our first choice. But this is business, Nick. And the point of business is to make profit."

I turned off the tape recorder. I envied him the conviction of his philosophy.

"Got what you need?"

"I think so." I sipped at the sparkling water I'd neglected. "I appreciate this. I know it's a brutal time for you. Your son. I don't know how you do it."

He swallowed emotion. Maintained eye contact. "You have children?"

"I don't."

He nodded. "I work hard to maintain a separation between my personal and professional life." He shrugged. "Right now, that's the only way I can function."

"My thoughts are with him. And your family."

"Thanks."

He stood up. I followed suit.

"Despite where your sympathies lie," he said, "I'm not giving up on you."

"You've got me wrong. I've got no agenda here."

"All due respect, Nick. That's bullshit."

I had a sort of half-grin. "Nah. Just old-school."

"Old school died, and for good reason. It was disingenuous." His smile was genuine. "But that's an argument for another time." We shook hands. "It's good meeting you. And good luck with the piece. Let me know how I can help."

I rode the elevator down alone. The buzz of commerce quieted for the day. I had voices in my head. Bo and Tillman. Each a passionate advocate for his perspective. I could see truth in both, and wanted to connect them – be a bridge – but couldn't see how. Or how it would matter. Instead I walked the streets – Fort Point, the ladder district – making masochistic comparisons in my head. Tillman and I were the same age. I knew something of what he had. What did I have? Early potential. A high-life marriage, then a black hole.

Chinatown. Downtown Crossing. Dusk turned to dark. My

legs – and mind – kept churning. Into the lost years. Truth is, I don't really know what I did after my divorce. Drive to the beach. Run. Late breakfast. Read the paper. Stare at the ocean. By then it would be three or four o'clock. Hit the day's last matinee. I drove a lot. Explored the state. That was the first year of five that vanished. It wasn't a good time.

Back through the financial district, where lights still burned on most floors, the unending churn of commerce. I crossed Atlantic and had a vodka tonic in the courtyard at the Harbor Hotel, where a sea breeze cooled the evening and a cover band played polite blues. Five years. Even I couldn't believe it.

In addition to the broken heart, there was the realization I'd pissed away a promising newspaper career, then failed at the two things I'd tried after: marriage and the magazine. What would I do? Nothing, apparently. Teresa made sure I had a golden parachute – the price tag for her freedom from guilt – and I was proud enough to limit myself to a small stipend, but not proud enough to turn it down. On some level, I believed I'd earned it. I'd played some role in her success. Anyway, I'd been more or less living off that ever since.

I needed a serious drink. In a serious bar.

I found both. A small, dark place on Tremont. Watched three innings of the Sox (down 4-1 in Seattle) before I dialed the ex-wife. "Hey."

"Ooh, you're in a mood."

"Tell me a story, Teresa."

"Good news, I think. I got the part. The old broad. But it's a part, right? That's what I'm telling myself. Listen, I'm meeting a friend for a movie. Right now. We'll talk later." A beat. "Be kind to you."

I followed her advice and bought myself doubles from that point on. The bar closed shortly after the Sox lost out west in extra innings, and I left under my own power, which surprised the bartender. Even walked back to Kenmore, where I'd left my car before the Tillman meeting. But I was in no shape to drive, and besides, I was tired. Closed my eyes for a minute and woke when a bus buzzed past and shook the Dart. The sun was up. That couldn't be good. That would mean I'd slept in my car on Brookline Avenue.

I rubbed my face. I needed to pull my shit together. Start with a diner breakfast. I searched my pockets for cash. Nothing. I had an unbreakable personal rule about cash at diners, so I walked in almost competent fashion two blocks to Kenmore and an ATM. Staggered into the bank lobby, where I couldn't get the machine to take my card. Five tries, I couldn't get it in the slot. Fine. Found another bank with a kinder machine, and in 20 minutes I was eating crisp bacon, scrambled eggs and toast, and doing my best to put a bad night behind me. Chris who?

Half an hour later I staggered into the house that wasn't home, blinded by the brightness the now-curtainless windows let in. That's okay. I had an eight-inch elite coil futon mattress, a supply of anti-hangover vitamin water in the fridge, and two messages on Thomas's ancient answering machine. 7:09 AM. That meant I was also in time for the morning news shows, with perky anchors who helped good citizens prepare for the work day.

I scraped my foot on a stray carpet tack, grabbed a vitamin water, pressed the power button on the TV remote, and the play button on Thomas's machine. Dust motes still lingered in the air, toxic with memories.

85

Answering machine: Hi, this is Spencer Adams from Suffolk Mortgage. You may not realize that interest rates have dropped...

Erase.

On the TV, a bright-eyed anchor I didn't recognize was talking about anti-globalist activism. I could tell because the graphic behind his head read Anti-Globalist Activism. I paused the answering machine.

"Activists attacked twenty-seven bank branches in a well-coordinated action," Bright Eyes said. "ATM slots were glued shut and screens smashed." Ah. I felt relieved it hadn't been a problem with my motor skills. "A group called Seattle10 – named for the anniversary of the 1999 World Trade Organization protests – has claimed responsibility for what they called night banking." Good one. I could feel Bo gloating a mile away. Bright Eyes moved on to a warehouse fire in Lowell, and I hit play again on the answering machine.

Answering machine: This is Brianna from Newton-Wellesley Hospital.

Nick (sips vitamin water): Fuck.

Answering machine: Your account is past due.

Nick (shakes head, sips)

Answering machine: Please call us at your earliest convenience to discuss payment.

Nick (sips water): Fuck. Go away.

Erase.

My cell phone rang. Not registering the time, and thinking it was Terry, I jumped right in: "Congratulations, kiddo."

"Nick?"

"Bo?" That didn't make any sense, either. "What's up?"

The TV announced deals on new and certified pre-owned Toyotas and Hondas.

"I called Marcela last night," Bo said. "And get this."

The answering machine made its ending beep and reset.

"What are you doing up? Why are you calling so early?"

"Early track. Coach is punishing us. Listen, Nick. Her cell phone's disconnected."

"What do you mean?"

"Disconnected. You know, *the cellular number you have called is not in service at this time.*"

Uninvited, Marcela Pruett's gorgeous body danced into my mind. I needed more eggs. I scratched my head and tried to redirect. "So she switched phone numbers."

A few seconds of dead air. "This is not right."

"Bo, I can totally see her disconnecting. She's this completely hot –"

"What the fuck, Nick."

"Fine. She's an attractive young woman with – excuse me – more than one guy on her tail."

"Thanks for your support."

I shrugged. I wanted to bond with my futon. I wanted to tell him to get over Marcela. Leave her alone. To leave me alone. But I didn't.

"So I called her sister. The one she's supposedly traveling with."

I rubbed my forehead. I was too hung over for this. "And?"

"And she was *home.*"

"So they're back. Congratulations."

"But she wouldn't tell me anything."

I told myself it was fatigue, but the dancing Marcela in my mind gave me a rush. The delicious curve of her. That glorious clavicle. Reset. "There's nothing to tell, Bo. Truth hurts. Love's a bitch."

"You're not listening. You have to talk to the sister."

I was angry with him. I felt he was responsible for the Marcela in my mind. "No. Wrong. You have to run races. And I have to sleep."

Before I clicked the TV off, Bright Eyes got my attention one last time.

"In Newton, police are getting heat for the almost total absence of leads in the Tillman robbery."

Click. I would hope so. It's a robbery. In Newton. Isn't that why people live in Newton – so their houses don't get burglarized and their kids don't get assaulted?

I wasn't sure who I was asking, but no one answered.

6

"Last time I saw you," I told Larry Hines, "you were drunk and hanging off the top of a parking garage over the Mass Pike."

We sat four rows behind the Red Sox dugout. In the fifth inning, the Sox trailed Cleveland 3-0 and Tim Wakefield was about to walk his sixth batter.

I'd met Larry and Seth outside Fenway. We slapped backs and hands and joked about how great we all looked. Seth looked exactly as I'd remembered him, only bald. Round, energetic face, eyes that read into things. Thick eyebrows still sandy, not gray. You always had the feeling he was moving fast, even when he wasn't. Larry seemed smaller, healthier. Handsome. His mop of black hair now neatly trimmed. Slicked back.

"I can't explain that," Larry said. "I guess I did some growing up."

Right. Me, I was trying to keep my nether parts connected. I felt a certain queasiness on seeing my old friends; my stomach performed acrobatics in some twisted survival response to the question of what the fuck I was doing there. *Go, Nick. It'll be good for you. Spend time re-establishing adult relationships.*

Wakefield walked the guy. The Sox pitcher had been on the ropes from the start, but somehow he was still out there. If he could survive, so could I.

"Larry's in demand around the world," Seth said. "Who would have thought?"

Not I. Larry had careened so wildly through high school and college that even we, his degenerate friends, considered it a minor miracle he'd survived. He had figured out how to make better choices and parlay those choices into perceived value. I wondered how, but that wasn't the kind of thing you could ask.

Seth sat between Larry and I. Beyond Larry sat Chris Tillman. It was supposed to be AJ, but AJ bailed at the last minute. If only I'd known. Instead, there I was with two guys I'd known a lifetime ago and one who was at the center of the city's news. I couldn't fathom what Tillman was doing there, either – a night out with friends while his son lay critical in the hospital. Tillman arrived in the bottom of the third and spent the entire fourth inning on his phone. I spent it dreading the inevitable inquiries into my life and the awkward silence that would follow. My stomach flipped at the prospect. I could hear it gurgle. I'd managed to avoid the first wave of inquiry by painting myself the good samaritan son tending to Dad between projects. But it was only a matter of time before talk – *what happened to you, you had such potential* – cycled back to me.

We each negotiated a hot dog and a beer. I wondered briefly whether hot dogs were a wise idea under my digestive circumstances.

Wakefield got Ben Francisco to flail uselessly at a third strike, then fell behind the next hitter, 2 and 0.

"This is the guy who has a story," Larry said through a thin beer-foam mustache.

Excellent. A story.

Larry gestured at Seth. "Blows me away. Six months in traction. Doctors said he'd never walk again."

Wakefield lost the batter. Four pitches. None close.

Seth smiling and blushing at once. "I was lucky." Seth was a database guru. Created an enterprise application that Microsoft got behind. Right idea, right time. He sold that, got deep into the development of an Internet database tool. Huge. I had no idea what Larry referred to.

"Puts me to shame with all he does," Larry said. "In business. For the community."

Yes, it was only a matter of time before one of them revisited the what-have-you-been-up-to question. That didn't mean I couldn't encourage delays. It was one thing to be humiliated in front of people I'd once known. It was another to be exposed in front of a story source. At the end of the row, Tillman scanned email. I'd spent much of the day transcribing my interview with him. Still had his voice in my head.

"So tell me," I said. "I'm intrigued."

Wakefield got Ryan Garko on a grounder to first to end the inning. Seth set up the story: running his second company with a partner, on an annual R&R/planning trip.

"We were coming back from skiing," Seth said. "A great weekend in Waterville Valley, just Brian and I. No wives, no kids. Raced our asses off all day. Drank good wine. Plotted a new direction for the company."

Varitek led off for the Sox. Got the crowd hopeful when he drilled one down the line to left, but it hooked foul.

"We were stoked, and sleepy, and eager to get back to work."

Varitek singled to right.

"Maybe I was following the truck too closely, I don't know. I've asked myself a thousand times. Truck didn't signal, tried to exit. There was black ice."

Ellsbury grounded into a double play.

"I had dozed. Half a second. Then the back of that trailer was in my face and I hit the brake too hard and got nothing." Seth swallowed, took a breath. "I clipped the trailer. Sent us into a spin. The truck's brakes caught and mine didn't and I could see us going under him and I couldn't do a thing about it."

J.D. Drew hit a fly to deep center that got caught.

"Brian was dead when the ambulance got there. They got me out and to the hospital. Broken neck. Broken leg. Couple of ribs."

This wasn't just another peer success story. This was TV movie material. "I had no idea."

"Once I got back on my feet, I cashed out the company. Set up trusts for Brian's family. Took a year to get my shit together. Think about what I wanted to do. Waiting to see what would matter. Answer was nothing would, not in the same way."

A depth charge went off inside me. This I understood. *Say more, Please.* "So what happened? Did things get to matter in a different way?"

Larry shot me a look, but I wasn't being an asshole.

"I'm serious, Seth. What did you do with that?"

Seth looked puzzled by the question, as if it wasn't tied to the data points he'd presented. He shrugged. "I started another business. Looked for a useful way to apply my skills."

No.

"He poured himself into the community," Larry said. "Made meaning there."

Shut the fuck up, Larry.

Seth looked thoughtful. "That's not how it felt," he said.

There was more there and I didn't know how to get to it. Somehow I had finished my beer. Somehow Wakefield was back on the mound. I nodded encouragement at Seth. It didn't register. I watched whatever opening had been there sail away like smoke.

Tillman leaned toward us. "He hates to hear this, but he's an inspiration to me."

"What'd I tell you," Larry said.

"Guys," Seth said. And it was gone.

From the respectful silence that followed Seth's story, we drifted into a relaxing focus-on-the-game groove. I bought a round of beers. We sipped them while the Sox went down quietly and then Wakefield struck out the side. The lights, the grass. The slap of ball in glove. It was nice. It was empty.

During a Red Sox rally in the seventh, I got a text from Unitarian Paul. BAFA planned a demonstration to call attention to the strike. "Thursday afternoon," it said. "Traffic blockade in the Back Bay." Weird getting strike news with Tillman not ten feet away. "With Delfi and Pollard threatening scabs, we're counting on Thursday to shift the pressure. Hope to see you." I put away the phone and sipped my beer, feeling vaguely conspiratorial.

Two outs later, after taking a call that clearly annoyed him, Tillman made his exit. He apologized. Shook hands all around. Lingered a moment with me. I got a chuck on the shoulder, a meaningful glance, and a "we'll be talking." I guessed he now had the news I'd gotten earlier in the inning. He disappeared down the tunnel and I savored being recognized as a player, even if that recognition was misplaced.

It wasn't until the eighth – and another Red Sox rally – that Larry turned the talk back to me.

"What about you, Nick? What's your story?"

No stomach acrobatics. Hardly a flutter. The question was obligatory. Polite. With Tillman gone, it was almost easy. After I swallowed back my sarcastic first impulse – *well, the other night after I left Chris' office I went on a bender and slept in my car* – and made a mental note to harangue AJ for abandoning me, I flung out a few almost painless sentences about the demise of the magazine, and the rise and fall of Nick and Teresa. How I was madly in love, how she was this terrific actress who couldn't catch a break, and how I thought I could help.

There was an uncomfortable silence. Ortiz singled home a run for the Sox. Cleveland changed pitchers.

"What about newspapers?" Seth asked. "You ever think about going back? You were good." He leaned forward, elbows on knees. "I could never figure why you left."

I felt myself flush. "That's one I can't explain." Okay, could. But wouldn't. Add it to the list of things we'd never talk about.

The Sox scored five in the eighth, Wakefield went all the way, and the home team held on to win, 7-4. We promised to see each other again. All in all, the company of accomplished adults was a strain. I'd rather have been with Bo.

By the time I dragged myself off my futon at eleven the next morning, my industrious age-peers were well into their days, having impacted the world in new and no-doubt profound ways. By the time I ran, showered, dressed, and headed for Coolidge Corner, it was early afternoon. No matter. I was on my way to the Council on Aging with a shopping bag full of medical bills. It seemed like something an adult would do. My night with the captains of industry had inspired me. If they could conquer vast chunks of the planet, I could haul my ass over to learn what kind of ally I had, and what options there might be to address my father's mountain of debt. While the prospect held a certain terror, today the guilt of not acting was worse. So I persevered through road construction, trolled for parking, and toted the bag of bills across Harvard Street toward Green.

A glint of sunlight off a passing car drew my eyes ahead a block, where a young woman crossed to the sidewalk. I caught a glimpse of a face, long dark hair, long graceful neck. Two minutes, I told myself. I hustled along the sidewalk in her wake, feeling a warmth course through me that I chose not to dwell on. I had purpose: put to rest Bo's paranoid fears Marcela was dead or disappeared. I bumped a woman with two Trader Joe's bags and breathed an apology as I passed. Smelled cinnamon bread from Great Harvest two blocks away. *Great news, Bo – Marcela's in town. You* are *an unwanted ex-boyfriend.* At least he'd be able to stop worrying and begin his doomed campaign to win her back.

Just before she reached Beacon Street I threaded through my fellow pedestrians and moved up beside her. Across the street a Green Line train screeched to a stop. I gathered my slightly short breath and glanced over, all casual. She looked back. Took a moment before I had the presence of mind to look away. Not Marcela. Just a pretty college student minding her own business. I stood stupid while the light flashed Walk and the pedestrian herd crossed toward the T. I watched the young woman who wasn't Marcela stop at the near side of the T platform, westbound toward Cleveland Circle. Got bumped by people with somewhere to be. *Enough. Remember the captains of industry.* I marshaled my flagging resources and marched myself back across the street.

The Council on Aging was in a single-story brick building that also housed a Jewish Community Center. Two entrances, side by side. And the one I wanted was locked. I peered in the window. Empty. Tried the door again. Saw the hours stenciled on the glass: 9-2. Two? Who closes at two? I caught the eye of a woman in the JCC and shook my arms in a gesture that meant *what the fuck.* She shrugged back *what do you want me to do.* I stood stupid another minute, wondering what a captain of industry would do. But the answers were too many and too obvious, so I hung my head and left. I told myself it wasn't the worst outcome. Information was dangerous: if they had no answers I was screwed – left to my own meager devices; if they had answers, I'd be obliged to act on them.

I ditched the bag of bills in the Dart and got myself coffee and a bagel. Inspiration had faded to futility. I couldn't handle the thought of another lost day. Work wouldn't save me. Long cycles are a trademark of magazine journalism, and in my current situation,

I was waiting for events to unfold. I'd begged a favor from Brad Mighty, a veteran beat reporter I had history with, who opened his notebook to give me credible sources. I had callbacks coming. I had a traffic blockade to attend in two days. Until then, I could attend noon rallies to give myself something to do. I was sick with waiting.

On that discouraging note, I went to visit Thomas. Skulked past the hallway rogue's gallery: the Babbler, the Weeper, the Whiskered Woman. For a change, my father was both lucid and gracious. Yes, I should have talked finances, swayed him toward roommate-reality. No, I didn't do it. I took refuge in small talk. Regaled him with my trip to Fenway, fed him first-hand details of the Red Sox comeback. We compared notes on pitchers, and I indulged the illusion that I had a life, a father. It was an easy visit, and I let it be that. Told myself it would do him good. Maybe that was true, but I left feeling conflicted.

Some captain of industry.

What?

Captains of industry don't avoid problems, they confront them.

Yeah, well, captains of industry don't have to smell death in the hallway, or face the Weeper every day.

That's a cop-out.

Fuck you.

I needed a reset. An adult perspective that wouldn't trash me. I called Teresa, got voice mail. Same with Lin. Took a long shot and drove to Newton-Wellesley Hospital, planning to wander the halls until I ran into her. She couldn't turn down coffee with a needy friend.

The automatic doors at the main entrance spit visitors into an anonymous lobby. From there, you passed a row of billing cubicles so you couldn't forget what's really important. On my way past, I had an inspiration and circled back to a cubicle where a bored young woman sat sliding a mouse in front of a computer monitor. Her nameplate said Cynthia. The day held renewed opportunity. I could be a competent adult. I could make progress.

"Hi," I said. "I'd like to check on a past due account." Something changed in her face with the words past due, but I was going to overlook that. "The name is Thomas Young. I'd like a printout of the most recent balance."

She had the kind of job you wear sweaters to even in summer, because of the air conditioning and the fact you never move from your desk. "Is this your account?"

"My father's."

She shook her head. Her eyes flitted to the monitor. "I'm sorry. Do you have power of attorney?"

"Do I have what?"

Eyes on me, like I was stupid. "Are you legally responsible for his affairs?"

"Hell, no."

"We can't give out that information."

"I'm his son. I take care of his finances." A horrific thought, and close enough to true. "I've got a shopping bag of medical bills at home, many of them from this fine establishment. Then there are direct bills from specialists, anesthesiologists, and the like. There appear to be some duplicate charges and it's just hard to tell what's what. All I need you to do is look at the screen and tell me a number. If you don't want to say it out loud, you can write it down for me."

Cynthia's face pinched at my sarcasm. "I can't do that. Also, this sounds like a matter best taken up with a patient advocate. They can often work out payment plans. But you'd have to make an appointment."

"All I'm trying to do is find out how deep is the shit my father is in." My face felt hot. I wanted a fight. Wanted the pure physical release of hitting someone. Foist pain off on another. I settled for taking a verbal swing at Cynthia to try to feel better about myself. "We won't even get into the fact that you people can't send out a coherent invoice. I mean, from how many different sources do you generally bill the same procedure, anyway? And how many seniors' lives do you ruin a week, you figure? On average?"

I looked at Cynthia. Cynthia looked at me. I leaned my forearm on the counter.

I did not feel better about myself, and Cynthia had run out of things to say to me. I almost apologized. I almost spilled my guts and sought understanding or pity, or some comparable human connection. In the end, Cynthia had more experience with assholes like me than I had with tools like her, so I slithered away to the cafeteria to regroup over some mint tea. It's supposed to have a calming effect. It's never worked for me. Twenty minutes of slow breathing and a silent apology to the universe substituted well enough, and I went to look for Lin.

Hospitals are bigger places than you realize until you're pursuing some bright idea like bumping into someone. Half an hour of hall wandering convinced me I was a pathetic loser. Another ten minutes convinced me the rest of the hospital knew it. I was set to head out when I passed the critical care unit. I paused. Pondered. Evan Tillman was, after all, a patient of Lin's. Worth a stroll. I half expected someone to stop me – I didn't know CCU protocol – but I ambled past the deserted nurse's station and made a full loop around the unit. No Lin. Several empty beds, and a few rooms crowded with visitors. The Tillman room quiet and still. The steady beep of electric monitors. I did another loop and found myself stopping outside Evan's room. TILLMAN, E. in grease pencil on white plastic.

Through the window I watched the boy's chest rise and fall with his breath. I felt weary of lost causes. Unrealized potential. How the world seemed stacked against certain people. I wondered what constituted Evan's membership in that sad club. Curious what he looked like, I stepped inside. Between the bandages and the oxygen tubes, it was difficult to say. He was young, far away, and alone. Fluids dripped from an IV bag suspended on a pole at his side. Monitors tracked his heartbeat, his pulse. His eyes were closed. Hands at his sides. Almost peaceful. I found myself wiping away tears. *Great.* Where the fuck was his family. I condemned Chris and whoever else for not being there to keep vigil. *Time out, Nick. Take a breath. You know nothing.* They could be on their way. In the elevator. How would I explain my teary-eyed presence. To them. To myself. I touched the kid's lifeless hand and got out of there.

The next morning, I woke up thinking about Evan Tillman. Kid stretched out in a lonely room, his body fighting to find a way back. To claim a future. Some of us pissed away potential and didn't deserve an advocate. But others had it taken from them. I did some research on crime stats that fueled my frustration, and on my way for an early afternoon visit with Thomas, I found myself pulling into the parking lot of the Newton Police Department. Heat, raging humidity. I needed to tweak someone. Armed with facts and curiosity, I aimed to thrust myself upon whatever passed for a public information officer.

Five minutes later I sat in a cramped office across a cheap desk from Officer Scott Halverson. Dark hair parted on the side. Thick-frame glasses. Early forties, but he still looked like the kid who'd been president of the math club in high school. I had no plan, but I had my research.

"Newton Police made eighteen arrests in seventy-two cases of robbery, rape and aggravated assault last year." I smiled as I read my notes. "Eleven arrests in 225 cases of burglary." A coffee mug on his desk proclaimed World's Greatest Dad. "Are those numbers right?"

"They are." Halverson adjusted his nerd glasses. He was a uniform cop. A perpetual boy scout. His smile condescended. "Those figures are comparable to other good law enforcement agencies around the country."

"You're shitting me," I said. "How can that be?"

Maybe he didn't understand the question. He stared at a file folder on his desk. Cool air blew from somewhere.

"No offense," I said, "but it seems like you could get that kind of arrest rate from people turning themselves in. Do you solve *any* cases?"

He made a show of looking amused. "Do you have an emotional interest in a particular case, Mr. Young, or are you just naturally acerbic?"

Fuck him. "Heard of Evan Tillman?"

His smile went away. "Of course." His face got a little red, his tone a little defensive. "You a friend of the family?"

"Concerned citizen." I pocketed my notes. "Blows my mind. It's what, three weeks in and all you've got is a car seen in the neighborhood. A black Lexus. For real?"

"The department is fully engaged on the case, Mr. Young."

"Yeah, it shows."

"Why are you here, Mr. Young?" I'd got to him a little. He moved the file folder from one side of the desk to the other. I watched him do it. "We are not in the habit of disclosing the details of ongoing investigations."

"So you do have more?" I was in the zone. "I hope so. 'Cause it'd be really great if when the kid wakes up you could tell him you got the people that did it."

It was a little satisfying, but only a little. Halverson wouldn't give me anything, and wouldn't punch back. I went another meaningless round and thanked him for his time.

At five o'clock on Thursday, I was due at a traffic blockade in the Back Bay. Sponsored quietly by BAFA "on behalf of the janitors," the blockade hoped to snarl traffic at the Dartmouth Street entrance to the Mass Pike and generally clog one of the city's busiest intersections during afternoon rush hour. Good for visibility, and it was still all about rallying the public behind the cause. Surely if public outcry got loud enough, the companies would bend. I'd spent a couple hours with Paul and other BAFA leaders that morning, getting their take on the state of the strike: encouragement at the level of public support, optimism at the companies' failure to find willing replacement workers. I rode the D branch of the Green Line toward Copley. I'd run, showered and returned videos to the library. Got another – *The Set-Up*, with Sterling Hayden as a worn-out boxer who dooms himself by defiantly refusing to take a fall – and while I was there, checked statistics on the percentage of robberies that got solved in Newton versus other cities. Wanted to justify my growing disdain for Newton cops. But discovered that crime seemed to be a better business proposition all around than I had thought. So I resolved not to think any more that day. To live in the moment.

In the moment, my phone rang: my gorgeously unavailable ex-wife, who was employed and terrified about it. She was also on a talking jag.

"Nicky! Yes, I got the job, yes, that means they think I'm old, no it doesn't close the door to the TV series possibility –they're still considering me and my agent says it's down to me and two others, only one of whom has done anything in movies. So it still feels possible, which would be great exposure, show the world that I can do more than sigh in exasperation and die, and not least important, would keep me in grilled cheese and tequila. And while I don't get to shriek like a terrified teen, I do get to let loose once before they slit my throat. Wanna hear my scream?"

"Hi, Teresa."

"Hey, kid. I'm a little wound up."

"What TV thing? You never told me about a TV thing."

"It's one of those divorced mom and teen daughter shows for the WB, but at least the guy who created it can write."

"Good. What's the angle? Mom secretly an alien?"

"No angle. Just that she moves back to her hometown after the divorce and has to confront her ideas of what she thought her life would be."

She stopped talking. I wondered if I'd lost the call.

"Oh," she said. "Maybe that's why I hadn't told you."

"Thanks. I appreciate that. I'm not sure I could handle hearing that my life is a TV cliché."

"You're not a cliché. Anytime you find yourself in an ordinary human situation, you think you're a cliché."

She was scheduled to start shooting the horror movie the next week. "Which should be easy," she said. "I've got eight lines and one scream. You sure you don't want to hear the scream?"

I filled her in on the Dad situation and the magazine piece, which she was glad (and relieved) to hear about. Now that we're divorced, she likes to worry about me.

"I'm proud of you, pal. Many fine actors have done screamfests."

The D Train filled by Kenmore and crawled the last two stops. But we got there. I squirmed my way off, up the stairs, and emerged out into a scene that surprised me. According to my phone, it was four-fifty. The sidewalks on both sides of Dartmouth Street were jammed with bodies. As was the stretch of median that ran between Boylston Street and Huntington Avenue. As was the narrow stretch of sidewalk that wrapped the entrance to the Westin Hotel and the island that separated Huntington from the Turnpike on-ramp. There were even a few dozen people at the corner of St. James, in front of the Copley Plaza. Thick clouds had rolled in over the last hour. There was a forty percent chance of thunderstorms. A handful of homemade "Justice for Janitors" banners painted on sheets and stapled to dowels. A handful of cops scattered about. Faces a mix of curiosity and concern. I scanned the crowd for people I knew, or major players. Found neither. Scores of purple t-shirts. I parked myself at the corner of St. James. To my left a boy worked the crowd with a clipboard. Black t-shirt, curly hair, mutton-chop sideburns.

Cars clogged the intersection. Commuters heading home. Cabs heading wherever. Drivers looked warily at the gathered crowd. The mutton-chop kid had worked his way behind me. "Do your part for workers," he said. "Participate in a Day of Chaos." Whatever that meant. He didn't approach me. A girl with a lip ring thrust a flyer at me: "The action doesn't end when the strike is settled." An anarchist broadside, some group called SLAM encouraging destruction of business equipment. At the bottom, a simple black-and-white logo of a clenched fist – presumably slamming down on injustice – and an anarchist A in a circle. Seemed to me the janitors could only be hurt by any implied association with radical groups. I got jostled. In front of the Westin I spotted a hand-lettered sign that said "It Won't Stop with Seattle." Near the sign, I thought I saw Bo.

Then, as if on some invisible command, the wave of people hit the streets. Everyone moved toward the point where Dartmouth met Huntington and the Turnpike on-ramp. A walk light held traffic. A woman behind me cracked, "Welcome to the commute from hell." A ripple of laughter. Horns honked as drivers put together what was happening. What it meant. Shouts of *"Assholes,"* *"What the fuck."* One plaintive voice called, "Come *on."*

Banners unfurled, hundreds of bodies moved in what seemed like silence, and by the time the folks on Dartmouth got the green, the whole area was a sea of cars and humanity and there was nowhere for anyone to move.

A cacophony of horns; the few cops on the scene all called the mess in at the same time. Four news vans with camera crews appeared from out of the Westin garage. Cars closed up whatever cracks had existed between them and standing bodies. A stalwart soul in an SUV tried to climb the curb on St. James, but there was nowhere to go.

Voices added the now-familiar chant: *What do we want? Justice. When do we want it? Now.*

More signs appeared – "People Before Profit" was back, and "Note to Cleaning Companies: We'll Move When You Do." *"Que Limpein Los Jefes* – Let the Bosses Clean." I liked that one. Along with the car horns and voices came sirens. Then a familiar voice beside me.

"This worked out well." There stood Bo, tall and proud, as if he'd orchestrated the event.

"It's quite a thing."

Sirens grew louder. Five police cars, three abreast and two behind, crested the hill on Dartmouth and stopped in front of Back Bay Station, where a line of people – hundreds – closed off that side of the square.

"How was track today?"

"Coach kicked our ass. I have no idea what pissed him off."

I kept an eye on the police cars and the officers who emerged from them, tentatively and with nightsticks.

"Getting up at six definitely cramps my style."

I envied him the structure and the unabashed hope of his situation, but I did it silently.

The crowd was an odd mix – kids, ex-hippies ready to join any demonstration, a bandannaed Willie Nelson look-alike. The young anarchy crowd. A surprising number of regular folks who looked like they had jobs.

The buzz of voices got louder when the cops fanned out, but no one gave ground. A press of people faced off. Bodies jostling.

Someone stepped on my foot. I grumbled. Bo was tall enough to breathe above the fray. He looked happy as a kid at a birthday party.

"You feeling the solidarity?" I said. "You suburban anarchists must be psyched."

"The janitors are right," Bo said. "It's nice to see people support that."

Cops stretched a wary, thin line across Dartmouth Street. Alert. Tense.

I watched the cops the same way. "Is this going to get ugly?" I asked Bo.

He shrugged. "Hard to say."

Somehow in the drift of things we ended up on Dartmouth near the Westin. Two blue sawhorse barricades on the sidewalk behind us.

Cops' faces coiled to spring into action.

I turned to Bo. "Once you tear it all down, what do you build in its place?"

A mischievous grin. "How should I know? I'm seventeen."

The nature of crowds: energy builds to crescendo; something has to happen, or it leaves a vague disappointment.

Bo bounced on the balls of his feet. He went to the sidewalk. To one of the barricades. "Grab an end."

"I'm an impartial observer. A professional."

"Fuck you. Grab an end, Nick."

I did, and we wormed our way through the crowd to a couple of cheers, some laughter. The Fox News crew shot us in action. Not something my ersatz employer would appreciate. The tangle of humanity made me feel distracted, irritable. Behind us, a group chanted for the cameras: *Marcus Gregory, you've got cash. Why do you pay your workers trash?*

Traffic was solid down Dartmouth and around Boylston. Southbound motorists, seeking a way through the tangle, had filled northbound lanes. A lone cop planted himself in the midst and attempted to direct the gridlock. Distant thunder. In all the humidity, I'd sweat through my shirt.

Bo stopped. "Here's good." We bounced off bodies, set the barricade down in the street maybe thirty yards in front of the Turnpike entrance ramp.

A pair of police vans pulled in going the wrong way on Huntington. They stopped at the entrance to the Westin garage, where the human tumor had swelled closed the fourth side of the square. A half-dozen cops poured out of each van. Riot gear. Helmets. Shields. The serious sticks. "We should get out of here," I said.

Bo's face animated, the excitement of the new. "You kidding?"

The first cops must have been waiting for the riot squad. Both groups advanced into the crowd, using clubs as prompters held crosswise between their hands.

Three SUVs jumped the curb at Dartmouth and started down the sidewalk in front of the Copley Plaza, where the uniformed doorman remained dutifully stationed.

Cops methodically prodded people, row by row, back to the sidewalk.

Impatient motorists shouted out car windows, amped up the honking. A line of cops started in our direction.

We drifted slowly north, bumped toward the corner of Dartmouth and St. James. Carried by waves. Jostled. An elbow here, a shoulder there.

One of the police cars from Dartmouth nudged into the crowd. Boylston Street was a parking lot. In the press of people, we drifted fast enough I had to concentrate on my feet.

We reached the sidewalk. A little amped, a little short of breath. The cops got St. James clear enough for a line of cars to escape onto Huntington and the Turnpike. Like most by then, Bo and I watched in silence. The crowd thinned fast. By any measure, the action had to be considered a success. And a powerful message. But there was something else in the air. A tension Bo and I would differ on: an explosion narrowly averted, or an exhilarating and necessary first step.

That night I made notes, then settled on the sofa with a Newcastle and a sore shoulder to watch the ten o'clock news. Channel Five, because I was hot for anchor Camille Oliver and their promos were the least annoying.

"The weather's not the only thing heating up," Camille said. "Both the action and the rhetoric got hotter today in the two-week-old janitors' strike. An estimated three thousand protesters blocked traffic during afternoon rush hour in Boston's Back Bay. Pat Andrus was there."

The footage was impressive. Crowds and angry drivers and even police presence looked more intense edited into a 30-second montage. Concentrated drama. I wondered if Bo and I had made it onto Fox's evening broadcast. If we had, I'd hear about it from AJ.

Camille reprised the highlights and it was time for the battle of the talking heads. The union disavowed responsibility for the event. *While we appreciate the outpouring of support from the community,* blah blah. *Presence of union members at the blockade did not constitute sponsorship,* etc. *We cannot – and will not attempt to – control the private actions of concerned citizens.* That was Sam. Then it got good. Tillman.

"These actions are inappropriate. Thuggish." His face strained. You could see fatigue etching itself there. "I know the union says they're not behind this and I sincerely hope that's true. None of this changes the facts. Discussions are closed. Our best offer is on the table." No Gregory. He stayed at a remove. Above the fray.

After Tillman came Juliana.

"The companies tell us the time for talking is through. We will continue to show our strength and let them know the time for *serious* talk has arrived."

Feisty.

But Camille had more. "While cleaning companies Pollard and Delfi have said they *intend* to hire replacement workers, Endicott today took action. Replacement janitors arrived at the company's downtown headquarters under heavy security late this afternoon."

The screen showed the arrival of the timid scabs, who were hustled past the few remaining pickets and captured by a horde of TV news types, which could mean only one thing: Endicott had primed the coverage, treating the occasion as a photo op. Was that why Tillman was glued to his BlackBerry at the Sox game? Planning this?

"Mayor Norm Reeves denounced the move," Camille's voice said as the picture cut to our city's illustrious leader, "calling it a step backward."

The picture changed to Juliana Reyes, who shrugged. "It's a circus act," she said. "A publicity stunt. It's insulting toward the janitors and the entire process."

She was sexy when she got angry. A little haughty. I liked her. Felt bad for her. For the janitors. Public support was a mixed blessing. BAFA had helped make the cause popular and kept heat on the companies. It wouldn't help that cause to be adopted by – or confused with – the anti-globalization radicals or the anarchist crew. Those groups were stoking the fire. I feared the janitors would get burned.

7

"You may want to come down here, Nick."

I dimly registered the voice on the phone as AJ's. "Where?"

"Office."

I rubbed sleep from my eyes. Tried to blink my way toward consciousness. "What time is it?"

"Six-thirty."

"You're shitting me." I reveled in my elite coil mattress and the den of darkness I'd re-established with sheets and duct tape. "I'll meet you at nine, nine-thirty. We'll have coffee."

"An hour, it will be on the news. In two, it will be cleaned up."

That got me. "Be right there."

The Washington Street lobby of the FirstBoston building was long, narrow, and impressive. Marble floors, brass trim, and pristine cream-colored walls. The effect lost something when it was knee-deep in garbage. The stench nearly overwhelmed me. Rotting food. Old coffee grounds. A clean-up crew had begun with shovels and the police had crime-taped the main entrance. AJ got me in the back way as an employee. We stood two steps down from the main carnage. A staggering number of coffee cups, take-out food containers, plastic bags, soft drink bottles.

"You guys throw a party and not invite me?" I was wobbly from a late night at the Middle East. A ska double bill I couldn't resist. A dose of young women dancing had done its part to stave off the lonely for one night.

"I figured you'd want to see this." AJ sipped coffee.

"When did you get here?"

"About two minutes before I called you." He offered his paper cup. "Want some decaf?"

Too many years of deadlines had eaten at AJ's stomach. He was off caffeine. "Thanks. I'll wait."

A half-dozen Boston cops lined the lobby, looking less than thrilled. A bunch of teens from the Boston Youth Conservation Corps, clad in peach cotton jumpsuits, were armed with shovels and equipped with two large gray trash bins on wheels. The kids looked even less thrilled than the cops. They'd signed on for summer jobs cleaning city parks. Near us, a black kid with a full-on '70s afro poked at one of the piles with his shovel. A rat skittered in search of refuge.

"So what do you know?" I asked AJ.

He sipped coffee. "Item one you're looking at." The cop nearest us, fifty-something Irish, had eyes half-interested in our conversation.

AJ gestured toward the doorway behind him. "Item two, dumpster in the back alley was empty."

"The janitors will get accused. But I can't imagine the union being stupid enough to pull this." For a sobering view of your culture, take an archaeological perspective on a truckload of trash.

113

It was hard not to do the math: how many buildings, how many days, how many barges headed out to sea with shit that would take a lifetime – or ten – to decompose.

"Item three, activist groups claimed responsibility already. Acting *on behalf of* the janitors."

"Seattle10."

"Yeah. And another."

A bad meat smell wafted past. "SLAM? Student Labor Action something?"

He sipped decaf, poor guy. "You're well-informed."

"I used to be a journalist."

The youth corps kids worked in twos and threes. Some with shovels, some just with gloves, all with anguished faces.

"Of course," AJ said, "that doesn't mean the union *wasn't* involved."

I shook my head. "The union runs a pretty tight ship. They've got folks motivated, believing they can win. They wouldn't do this."

AJ finished his coffee, went to throw his paper cup onto the trash pile, then didn't.

I watched the cops watch kids clean. "The 'battle in Seattle' crew, on the other hand. They're antsy to make something happen, they've got a popular cause in the janitors and this is exactly the kind of thing they like to do." Violence against property. I'd bet I knew where some of my favorite teens had spent the night.

Workers trickled in. FirstBoston folks, couple of nonprofits, maybe a law firm, that mix of light suits, oxfords, polos, and khakis that spelled summer professionals. Most looked annoyed, some vaguely amused.

AJ: "How's the piece coming?"

"Good." Maybe the odor had started to dissipate. Maybe I was waking up. I craved coffee. "I've talked to all the major players, been to a bunch of rallies. I've got the background I need."

AJ tossed his cup into a passing gray bin, called thanks to the peach-clad kid pushing it. "Well, you've got a story. I'll send out the contract today."

"That's the best news I've heard this week." Actual money. Earned money. What a concept. I felt a glimmer of something I almost recognized as self-esteem.

It would be a few hours before the custodial staff could douse the lobby with disinfectant, but the youth crew had cleared a path from the back entrance to the elevator bank. A steady stream of people now made their way to work, not categorically grumpier than any other day.

AJ geared up to join the throng. "The double issue is kicking my ass, and standing here, while aromatic and entertaining, isn't getting me any closer to production." He headed for the elevators.

I left the way I came. Out on Water Street, Boston air never smelled so sweet.

Two coffees, a cranberry nut muffin, a shower, the Globe sports page (*Sox top Indians 7-2 behind Lester*), and a message to Terry's voice mail (*I know you're either asleep or on set, and I have no doubt you are the sexiest, youngest-looking, most talented horror mom in movie history, but I want to hear how you're doing with this*), and it was off to see Thomas.

AJ was right about the news. On the drive over, the dumpster incident was NPR's top local story. "While the two activist groups have claimed responsibility," the news anchor's voice said (it was that annoying one, the woman who sounds as if she's enunciating for fourth graders), "a link to the janitors is also suspected. Union leaders could not be reached for comment." That meant they hadn't tried to reach Juliana or Sam. I didn't like it. This kind of stunt – and irresponsible coverage – could only escalate tensions and confuse the issues. Not to mention fuel the imaginations of certain idealistic teenagers.

Thomas sat in his green chair, engrossed in the television. Some talk show host I didn't recognize. A half-eaten bowl of lime Jell-o on the end table.

I dropped into the chair beside him. Caught a lingering whiff of coffee grounds. "How you doing?"

Time delay. I watched his eyes shift focus. "Hi, son."

"How you feeling today?"

A beat. Two. "Paul was in yesterday."

I waited to see where this was going. I thought I heard someone on the tube say something about hermaphrodites.

"He's got nothing to say to me. Just that smug face. Breezes in, checks my heart, disappears. Looks in my eyes like he can read everything."

"That's Dr. Stern," I said. "The doctor's name is Stern."

"Making progress," he said. "What does that mean." His eyes on the television. "He doesn't listen. Young people."

True enough. A few seconds went by. Applause on the television. Outside, gray. Humid. Felt like thunderstorms. Time to deal. "We need to talk money, Dad."

116

I waited.

He stared at the TV screen, where the topic was in fact celebrity hermaphrodites. "They're stealing from me."

My day had begun too early to indulge this. Deep breath. "The medical bills, Dad."

"Listen to me." Anger in his voice. "She takes things. A hair brush. A flannel shirt. Small stuff, but still."

"What are you talking about? Who takes things?"

"The fuck she going to do with an old man's hair brush?"

"Dad – who took your hair brush?"

"That nurse. The bitchy one. Named after a state."

Word scramble from another planet. States. Virginia? "We'll take care of that later. I promise. Right now we need to talk about money. We need to do something about these medical bills."

His mouth got small. I swear his eyes sunk deeper into that stubborn skull. "You didn't win the lottery? Cash out your publishing empire?"

"Funny." So much for self-esteem. I had $2k coming to me – in a couple months. What I needed was to spin that into ten, twelve, sixteen. Deep breath. "We have to figure this out, Dad."

"The hell we do." He watched the TV screen. "Fuck 'em."

"Fuck 'em?"

"You heard me."

Breathe. "You owe thousands in medical bills."

He looked at me. "What are they gonna do, kill me?" Thunder in the distance. "Throw me out?" Out the window, storm clouds hovered.

I wanted a one-way ticket to anywhere. "They might."

"You wanna let that happen to your old man, go ahead."

I swear a hint of a smirk flashed across his face.

"Great," I said. "Perfect." On TV, the talk show host had moved up into the audience, where a woman asked for the medical definition of hermaphrodite. "So it's my problem."

"Problem, whatever." His smug glare. "I'm not dealing with it. You deal with it."

He turned away. I watched the sky turn black. Applause from the TV was the only sound in the room. We let it fade.

"I've never understood you," my father said. "Why you didn't make more of yourself."

Nurse Joan had warned me. *Bear with him. He may make sense one minute, and not the next. He may say things that are flat wrong, or hurtful.*

Either he had changed the channel or the talk show had somehow become a game show.

"You did that one thing," my father said. "Got a big head." Looking at the TV.

I told myself it was a riff in his brain. Nothing personal. Told myself I was an adult and he didn't matter anymore. I saw myself as in a mirror my father had invoked – no career, no family, no prospects. The game show host bantered with a new contestant.

"You always thought you were too good for the rest of us." He looked over at me again. "I don't know where you got that."

It was the looking over at me that did it.

"You weren't *exactly* the best role model, you know." My jaw tightened. "The invisible man."

"Your mother and I had our troubles."

118

"That's not what I'm talking about." For two years, my father hadn't lived with us. He took a job in New Hampshire and we didn't see him much. The occasional weekend. A summer vacation my mother decided not to go on. *Don't do this.* "Never mind."

His ears red. "You know what it is to be a father? You some expert husband?" His breathing strained. "We stuck it out, at least."

I bit my lip, told myself to count to ten.

Four. Five. Outside, thunder.

"Why don't you leave me alone," my father said.

We sat in staredown mode. On the TV, a guy won something.

"Because I won't have you haunting me from beyond the fucking grave." *Nice.* I leaned back in the chair. Rested my head against green vinyl. Started counting again. Got to ten. Did it over.

Dimly, my father's voice.

"What?" I asked.

Vinyl squeaked. Thomas shifted in his chair, looked around the room. "Where's your mother?" he said.

The black hole of his empty gums.

"She's dead. Eight years now."

He nodded. "Never mind," he said. "This guy I worked for, Charlie Rome, he saw the future of machine shops was automation. Saw it before anybody."

"I know. You told that story."

The TV was giving me a headache. The way it dinged when a contestant gave the right answer.

Back at Thomas's place, late afternoon. Nothing to do, no one to do it with. The clouds had passed without rain, without relief. I

119

wanted to go to sleep and wake up somewhere simpler. That wasn't going to happen. I wanted to knock some sense into my father. That wasn't going to happen either. I could threaten to pursue power of attorney. But then he'd give it to me, for spite. I did fifty angry sit-ups in good slow-burn form. Tried to think like an adult. Maybe I could run my troubles away.

I found my shoes and headed out into the heat. East coast humidity sucks; give me dry LA summers any day. The blacktop felt like fire and the moist air had me sweating before I'd taken a step. I ran on leaden legs. Started off fast to shake out the stiffness and sweat fatigue out through my pores.

A mile and my body started to feel good. Found a rhythm and welcomed the heat. Two miles and it felt better. *I don't want to deal with it.* Fuck him. I didn't want to deal with it, either. I felt so good I tackled arduous Medicine Hill, around to Cottage Farm, out the Riverway into Jamaica Plain before doubling back into south Brookline. Almost stopped at Steven's, a little neighborhood market, for a sports drink, reminiscing about long summer days playing baseball, farting around.

Ran past the playground on Cypress and got a chill. A kid walking across the outfield looked familiar. That idle summer pace. He was stocky, early adolescent. Brown curly hair. *No.* I checked myself – no more chasing phantoms. We moved toward the center of a clock, me from six, him from three. Adrenaline confirmed my suspicion. He cocked his head, checking me out.

I watched him put it together. Veer course casually away from me. He did a quick scan, as if for backup. I angled across to the playground side of the street, slow, as if that had been my plan all along. He neared the gate, but I was gaining on him. He picked up his pace. Looked over his shoulder. When I hopped the low fence, he ran. I sprinted after him, no idea what I planned to do. Riding the moment. I could smell his fear. He fumbled with a latch on the gate, muttered a curse. I had him. I grabbed a fallen branch off the ground. I thwacked the stick against the fence next to his head, which got him to turn and face me.

"What's the matter?" I had endorphins flowing. "Gate locked?"

"What do you want?" Thinking about how to play it. His cheeks bright red. Puffing. Kid wasn't a runner.

"Remember me?"

"Yeah. So?"

It was a good question. I wanted to scare him. Now that I had him, I didn't know how.

"So I've been looking for you. You and your punk friends." He was cornered. Two fence sides and I formed a loose triangle around him. But I was losing the intensity of rage to uncertainty, even embarrassment. I watched his fear melt. He grinned a little.

"What are you gonna do, man, hit me?" He gestured toward the stick in my hand. No deference in his brown eyes. "With that?"

It wasn't much of a stick. I hated him for his confidence. I'd had enough of feeling played.

"That cop, he talked to us. Guy's a joke. Can't do shit. And you? You think I can't go through you?" Eye to eye. He knew I wouldn't touch him.

I wanted to strafe his face. I wanted the stick to be stronger and sharper. "I'd love to see you try." *No. Breathe. Be a grownup.* "How old are you?"

"Twelve." He had a pouty little mouth.

"What do you get out of killing a dog? Make you feel strong?"

"What do you *care*, man? Not your dog." He worked his fingers. Shifted his weight foot to foot. Slow, but always moving.

We were at an impasse, and he knew it. I wiped at my brow. Shook the stick in his face. "If this was re-bar."

The kid laughed. Swiped the stick away. "Yeah, and if you had the sack."

I stepped back. He started forward, a swagger step, on his way past me.

I reacted. A forearm hard to his face. I felt cartilage give. A blow against words, reason, passivity. The kid went down. My arm tingled. Stung. I saw blood.

The kid's voice. "*Fuck.*"

I didn't look at him. I sauntered toward the open gate, a little swagger in my own step. "I don't want to see you again."

The air cool against my skin. I walked home invigorated, ashamed at how alive I felt.

I'd never hit anyone before. Not ever. Not a single fight.

I showered. Shaved. Sat in my father's recast den feeling wilted and restless. The air stagnant. The room was no longer Thomas', but it sure wasn't mine. A long night loomed, and dusk still a couple hours away. I drove to the video store, rented *Kid Galahad* with Edward G. Robinson. Knew I wasn't in the mood even before I got to the house. My forearm hurt and there was an element of don't-fuck-with-me pride. Until I remembered the person I popped was twelve years old. A clueless kid.

I pulled in the driveway. Dialed Bo. "Let's do something."

"I am doing something." Voices on his end.

"Don't be difficult." Heat hit me from the door frame. The dashboard.

"I have a shit-ton to do. You want to do something, give me a ride."

My shirt stuck to my back. My arms. "Where are you?"

"Church."

"Fuck."

"It's practically on your way."

"On my way to what?"

"Just come get me."

Bo was part of a youth group in what he called a progressive congregation on Mission Hill. I made two circuits of Tremont Street before I got lucky and found a broken meter on Parker Hill Ave. Some kid leafleting windshields. He shoved one in my hand. I recognized the Seattle10 logo. The headline: *Summer of Strife – Undo Corporate Capitalism*, and under it, *Top 10 Ways You Can Help*. My stomach tensed. There was too much combustible material in the city, too many people trying to strike sparks. I shoved the flyer in my pocket and pushed through the rickety wood-and-glass side door into a musty church basement where Bob Marley sang from an old stereo and a dozen or so teens sat in clusters. The place smelled of stale cigarette smoke. Cheap linoleum floors. Industrial gray walls. Kitchen at the back. It felt like a nursing home. I didn't want to be there. I scanned for Bo. He and another kid sat on stools, working with needle and thread next to a dressmaker's dummy. Adam sat beside them on a formica counter.

I walked over. "I didn't know you could sew."

"Hey, Nick." Bo's fingers kept working. So did the other kid's. Adam nodded hi.

"It's not hard," Bo said. "Just attach one piece to the others."

On a folding table beside them was a pile – hundreds – of cloth labels from clothing items, the made-in-wherever tags. Bo and his pal were sewing these tags together.

"Nick, Ruben. Ruben, Nick." Ruben had short black hair, black frame glasses and a regular-boy grin.

We nodded hellos.

"Okay, I'll bite. What are you doing?"

"Fashion project," Bo said. He pricked himself with the needle. Sucked at the tip of his ring finger.

Bo had a lot of projects. I distrusted his use of the word. "Decode, please."

Adam pushed off the counter, circled us.

Bo and Ruben held their handiwork in position on the dummy.

"An outfit made of labels from clothing produced in countries where there's sweatshop labor," Bo said. The silver-and-white hodgepodge of cloth tags was on its way to becoming a tank top and miniskirt. They showed me two color sketches of how the finished product would look.

I felt old. Implicated. My forearm throbbed.

Adam skulked behind us, loud unhappy sighs.

A girl came in from the kitchen and joined them.

"This is Monica," Bo said. "Her design."

Monica wore a denim miniskirt over black leggings. T-shirt. Rust-colored hair.

"Impressive," I said.

"Thanks." Monica had killer dimples and a wide smile. If I kept hanging out with teens, there was a good chance I'd be incarcerated.

Bo continued, "The outfit goes on the dummy, the dummy goes in a display case we're building tomorrow night–"

A loud grunt from Adam. "This accomplishes nothing," he said. "I'm gone." He stalked out.

Ah, teens.

Bo and Ruben led me to a back table which held a dozen brightly colored masks. "These will hang from fishing line all around the dummy. One for each country victimized by sweatshops, painted in the colors of that country's flag."

A few of the face flags I recognized – Mexico, Nicaragua, Venezuela. The kids had facts – average prices of Newbury Street fashions, average earnings of sweatshop workers by country. Their industriousness exhausted me. I wanted to be done. Monica moved on to another cluster.

"It all gets unveiled on Friday," Ruben said. "Newbury Street."

I laughed. "How long you think it's going to last on Newbury before the cops take it down?"

"Exactly a month," Bo gloated. "It's church property. Another BAFA congregation. This is a sanctioned youth group activity."

I had to smile.

Ruben headed for the bathroom. I hugged the dummy and watched Bo. If it was possible to sew frantically, Bo was doing it. "Grab a needle and thread," he said.

"I'd love to, but I was on my way somewhere, and you called looking for a ride, remember?"

"A few minutes. You can spare a few minutes."

"And you had stuff to do, remember?"

"A few minutes, Nick. What the fuck."

Bob Marley sang about buffalo soldiers. Why couldn't these kids get their own music. "What the fuck yourself. You want a ride or not?"

"Fine, *Dad*. I'll get my stuff."

Oh, kid. You have no idea. I considered leaving him there. It had been too long a day and I blamed Bo that I was dragged out of bed early.

We walked toward the car. The heat hadn't quit.

"Bet I can guess where you were last night. Clothes at home have that rotten egg smell?"

He beamed. "You heard? Pretty great, huh?"

"Pretty effective." Somewhere behind us, an ambulance. "You know you're getting into shit the cops will take seriously."

"I'm acting on what I believe." Only a teen could make that an accusation.

"Admirable, but not reassuring."

"I'm also not stupid."

"So I shouldn't worry?"

"Sweet of you to offer, but no."

We turned onto Parker Hill Ave.

"I don't get it," I said.

"Get what?"

The idea of an activist church was new to me. I put my hands out, mimed the trays of a scale. "Anarchist. Episcopalian. Seems a little disjunctive."

"I don't know that word."

"Doesn't add up."

He shrugged. "Only adults need to make shit add up."

Fine. We got to the car. The leafletter had double-dipped. Another Seattle10 flyer on the windshield. I handed it to Bo. "You'll want this."

"Got tons. I printed them."

"Excellent." I reminded myself I shouldn't worry.

All I wanted was to get in the Dart and drive, fast and far. Music cranked. Windows open. Blow it all away. I dropped Bo off and did just that.

My worry returned with the morning paper. I read the headlines with a sore forearm and a strong coffee.

GoodBuys Thwarts Hackers

Activist group claims responsibility for near-miss e-commerce sabotage

According to the article, the national box store chain had narrowly averted a major hack which would have re-routed funds from the company's e-commerce sales to a number of social justice-oriented nonprofit organizations. I liked the style. What worried me was the Seattle10 branch that nearly pulled this off – or at least laid claim to it. According to the Globe, Boston was emerging as the growing movement's most active and effective arm.

Worry turned to something worse when I scanned to the bottom of the page.

Two Janitors Killed in Fiery Crash

One considered key agent of union growth

Marcos Najera and his cousin Eduardo Mendoza, both
of Dorchester, were killed last night in a fiery hit-and-run
accident on Morrissey Boulevard.

The pair were driving north from Quincy, where they had
just dropped off a co-worker, Roselia Suarez, after a janitors'
rally at Old West Church.

According to police, Najera's car was struck from behind by a speeding vehicle traveling in the same northbound lane of Morrissey Boulevard. Najera's car burst into flames, trapping him and Mendoza inside. Najera was considered a leader among janitors in Service Workers Union International Local 13, which recently went on strike against Delfi, Pollard, Endicott, and others.

Friends of the victims said they were shocked and reeling.

"Marcos was more than my friend," said union leader Sam
Abigail. "He was like my brother. This is a devastating loss
in human terms and a terrible blow to the cause of justice
for janitors in Boston."

I figured there was a limited pool of janitors named Eduardo in Dorchester. I figured right.

8

A sleek black Lexus turns the corner onto Randlett Park, moves slowly up the small hill in early afternoon heat. All is still. Adults at work. Kids, newly free from school, at camp or mall or pool. Even teens up and out. Backyard swing sets and climbing structures. Up Randlett to Waltham Street, across to Fairway Drive then down to Watertown Street, across to Warwick Road. It's deserted. They knew it would be. Maybe deep inside a house there's a Guatemalan cleaning woman making a kid's bed, picking up underwear. Up Warwick to the house. They could be family from out of town, arrived earlier than expected. They could be real estate agents or architects come to appraise the house or double check a beam placement on a planned addition. Into the driveway, around to the side door. Who would notice? Who would think anything?

Bo's janitor friend Eduardo was dead, and the kid was shaken. Sat vigil with the family. Skipped track. Skipped eating. The union had declared a three-day moratorium on strike activities and asked all supporters to respect it. I spent the first day researching recent US labor actions and making appointments with story sources: a workforce economist at Tufts, a labor relations expert at the Kennedy School. By day two I was looking for things to do, so I marshaled my impotent anger and decided to solve the Tillman robbery.

Two kids play basketball in a driveway. One of those free-standing hoops on a roll-away base. They're brothers, you can tell, 'cause the older one looks like he'd rather be off with his own friends. You can read it on his face: the pout, the dead eyes, even from a distance. The vaguely disgusted way he bounce passes the ball to his kid brother who keeps knocking down shots. And even if they notice the car, they don't think anything of it. They just play ball and the little one keeps knocking down jump shots hoping to impress the older one, who keeps sending the ball back out, not looking, hoping some friend – any friend – will come by. The people in the Lexus know the neighborhood. They know the houses have alarms. They know the alarms only work if you turn them on, and why bother: it's a quiet neighborhood.

Wait. The robbery was early June. Kids were in school. And it probably wasn't hot. Damn. I liked the image. Anyway, the Lexus.

They didn't expect Evan to be there. And the surprise as much as anything makes one of them pull the gun from the waistband of his pants and sweep his arm, before he thinks about it, across the kid's face. Blood on his hand, his forearm. The way the bone gives so easily. He's angry at this obstacle. Wants to get in and out quickly. And there's the kid, lying on the floor, screaming or moaning. The fact of the kid on the floor and the blood just makes him more angry, so he kicks hard a few times in the vicinity of the ribs and his partner

gives a few kicks in the head for good measure, and then the kid is
quiet and they get on with their work and get the hell out.

I got my contract in the mail from AJ. Another bill from Newton-Wellesley Hospital. I called – finally – the Brookline Council on Aging. Found out they had a consultant specifically devoted to seniors having trouble understanding and paying medical bills. Also that he was only in two mornings a week. Made a note to call him back. Spent time with Bo. Listened to what little he would say. *–I don't want to feel like this, Nick. –Like what? –Like everything sucks and I can't do anything about it.*

The *Globe* eulogized the dead janitors. I remained mystified by the inability to solve what looked like a simple robbery. How hard could it be? Maybe it spoke to the quiet vulnerability of sleepy neighborhoods. Maybe all it took to penetrate them was the willingness to do it in broad daylight.

Forget the Lexus. Why not a delivery truck, or beat-up panel van that might signal a contractor. Remodeling a basement family room. No neighbor would think twice. They find a basement door, quietly force it in. Shoulders against wood. Tough-guy stuff. Only when they get in, there's Evan, come to find out what all the noise is.

Maybe he's an annoying little shit that no one likes. One of those kids targeted by bullies, by all boys because he's a pain in the ass. Maybe he gets mouthy, his own house and all. Someone hits him in that mouth, and likes the way he reacts, or doesn't. Maybe gets off on the way it feels. Then again, maybe a kidney shot, or ribs. And maybe Evan, hurting now, gets a flash of anger – my own fucking house – and maybe hits back, or says something smart, sharp. And maybe there's a sculpture on a table by the door, and maybe someone starts to pick it up and turn it over in his hands, and ask how much it's worth, and maybe Evan suggests they put it down, and go fuck themselves, or maybe he kind of yells it, blood coming down from his nose, pain and a little panic pushing his adrenaline, making him dizzy, and when he says or yells it he's also spitting a little blood and saliva with the words, and maybe that makes the guy with the statue kind of grossed out and pissed off at the same time, and before he realizes what he's doing his right arm, the one with the hand holding the sculpture, is moving hard toward Evan's head.

Yes, I felt bad about busting that kid's nose. I also felt good about it. Satisfied. Proud of my bone-bruised forearm. My whole life I'd been a words-only warrior. Relied on reasoning to a fault. I remembered as a kid, playing freeze tag on the way home from school. How one time I got tagged – frozen until the game ended or another player freed me – and Andy Mulray came along, a bully with a limp from infant polio and a nose for human weakness. I explained about the game. He got that bully grin of pure glee. Somewhere around me, other boys evaded chase. *-So you can't move? –That's right. -Even if you knew I would hit you as hard as I can in the stomach if you don't walk away now.* I didn't move. Bound by some code. Instead I explained again, as if he'd merely failed to understand.

In the enforced semi-darkness of my father's house, I paced the den. The kitchen. Got out the bills and re-counted them, as if the total might magically drop. As if my counting them would prove me conscientious. Outside, rain. Perfect.

I made a smoothie in the old metal-base blender – strawberries, bananas, milk, protein powder. I'd shed a half-dozen pounds and made a dent in my baggage handles. The smoothie didn't taste very good, but I drank it. My phone rang and I thought about not answering it.

"Nick?"

"Yeah."

"It's Eric Grunow."

"No, it's not. I haven't talked to Eric Grunow in ten years."

A pause. I drank my smoothie.

"More like twelve," Eric Grunow's voice said. Eric had been the assistant managing editor at the *Weekly* when I was there – the guy whose job it was to shape the final drafts of longer pieces with reporters and push copy through to production. Eric had known me when – and only when – I was a serious journalist. "I heard you were back in town." Static. Reception was spotty in my cave. "I also heard you're doing a piece for AJ."

"I guess that's true." Immediate fear – expectations. Hearing Eric's voice brought back sense memory of a younger, idealistic Nick. It gave the smoothie a sour aftertaste.

"Welcome back. How've you been?"

How do you answer that after so many years? "You know. Marriage. Divorce. Couple of careers. You?"

"The wife finally got fed up. I stayed at the *Weekly* a year too long. Kicked around the state house. Did a *Globe* stint. Now I got a snazzy title. Editor of *The View*." *The View* was the free daily newspaper that commuters read on the subway.

"I've seen your name on the masthead. Congratulations."

"Yeah. How the mighty have fallen. But the offer was too good to turn down."

133

I finished the smoothie, rinsed the glass in the sink.

"I got a proposition," Eric said. "I'd like you to do some work for us."

"You're kidding." The unfinished wood floor smelled musty, and I'd already cut my feet twice on protruding tacks.

"You can still do whatever you're doing for AJ."

"I'm only in town a little while, helping my father." *Interesting use of the word helping.*

"I like your work, Nick. Always did."

I paced. The den. The kitchen. The bills on the table. "You're all about those ultra-short articles. I'm not a short piece kind of guy."

"It's not all McNews. There's a substance piece in the center spread, every day. Do a series on the strike. Then, if you're still here, see what else grabs you. Or try a column."

That tweaked me. I'd long harbored a desire for a column: a license to rant; a stamp of credibility.

"I'm not a journalist anymore, Eric. I just mess around once in a while for AJ."

"Lot of people would tell you I'm not a journalist anymore, either."

I didn't much like the idea of writing for a throwaway. I preferred the moral high ground and a patron. On the other hand.

"Try it for a few weeks, a month, see if it gets readers. It'd be an honor to have the Nick Young byline."

"Like anyone remembers."

"I do." A pause. "Think on it. We'll talk later in the week."

I tossed the phone on the counter and joined the bills at the kitchen table.

Eric and I had covered the Ashton-Cooper scandal together, a high-stakes drama that gave me my fifteen minutes of local fame and was at least a cog in the wheel of reform that rolled through the Massachusetts State House in the mid-nineties. Three state officials were indicted and prosecuted, public contracting procedures changed, new state offices established to prevent abuses. The creation of the State Inspector's Office and the Governor's Council on Ethics were a direct result of the work we did. Cloistered in the state house basement for weeks on end digging through files, huddled in Eric's office night after night haggling over phrasing that wouldn't get us sued, checking facts, confirming sources.

State contracts were going to builders who clearly weren't up to the work. Eric and I started looking into the process of how those contracts were awarded, and from there into specific bids and decisions. We looked at key legislators on the Appropriations Committee whose campaign contributors included prominent construction firms. Firms whose projects resulted in unusable libraries and other deeply flawed public facilities. We followed the connections one way or another back to Ashton-Cooper, an engineering consulting firm which had played a role in a majority of these ill-fated building projects. We started our investigation with Mickey Connors, a state rep from Saugus and the youngest son of a legendary Boston political family. Mickey's connection to building firms that got – and mismanaged – state building projects was my first piece in what became a series which tunneled wider and deeper.

We documented examples where the influence of Connors and two other legislators led to the awarding of contracts involving

135

Ashton-Cooper and one or another of their favored builders. Then an aide let slip a comment that helped me trace a direct link between Connors and a check from Ashton-Cooper. Turned out it wasn't the only one of its kind.

For weeks I practically lived in the State House archives, substantiating instances in which mysterious checks appeared in legislators' bank accounts – checks whose sources led back, directly or indirectly, to Ashton-Cooper. Other reporters picked up the issue and made contributions of their own.

Connors resigned and managed to avoid prosecution. A legislative task force looked into the process of public contracting. A grand jury indicted two state senators, who were convicted of accepting bribes and sentenced to jail terms. The State Inspector's Office was created and charged with the investigation and prevention of mismanagement in state contracting. The Governor's Commission on Ethics, in its founding report, charged that "corruption was a way of life in the commonwealth" and that "political influence, not professional performance, was the prime criterion for doing business."

There were other good results. Tougher bidding laws. A contract process with accountability. A few bad apples wormed out of administrative office. And a hit of short-lived celebrity for me. TV news and talk shows. Job offers. I rode the attention, followed the story to the end. I was no better a reporter than I had been six months before. The level of corruption was rampant and Beacon Hill's notorious disdain for accountability had simply made legislators sloppy.

But there was another side. A contingent of business leaders and elected officials called it a witch hunt. We were accused of muckraking. Fabricating evidence. Ashton-Cooper and two of the four construction firms refused to ever acknowledge what lay in plain sight; while they were slapped with fines and reduced to a level playing field, their influence on Beacon Hill was strong enough they avoided major consequences.

The excitement waned and I started looking for the next thing, weighing offers. I acknowledged to myself the *Weekly* was no longer the *Weekly* I'd loved. An air of self-satisfaction had infected the paper and begun to infect me. A steady decline in ad revenue made investigative work prohibitively expensive, a rare indulgence. Eric and I talked about moving on, but neither of us knew where. We'd worked hard and done some good, but too many of the same assholes still manned the controls, able to twist that good and erode the ground that had been gained. Besides, it was clear to anyone who stopped to look that progressive journalism was in its death throes. It was another few months before I resigned without taking another offer.

Hearing Eric Grunow's voice brought it all back. Cast into relief the span of years, the chasm between what I had done then and who I was now.

If I was going to consider a column, the city offered no shortage of material.

"In Malden last night, vandals attacked another Berkley's. Plate glass windows were smashed and anti-globalist slogans spray-painted in the store. Sport utility vehicles vandalized in the area. It all fits a recent pattern attributed to activists."

Moratorium, day 3. July 3. I camped in front of the tube, watching the late news in my Aloha boxers with a midnight snack of raisin bran and a Cairn terrier named Archie. AJ had left for a long holiday weekend with his in-laws. He'd planned to skip out on it but couldn't: after all his anxiety, he finished the double issue on time. Since the kennel was full and I owed him, I got the dog.

Natalie Noone anchored for Channel Five. She was no Camille Oliver, but she was alright. "Well, it's a wild summer in Boston and police are talking tough about the recent spike in violent activism. Just last week, a traffic blockade choked the Back Bay, night banking radicals vandalized dozens of ATMs, and activists are suspected of the trash dump inside Endicott..."

"I don't like this," I told Archie through a mouth full of cereal.

Natalie intro'd a clip from the police commander.

"This is not mischief. These are criminal acts," he said. He was the suit sort of cop, not the uniform sort. "And they will be prosecuted to the fullest extent of the law."

I'd spent the day goofing around on the computer. Started and abandoned various column ideas – a broadside against the Newton cops, a tract on violence as a flawed political tactic, a tirade against our health care system, a paean to the manual typewriter. Talked briefly with Bo. *–You OK? –Better. –Eat anything? –Yeah. –For real? –(a laugh) Yeah.* Frolicked with the dog in Franklin Park.

Natalie again. "Boston Mayor Norm Reeves spoke out about the rising violence. Saying that whatever the connection – or lack of one – between all these incidents, police must act quickly."

Cut to the mayor. "We need to show people these acts of violence and anarchy will be punished."

"Not good, dog." Archie cocked his head. "They're making irresponsible connections." Like Natalie, the mayor, and certain Boston Police officials, Archie didn't seem to understand.

I have a bias against dinner-plate dogs. And there was this medicine I was supposed to give him – he's got a fragile heart, according to AJ's wife, and I'm thinking don't we all – and four walks a day 'cause the medicine makes his bowels loose. But Archie had spunk. A little spiked rubber ball he'd chase all day if you let him. After the park, we spent the evening with a Fred MacMurray noir double bill – *Above Suspicion* and *Borderline* – and an Indian feast of chicken vindaloo for two. I wasn't sure it was a good idea, but Archie seemed to like it.

Natalie returned from commercials. "And now, from violence to threats of violence. News Five has learned that in the last 24 hours, two Endicott executives have received threats."

"Fuck," I said to Natalie. "Shit." I dribbled raisin bran.

That morning I'd got an email from SLAM – Bo must have put me on their list. *The Student Labor Action Movement applauds the janitors' courageous actions standing against corporate greed.* I'd followed the link to their site, which highlighted the group's acronym and their clenched fist anarchist logo. I found a page about their past campaigns – a history of aligning themselves with causes toward which they felt sympathetic. I felt certain I was seeing their impact.

Archie lay between me and the TV so he could watch both.

"Chris Tillman would neither confirm nor deny the threats." Cut to a combative Tillman, all but leaning forward in a boxer's stance. "Am I scared? No. What I am is angry."

139

Natalie again. "Endicott CEO Marcus Gregory declined comment."

Of course he did. Marcus Gregory ran half of Greater Boston and remained virtually invisible.

I thought about the tough talk on both sides and how it only created more problems. I thought about my blacksmith grandfather and bare knuckles boxing. The toughness that presupposed. How visceral Stan's world, Thomas' world, compared to mine. The directness appealed to me. I felt echoes of something similar in Bo, in his friends.

My raisin bran had gone soggy. Natalie wasn't done. "The union may be taking a day off, but cleaning companies aren't. Replacement workers for Delfi and Viatron will start today."

Fuckers.

I'd picked an interesting summer to come watch my father die. Strewn on the couch were the last couple days' worth of *Globes*, *Heralds*, and *Views*, as well as the most recent *US News* and *Time*. Events in Boston had earned mention in the national news mags, and I'd spent the previous night comparing coverages.

I was torn between poles of anger. On the one hand, corporate greed had spawned the disillusionment whose fruit we were now seeing; on the other hand the destructive, violent acts of those whose sympathies I (and many others) might otherwise share could endanger an important cause. That sounded pompous enough for a column. I clicked off the TV. Adjusted my alohas. Almost called Eric Grunow to commit myself to a bully pulpit. Archie gave me a look. He was right. Time for bed.

The moratorium unofficially stretched on, because day four was Independence Day. Usually I took time to steel myself against holiday loneliness and scale down my expectations. But that year caught me unprepared. First strategy was to stay in bed and sleep through the day. Shame foiled that plan. Second strategy: be proactive. Live fully. That felt oxymoronic as a solo act on an iconic summer holiday. No matter.

Went for a long run. Showered and shaved. Cleaned the house some. Toyed with titles for my nonexistent column.

One o'clock. Sad. Restless. Called Bo, got voice mail. Called Terry, got same. About to be flattened by major lonely wave. Called Lin. Got her. But she was on rounds and couldn't talk. Then she and Bo were heading to a friend's for a cookout. Thought about calling Juliana Reyes to express my sympathy. But couldn't convince myself it was really about condolence.

No problem. I had options.

I could visit Thomas.

Picked up a blueberry pie on my way to Brentwood. But maybe Thomas didn't like blueberry, because he either slept or pretended to the whole time. So I ate the pie myself and watched New England Cable News mourn the two janitors. That's when the sad hit me. All of a sudden Eduardo and I had been bosom friends, kindred spirits, and the deaths of these two men signaled the end of all hope. I turned to my father for reassurance: eyes closed, almost smiling. As some desperate countermeasure, I dialed Eric at *The View*. Left him a message that I would do the column, that it would be about the strike, and that I'd have a draft to him within a week. Perfect. Now I was sad *and* screwed. A nurse I didn't know poked her head in, but ducked out fast when she saw me, as if the scene were too pathetic even for her.

All holidays eventually end, and the next afternoon I met Bo at Mars, our favorite used CD store. I came from an uneventful visit with my father; Bo came from his new summer job at a South End day care. He still wore his staff t-shirt, banana yellow.

I hugged him and he let me.

"Show-off," I said. My shirt, sweat through, stuck to my back.

"Role model." He surfed the bins, energized – caffeine, adrenaline. The old Bo. "Youths look to me for guidance."

Go with it. "Another sign of the apocalypse. So how's the job?"

"I like it. Goal number one is to help Milo lose his fear of the monkey bars."

He found an old Durutti Column disc and a new Anti-Flag. I found nothing I couldn't do without, so I ogled Liz Phair CD art while Bo browsed.

"Hey," he called. "Big Audio Dynamite. Which is the good one?" He held up a disc for inspection.

"The first," I said. "That's the one."

He made his purchases and we headed for the car. The air stifling. I was grateful for his company. "I'm thinking about some music tonight," I ventured. "You interested?"

"Can't," he said. "Meeting friends for coffee."

Fine.

I had nowhere I needed to be, and Bo had an errand to run, so I drove him. "Where we going?"

"Route 9 west."

142

We had the windows down on the Dart, a hot breeze blowing through. I had the radio tuned to NPR, where we caught the end of a story on the janitors' funeral.

"I wouldn't be surprised if they were taken out," Bo said. "Murdered."

Oy. "They died in a car accident, Bo."

"They died in a car *fire*, Nick. We don't know it was an accident."

"Righto."

"Think about it." Bo's arm out the window. "Union leaders. Strong voices. A strike that's gaining popular support. Kind of an unlikely coincidence."

Oy oy. "Accidents happen, Bo. Even to people on the periphery of public affairs." I drove west, locked in the passing lane. I didn't want to do this. "How's his family?"

Bo stared out the windshield long enough I thought he hadn't heard me. "Why does every good thing have to get shit on?"

I nodded, hugged a reverse curve.

He vented. "These people don't value workers. They're spare parts, to be replaced when they get expensive. Or troublesome."

Sure, it was a defense. But still. "That the anarchist line?" I stuck a fist in the air. "Fight the power."

"Don't embarrass yourself, Nick."

It took a lot to embarrass me. He should know that. Bo switched from radio to one of his new CDs.

The breeze flirted with my hair. I should have left it alone. "Have you thought about the major disconnect between anarchy and your alleged faith?"

"*Anarchism.*"

Big Audio Dynamite sang about the bottom line. I drove with one palm on the wheel. Exasperated. That smug tone. Self-righteous rhetoric. Sometimes I wished he'd accept my greater wisdom and experience. Have lofty notions of how things should be, grow bitter when they don't unfold that way. But for fuck's sake, don't *do* anything.

Still. Intense sympathies on the one hand, denial of any human qualities on the other. "Destroying someone's car because you don't like their politics?"

"Really? I got a dead friend and you're upset because some asshole needs a paint job?" He picked at a thread on his jeans.

"Fair enough. Your morality's a little inconsistent is all."

"Fuck you." Bo blew out an indignant breath. "The system has rotted. Revolution only begins with people who have nothing to lose."

I didn't disagree. The rich got richer, the rest of us got kicked in the ass, and the history would be (re)written to suggest that success came to those who earned it. I didn't feel like arguing. I just couldn't tolerate self-righteousness in anyone but me. "Inspiring rhetoric. But I've been to your house."

Traffic slowed to a crawl, killing our hot breeze.

"You're so full of shit," he said. "Your whole generation. You wake up one day and it comes to you. *Wow, we're destroying the planet.* Let's study the causes, hold a candlelight vigil then turn the whole fucking mess over to our kids. *Here. Sorry.*" Bo glared out the windshield as he spoke. "I'm not sure I blame anyone of my generation for anything they do."

A busy road, a slant-6 engine, new music, 400 percent humidity. A fine day.

Our destination turned out to be a third floor apartment in a massive complex in Framingham. A blonde head appeared in the door frame seconds after Bo knocked.

"Yeah?"

"Suzanne?" We stood in a cramped, poorly lit hallway on coffee-colored carpet.

"Yeah." Mid-to-late twenties. Hair in a loose bun.

"I'm Bo. Friend of Marcela. This is Nick."

Suzanne Pruett. Fuck.

Door open maybe a foot. She wore scrubs. She looked tired. Washed out. "What do you want?"

Good question.

Bo: "I've been trying to reach her – a week, ten days. Haven't heard from her." Errand, my ass. "None of us have. I'm worried."

Suzanne Pruett leaned against the door frame looking puzzled and not at all amused. She glared at me as if I were responsible, rather than an onlooker trapped at the scene of this accident. She spoke to Bo. "You're what, sixteen?"

"Seventeen," he said.

"I'm guessing an ex-boyfriend."

He nodded.

Arms folded across her chest, she addressed me. "You came here because my sister doesn't return the ex-boyfriend's calls?" Her eyes were small. Reflected in them, Bo and I were smaller still. There was no point clarifying my participation as involuntary.

Bo: "We came here because she was traveling with you."

"Who told you that?"

"Your grandfather."

145

In the doorway, Suzanne almost grinned. She didn't say anything for a minute. We waited through it.

"Okay." She spoke to me again. "Let's put aside how sketchy this is, you show up here with your teen pal." Somewhere down the hall a door opened and closed. "Let's say you don't know what it's like to be a smart, sexy young woman who likes to maybe not be locked in." Distant footsteps became more so. "These boys," she said, "They don't want to accept she might get bored and move on. They call, maybe a few times a week, maybe a few times a day." Her voice sounded bored, as if she were reciting a script. "First couple times, it's cute. Flattering. After that, just gets annoying. So you change your cell number."

I slouched in the dim hall, inadvertently idiotic.

"My guess," she said, "she'll be back when she feels like she can breathe."

If I got any smaller I'd disappear. "I'm sorry. I thought we were running an errand."

Bo undaunted beside me. "Why would your grandfather tell me that?"

"Because he feels bad for you. Because he's an overmatched ex-cop with an overactive imagination and it's what he wants to believe. Because for him the only alternative is some scary girls-gone-wild scene." She backed out of the door frame. "We done?"

On the drive back, we hit traffic again at mall hell in Natick. I seethed. "That," I said, "was not cool."

Bo stared out the windshield. "I don't buy it," he said. "Marcela wouldn't just shut down."

We were surrounded by satisfied consumers. "Bo, it couldn't be any clearer."

"I'm telling you, Nick –"

"*Enough.*"

The rest of the drive was silent. Bo needed a good sulk. I needed to plot my escape from shame. I had a plan: a noir double feature, *Out of the Past* with Robert Mitchum and *Pushover*, with Fred MacMurray reprising his *Double Indemnity* shtick. Dark, and just cynical enough.

"AJ, I've got an idea." Daily Grind. I sat at a window table with a morning mug served up by my favorite Goth queen. A new day. A fresh start. My erstwhile editor had come back for his terrier. Archie and I had our tearful goodbye, and now he dozed on AJ's back seat.

"Nick. We had this conversation." He set down his mug, his bag. Dog-eared papers poked out the top. "I said yes."

"I want to pitch you on another story, and I want you to bear with me."

It was a bright morning. Clear. Summer sun shone on our city; that afternoon another batch of replacement workers were slated to begin stealing janitors' jobs. The day, like most now, would get hot.

"Let's do this one at a time, Nick. I'm maxed out."

"I know. One minute. Hear me out. Because on the surface it's going to sound strange. Because on the surface it's about bare knuckles boxing during the depression."

"I'm leaving, Nick."

"Bear with me. Because it's really a story of mental and physical tenacity – the ways it showed itself back then, the ways it does now.

147

What that says about us as a culture." The Grind was quiet. Just AJ and I and a trio of Brookline housewives.

"What does it say about us, Nick?"

"I don't know yet."

"Next subject. You're working on a piece. It's the labor piece. It will be a good piece."

There are times you have to just ignore peoples' negativity and press on. "How there's a ruthlessness to us now – our business dealings, our social institutions – but it's all indirect. The grit of our grandfathers, the immediacy, it's gone. And Bo, his generation, they're rejecting our detachment. Looking for something more primal."

On the shop's sound system, strident feminist neo-folk. Couldn't AJ see it was all connected?

He looked at me like I was work.

My forearm hurt when I made a fist or clutched a mug. "It's a hell of an idea, AJ. You should think about it."

"There's a lot of things I ought to think about, but I've got no energy for those, either."

Fuck it. If AJ wouldn't bite, I'd salt it away for a future column. "What is it with editors? Is there some law that you have to develop a slouch, become timid and unimaginative old men?"

"Tough night last night?"

No more so than most. I'd run the gamut of late-night talk shows, then laid awake wondering why I'd said yes to Eric Grunow. How many days it would be before I was exposed as a fraud. "Okay," I said. "Here's one. What percentage of burglaries you think are committed in daylight? Aggravated assaults? You have any idea how many robberies go unsolved? Say, in a town like Newton?"

He stared into his mug. "Maybe you should ease up on the coffee."

I couldn't help it. If I didn't redirect my energy, all the shit I didn't want to think about would come crashing down. Then where would I be. "Take a guess," I said. "Percent unsolved."

"I don't know. Twenty. Twenty-five."

"Flip it around." The housewives left. AJ and Goth girl and I had the place to ourselves. "That's how many get solved."

"Really." Half-interested. Polite.

"Don't you think there's something wrong with that? How can the cops just quit on these cases?"

"I'm guessing other stuff happens they need to move on to." AJ sipped low-test.

"The Tillman case, the only lead they've got is a black Lexus that may have been in the neighborhood around the time of the robbery. How lame is that? I mean, there's gotta be more."

AJ shrugged. "I'm a business editor."

My mug was empty. That made me sad. I gestured at AJ's. "Want more?"

He shook me off. "No joy in simulacra."

Goth girl was sexily sleeveless. Soloing through the mid-morning lull in black tank top and pout. Her head buried in a textbook I craned my neck to read. Genetics. I went breezy. "Could I have more, please?"

She looked up at a spot past my shoulder. "Decaf?"

"Never," I said, stung. "Fuck, no." There was urgency, even passion, in my voice.

She rolled her eyes. Left her stool. Slid me my refill. A cynical soul would say my campaign was on the ropes.

When I got back to the table there was a stack of business cards on it, bound with a rubber band.

"What's this?"

"Street cred," AJ said.

It was a small stack, maybe twenty, but still.

"Don't fear them," AJ said. "They don't imply anything permanent." He squinted against the day's brightness.

I picked the stack up. It didn't terrify me. "Eric Grunow called yesterday," I said.

AJ tried to sound surprised. "Really?"

"Wants me to write for him. A column."

"Really?" He was a bad actor.

"So you gave him my number. If this was a charity call..."

"He called looking for you." He emphasized it. "People don't offer columns out of charity, Nick."

"I don't know." I clutched my mug.

"What's not to know?"

"I'm temporary, remember? Itinerant." Synonymous with *the guy alone in the coffee shop.* "Besides, I don't know if I want to go back to this."

"It's not marriage. Try it. Do what you do, for now."

Sure, there was that, but there was also this: one thread, then another and another, suddenly you find yourself bound. I shrugged. "I gotta think about it."

"It's hot. We're tired. Tired of asking for the same things and getting no answer. Our families are anxious, wondering how the bills will get paid."

Juliana addressing the janitors' noon march and rally. Dark hair pulled back off her face. July sun beat down. No breeze.

"But we are here, standing strong even in the face of tragedy. And we will continue to stand strong, and carry the memory of Marcus Najera and Eduardo Mendoza until we have justice."

The crowd was still strong. BAFA continued to impress me with both its commitment and ability to turn out bodies. But there were fewer purple t-shirts. You could feel cracks in the janitors' resolve, and you had to wonder how long that resolve would last in the face of dead colleagues, missing paychecks, and the looming prospect of lost jobs.

My phone rang. I ducked away to answer. Eric, excited about the column. "Let's do something worthwhile, Nick. Holler if there's anything you need."

I swallowed self-doubt and made my way back into the crowd of strangers, focusing on Juliana's voice. Her grit. She was wrapping up. Logistics. I worked my way beside the podium. I wanted to catch her and Sam, express my condolences. Caught Sam, and was turning toward Juliana when she saw me and approached.

"Juliana, I just wanted to say I was sorry to hear about the accident."

She took my hand. "Thank you, Nick." She held it just long enough for me to hope it meant something, then a man with a microphone shoved his way through, followed by a camera.

I recognized him from my former life. Alvin Fraser, Channel Five. Back when I knew him, Fraser had been an ambitious punk who bulldozed his way into other people's stories. Over the years he'd turned himself into a local celebrity with a style that left no doubt every piece was about him. He had the same parted-in-the-middle, blow-dried haircut and boyish face, now with crow's feet and gray at the temples. He was the kind of fucker who gave journalists a bad name.

"Ms. Reyes, Alvin Fraser, Channel Five. How do you respond to allegations that the union is quietly applauding – even encouraging – the trash vandalism in downtown buildings and the anti-globalist incidents around town?"

He thrust the microphone in Juliana's face.

She took a breath and stared him down. Sam walked away. "Who's making these allegations?"

"Ms. Reyes, how do you respond?"

"When I hear the specific allegations and the source of those allegations, I may have something to say."

Fraser wasn't about to quit. "Isn't it true the union is benefiting from the increased publicity these events have generated, that more attention has been focused on the strike, and that the push to connect the janitors' cause to a larger, anti-globalist economics movement has broadened your public support?"

I wanted the microphone. I had an answer.

Juliana waited. You could see wheels turning in her head.

"I do not believe that violence benefits any cause, that publicity for its own sake is a desirable end, or that threats are an acceptable way to negotiate. The Service Employees International Union has no specific grievance against the Endicott Corporation or any other company, nor do we have a desire or interest in expanding this cause, as you call it. What we seek, what we are demonstrating for, what we have been clear and consistent in calling for, is to sit down around a table with real options and come to a resolution that puts the janitors back to work under conditions that are just for both sides."

Fraser locked in. "How will you respond to the hiring of replacement workers? Couldn't your members be out of jobs within a couple of weeks?"

I wanted to shut him up. Argue him into embarrassment.

"We believe the hiring of replacement workers to be illegal and we will contest that move in the courts."

"Ms. Reyes –"

She cut him off. "That's all I have to say." Touched my wrist with her fingers and walked away. My wrist felt warm. *She's smart, Nick. Committed. You should pursue this.* A man's voice interrupted my musings.

"You sir. Are you with the union?"

Fraser didn't recognize me. It had been a long time, and people as self-absorbed as Alvin Fraser only remember faces that can advance their ends.

"No," I said, brushing past. "I'm with the press."

9

In 30 days – barring incident – my father would be booted from Brentwood Home. I had a certified letter that said so. I opened it, read it, and went back to bed. When that didn't work, I did strike research. People talk about denial like it's a bad thing. Me, I say it's the only way some of us get anything done. I learned, for instance, that since President Reagan fired 12,000 striking air traffic controllers in 1981, the threat of replacement workers had become a common strikebreaking tool. 30 days. Thomas didn't feel inclined to deal with his financial obligations. Fine. Maybe I wouldn't either. Fuck him. Let him deal when they dumped him and his meager belongings on the sidewalk.

In this frame of mind I went to see my father.

The smell of human decay struck me as I walked into Brentwood, and the rogues' gallery regulars – the Crooner, the Weeper, Hairless Sal – lined up in their wheelchairs by the nurses' station further eroded my angry resolve. I tunneled my vision and set a fast pace toward Thomas' room. Behind me, the Crooner sang: "Please release me, let me go." *Careful what you wish for.*

As I turned into the room, I switched from sulky to breezy. Call it compassion. Call it self-preservation.

"Hey handsome. What's shakin'?"

He sat in a green chair, a plate of foul-smelling food untouched on his table.

"You didn't eat."

He looked at the plate, then at me. "I picked the BLT," he said. "That look like a BLT?"

Gray meat and noodles in a congealed, creamy sauce. "Want me to get you something else?"

He shook his head.

I wheeled the table into the hallway so we could at least escape the smell. Came back and parked in the chair next to his.

"Paul. I didn't realize you were here."

I sat through the awkwardness – that first impulse to get the hell out. He came and went so fast I couldn't help wondering at times if he put it on. Forever wishing I was someone else.

"You remember that baseball game we played growing up?" My father said. "With the dice?"

Right. 30 days. *Barring incident.* The fuck did that mean?

He had sports highlights on the television. Tennis. Baseball. The Sox won, 5-2. It would be a couple weeks before they'd start their slow, steady fade.

"I'm doing this magazine piece, Dad. For *BusinessForward*, about the janitors' strike and what implications it has for labor relations around the country." Just talking. If denial was a river, could I catch its current. Had I really called Eric Grunow and committed to a column? Or was it part of a recurring nightmare in which I found increasingly extravagant ways to fuck up? Exposure as a fraud in a public forum. Excellent.

Anyway, nothing from Thomas. He watched out the window. Presumably, the grass grew.

A column. Fuck me. What did I have? I considered a rant against the Newton cops. A clever mosaic – the bare bones facts of the Tillman robbery juxtaposed against statistics. A litany of woes regarding the hometown police. Yes, it was a cheap shot. I like to think professional ethics would have eventually stopped me. Fear of exposure as petty and superficial got there first.

Footsteps behind us. A nurse I hadn't seen before, holding the lunch tray. Thomas waved a dismissive hand at her. "Take it. I don't want it."

She moved to set the tray on his table. "I'll leave it for when you change your mind." A short woman with brown corkscrew hair and a Caribbean accent.

"Take it away!"

The nurse's mouth got small. "Settle down, old man."

I tried to play peacemaker. "He asked for a BLT."

She eyed me. Sizing me up or staring me down. She spoke to Thomas. "If you waiting for this to turn into the Ritz, is not gonna happen." She took the tray and spun out of the room.

The smell didn't leave with the food. I looked around for likely causes. Didn't find anything. 30 days to figure something out.

"So," my father said, not looking at me.

Sometimes the chasm between Thomas and I felt boundless. Other times merely impassable. I couldn't remember a time it wasn't there. I'd first felt it as something permanent – elemental –

when he returned from his New Hampshire exile. It was as though he'd categorically disengaged from me, which only confirmed what I'd long felt: I was his kid and he'd deal with that fact, but he didn't want to be my father. We'd been staring across that precipice ever since.

The nurse reappeared. She had an ID badge. First name Florida. Thrust at Thomas a tiny paper cup containing a vitamin. "If you're not gonna eat, you gotta take this."

He looked at her, blank. Swallowed the pill with some water. She took the empty medicine cup and left the room.

"That the nurse you were telling me about? Florida? The one with the state name?"

"Huh?" He tugged at the knee of his pants. My father had a fondness for those heavy-duty work chinos – forest green, navy blue – that were virtually indestructible.

"Your shirt. Your brush." I kept my voice low. Leaned close. Yeah, I had concerns, but I didn't need to make enemies of Thomas' caretakers. They were willing to do a job I wasn't. "You thought they might have been stolen. Was it Florida?"

I got the hairy eyeball. "Florida? The hell you on about. I've never been to Florida."

Fine. So maybe she'd taken a hair brush. I'd never know the real story. *Thomas Young has come unstuck in time.* So it goes.

"You doing your exercises?" I grabbed the red rubber ball off the end table. "They'll help you get better."

He scowled. I still smelled something beyond the usual odors of decaying humanity and alleged food. I said so.

"Don't be so sensitive."

Whatever. I checked the counter, the wastebasket.

"Sit the fuck down, will you?" He tried not to watch me. "Christ," he scowled. "You always were fussy. It's nothing. It's in your head."

It wasn't. I'd prove it. I looked in the closet. Behind the curtains. Finally, I pulled back the covers on his unmade bed. Recoiled from shit-stained sheets.

"Jesus, Nick." Red-faced. "Satisfied?"

A wave of despair hit me, worse than the smell. "It's okay, Dad. Just ask someone to change the bed."

"I did," he said. "Twice."

"And?"

He shrugged.

I started for the hall. "I'll talk to Florida."

"Don't." His voice firm, almost a command.

"She can get it taken care of."

"Don't tell her." This time pleading.

"Dad, what?"

"She's mean." He spat out the words. We both sat with that. His look condemned me for what I'd forced him into. Close enough to feel the other's breath, and no way across. It had to get cleaned up. I asked at the desk for an attendant.

Half an hour later someone came in and changed the sheets. Meantime, my father and I watched nothing happen slowly out the window. This visit was shot. 29 days.

That afternoon the janitors' strike took a sharp left. I found out about it sooner than most via my *other* editor, Eric Grunow.

"Something's happening outside Endicott."

"What?"

"Don't know, but it's right now."

What it was: a couple hundred people seated peacefully in front of the main entrance to Endicott HQ. They had chained the doors shut and connected themselves to each other – and to the entrance – using a braided steel cable and Kryptonite bike locks hung around their necks. I made record time through afternoon rush hour and got there for the whole show. The police had no better info than I. We arrived simultaneously. The dozen or so cops unprepared for what they saw.

No signs. No purple t-shirts. No chanting. Just quiet resolve. People willing to be arrested on principle for something that didn't directly affect them.

I scanned faces – mostly young. Lots of students. I suspected SLAM and I'd turn out to be half right. In addition to the chain gang, another couple hundred bodies gawked and put themselves in the way. If I wasn't mistaken, this was about the time the replacement janitors were scheduled to start their day. The gathered cops threaded through bystanders to the chain. I threaded close behind them. Full-on summer. Hazy and hot. Stifling.

A text from Eric. *What's going on?* Then another, on top of it. *Send pix.* I punched back *Later* and put my cell away.

The cop nearest me, a short, solid guy with dark hair and a thick moustache, rolled his eyes when he saw what he was up against. He muttered something. I'm pretty sure it was "fuck this." The usual city buzz filled the air – car horns, squeaky bus brakes, the occasional airplane. The demonstrators might have been office workers on afternoon break. The cops now formed a rough semicircle between the inner ring of chained protestors and the outer ring of onlookers. Not one officer looked eager to deal. You see happier faces on root canal patients. I worked my way around the building to confirm my suspicion that other entrances were similarly occupied.

Yup. Outside a service entrance next to the loading dock on Franklin Street massed another crowd. Same deal there. Chain gang tight to the entrance. Onlookers crowded the passage, the sidewalk. Commuters had to swell into the street to get by. I felt a flush of righteous pride. Solidarity. On the sidewalk, a crew of blue-smocked scabs – a couple dozen, maybe thirty, mostly Latino. A half-dozen rent-a-cops no more prepared to deal with this than the real cops. A siren sounded the arrival of reinforcements down the block.

No one seemed sure what to do next. I smelled grilled chicken and craved a burrito. One of the rent-a-cops must have had a brainstorm, because he cleared a path and provided the smocked replacement workers unblocked access to the crowd chained at the entrance. It was a bizarre sight and the new janitors' faces wore anxious looks. A few laughed. Not one moved. You could smell their discomfort. I heard a van door behind me and turned expecting more cops, but it was Fox News, followed closely by Eyewitness News. Behind them a detachment of cops. The circus had officially begun.

I took a few instinctual steps back and watched it unfold. Fox's camera crew emerged fast, hoisted cameras, rolled tape. The Eyewitness reporter milled among the replacement workers keying into the vibe. The rent-a-cops used their bodies to maintain a path to the entrance that no one took. A few replacement workers turned to leave. If they'd been hesitant before, the arrival of news teams had made them downright allergic. Once the first few left, the others followed fast. You could sense the news crews' disappointment. When the scabs left, there was no need for rent-a-cops. It became the slow, dull work of real police cutting loose and arresting demonstrators. I was no veteran of direct actions, but the deference between the two groups impressed me. The cops surely would have met force with force. But they also met gentleness with gentleness. A hand under a tricep to help a young woman up. An arm guiding an older man into the van, making sure he wasn't shoved. Their distaste directed more at what they were being asked to do than at the protestors.

Score one for civil disobedience. A young man watched the woman next to him get cuffed and carted off. Waiting his turn. The young man looked familiar. With good reason. He was Bo. I phoned him. He answered.

"Hey, Nick. What's up?"

"You okay?"

A female cop approached him.

"I can't really talk now."

"I know. I can see you. You okay?"

I saw him smile. Scan the crowd. The cop cut Bo loose, unwound him from the braided cable. He let it happen. "I'm *good*."

"You gonna need bail?"

"Thanks. Not sure how this works. I'll call you."

The cop waited for Bo to adjust his untucked shirt before fitting him with plastic zip cuffs. I watched her lead him by the upper arm toward the van. Sharing his satisfaction. A touch proud. As if I'd instilled this. As if I could claim credit.

The police process was less than half done. Dozens of demonstrators still snaked from the entrance, chained to the doors or to each other. I thought about Thomas and Brentwood and how I could chain him to a radiator in protest. Time to go. I saluted Bo and his fellow agitators and headed for the house.

Archie met me at the door groaning. I'd forgotten his afternoon trot. Truth was, I'd forgotten him entirely. AJ's wife and kids had stayed on for a week at the shore with her parents, and AJ had been summoned to New York to see the money guys, so I'd inherited Archie again. To celebrate our reunion, we relived our night of videos and vindaloo; this time Archie got the shits, though, so I promised him we'd expand our palate beyond Indian. Anyway, I got involved in the day and forgot about him. So I let him go in the back yard and resolved to take him on a real walk once I caught up on the news.

It turned out the same scene had played out at all five downtown office buildings where replacement workers had been contracted, and that SLAM was only half the story. The scab shutdown was a joint effort with Jobs for Justice, another leftist labor group. The SLAM web site, which gave a shout-out to a true cost economics blog by someone named Marcela Pruett, told me what I already suspected: SLAM had officially adopted the janitors' strike as a campaign; Shutdown Scabs Day had announced their arrival.

Channel Five's Camille Oliver told me the rest:

"A dramatic scene downtown this afternoon as members of

two activist groups chained themselves across the entrances of downtown office buildings in a show of support for striking janitors." Camille wore a peach-colored jacket – not a good choice for her skin tone. I said so aloud, but Archie wasn't interested. He sulked in the corner of the den making weird noises. "More than 250 demonstrators were arrested at the five buildings where replacement janitors have been hired. Their goal: to obstruct the arrival of so-called 'scab' workers. It succeeded. By the time frustrated police cleared the scenes, the stunned replacement workers had gone home."

The footage behind Camille's head showed the doings at Endicott. Cuffed demonstrators filed slowly into vans.

"While the strike action was a success, neither side welcomed it. In fact, charges and counter-charges flew."

Cut full-screen to Chris Tillman with a microphone in his face – "not negotiate with those who endorse this kind of behavior." *Careful, Chris.* "These strong-arm tactics will not force our hand, nor will they intimidate company management or our new employees."

Looking at Tillman made me think of his son. Breathing tubes and a lonely hospital bed. *Go home,* I thought. *Keep vigil.* Let Marcus Gregory take the spotlight, and the heat. But when you're the bad cop and your work is the top news story in the area, maybe you don't get that option.

Back to Camille: "Andrew Sarkis of Pollard took the rhetoric a step further." Now a red-faced, red-bearded bald man commanded the screen. "By excusing if not encouraging the acts of these radicals, the union must be held accountable."

163

Not surprisingly, Juliana was pissed. She appeared next. "These groups do not represent the janitors. They have no connection with the union. They are independent citizens exercising their rights. To suggest a connection, let alone an endorsement, is not only wrong-headed, it's slanderous."

Yikes. Time for the voice of reason. Not in the sound bites, that's for sure. Got a trace of it in the mayor's response, criticizing Tillman and Sarkis for "incendiary language."

"Both sides need to calm down," he said. "Stop trying to demonize each other. Get back to the bargaining table and address the issues, the specific obstacles, and work toward resolution."

A good start. I wanted it to go further. It didn't. But I had the seed for my first column.

After an abbreviated but cathartic run, Archie and I walked to Jamaica Pond, down the hill to the little park where I threw the ball for him, a half hour, him still wanting more. The sun had begun its slow summer fade. To get Archie to leave I had to pocket the ball. We headed across Perkins Street toward home.

Along Cypress, I heard the distant sound of a phone. Took me three rings to realize it was mine.

Teresa.

"Hey."

"Hey yourself. What'cha doing?"

"Walking AJ's dog. You?"

"Just got back from the first day's shooting."

"Ah. How'd it go?" I crossed Archie over to the sidewalked side of the street. A majestic sunset had begun – purple-pink sky. A hint of breeze.

"It went great. Director's very respectful. Either knows and likes my work, or does a good job pretending. Right now, either's okay."

Archie stopped to sniff a shrub. I stopped with him. He peed and trotted along again, happy as a clam.

"So you think you'll like it?"

"I'm a professional. I'll do a good job and see what comes of it. And guess what else? Turns out the assistant camera is this guy Jake that I'd dated a few months ago, liked him, then never heard from him. Chalked it up. So he's thrilled to see me today, tells me how he was just getting out of another relationship at the time and regretted not calling."

"And you bought that?"

Across the street, a narrow driveway led up a tree-lined hill to luxury homes: Jamaica Plain's only gated community.

"It's possible. Anyway, we're going to dinner."

I had no right, but I felt wounded. Not because she was going out with this guy, but because she already had and I hadn't known.

"Cool. Keep me posted." I tried to sound upbeat and not reveal my vulnerability.

I missed what she said next because Archie stopped in his tracks, coughing-gasping. I thought maybe I'd pulled too hard on the leash. But it was getting worse. He wasn't getting any air.

"Teresa," I said into the phone. "The dog's having a seizure. I gotta go."

I scooped Archie up and hurried for home. His little body shook with convulsions. *Don't fucking die on me. I only missed one walk.* I stopped twice so he could puke. We got to the house and into the Dart and headed for Angell Memorial, an animal hospital less than a mile away. I wrapped Archie in a towel – I didn't know what to do for him – and talked to him all the way. "Don't die, Archie. Your father wouldn't like that. Hell, I wouldn't like that. Your people love you." I told him about Bo's noble arrest. Talked through my column idea. Wondered if I was a curse to dogs. Somewhere in all that, Archie's breathing slowed. The vet was quick and reassuring when I explained the situation.

"It's not his heart," he said. A wiry guy, he had a prominent nose and close-cropped black hair. He checked Archie out and declared him healable. "It's his stomach. He eat anything he shouldn't have?"

I looked at Archie, then at the floor. Okay, so the vindaloo wasn't the best idea. I fessed up.

The vet shot me a look.

"How was I supposed to know?" I explained my dog-sitter status. Even the medical tech – a teenage girl I thought I recognized as part of Bo's crew – gave me a look. The vet reassured me Archie would recover. He wanted to keep him overnight for observation.

I drove back to the house, kicking myself. *Dog food, Nick. It exists for a reason.* Wing it. Improvise and fuck the consequences. Right. I was not fit to care for anything. Anyone. But at least I hadn't killed the dog.

Restless. Thought about dinner, but didn't feel like cooking. Thought about calling AJ, but didn't want to worry him. Worked my notes from the interview with the labor relations guy for a while, but wasn't into it. Didn't feel like hanging around. Checked the *Weekly* club listings. No bands I knew. So go for the best name. Easy. Residual Funkitude were playing at 608 in Somerville. Across town, but what the hell. That stretch of Somerville Ave had become active, a hot place to hang in what used to be a desolate corner of town. The SkyBar and the B-Side Lounge right up the street.

I stopped at Doyle's for the fish and chips and a couple drafts. Sat at the bar with a handful of others. One 30-ish woman knitting, one eye on the news, a nearly full pint before her.

Juliana's face on the TV screen, though I couldn't hear which clip they'd used. Alvin Fraser doing his standard close-up high drama voiceover finish. I scowled. The bartender saw it and laughed.

"You like that guy?" I asked him.

He refilled a tray with peanuts for the knitting woman. "Fraser? He's a putz. Always has been."

I left a healthy tip.

I had time to kill. Called Angell to check on Archie. Sleeping peacefully. All signs positive. The medical tech thought it was cute I called.

Two used bookstores in Central Square, looking for a hardcover of Flannery O'Connor's *Wise Blood*. Futile, but a long-time dream and a constructive time-killer.

Drove through Somerville, then Everett, just to see what had changed. Once upon a time I'd done a couple stories on the trucking of liquefied natural gas through Everett. How these huge tankers traveled residential streets and a citizens group decided that was a bad idea. Fought it for a year, won for a while. The houses hadn't changed much since those days, but now there were a couple shopping plazas, huge parking lots, a Target, a K-Mart.

My phone rang. Bo the Worthy.

"Hey. You a free man again?" I waited at a light.

"Hundred bucks bail. On my debit card. How cool is that? *Own recognizance.* Judge actually used those words."

"You OK?"

"Good," he said. "See the news? We're getting to him."

"Who?"

"Tillman."

The light went green. I merged onto Mystic Valley Parkway. "Come do music with me."

"Can't. Long day. Early track tomorrow. Gotta crash."

The screen went dark. I turned left on Mystic Ave.

Back to Somerville. Found a parking spot in a strip mall a couple blocks past the club. Found my way in. Found a cold Heineken.

Opening act played. The Moon Unit. Lots of energy and a sexy lead singer who'd modeled herself on Kay Hanley circa Letters to Cleo. One of those nights. Kept trying – and failing – to tear my eyes away from a girl in a shredded white muscle shirt and jeans decorated with scraps of lace and black spandex. Big eyes and a dyed-blonde crew cut and attitude. A way of moving that made me want to jump her. I tried to remind myself I was the old guy. No need to invite humiliation. Or, for all I knew, jail time.

I found a wall to lean against and watched people. The Moon Unit set ended and the room, long and narrow and dark, got crowded. I hit the men's then found another beer. The room, and half the bodies in it, throbbed now to a DJ mix. My spot along the wall was still there and so was the sexy faux blonde, dancing. *When in Rome.* I drained the bottle, nonchalanted my way onto the floor and joined the groove. It wasn't that I danced toward her so much as the force of her drew me. Yielding to the gravitational pull of a heavenly body. Anyway there I was and the groove was good.

A knot of us, half a dozen, in orbit. We fed off each other. Smiles. She caught my eye and sidled close, joined my rhythm. Young flesh through the shredded shirt. Beat pounding my chest. Her ass grazed my crotch and we both laughed, kept moving. Locked. Trance. Hips and thighs in thrust and sway. Sweat. A woody to keep me warm. I was loved on the dance floor. Deliciously lost. I could go all night, and so could she. I smelled her. If I stuck out my tongue I could lick her neck. I spun toward the others in our little circle on a keyboard fill, closed my eyes to soak in music lights joy, opened them to an apparition moving beside me. Recoil.

"That's twice you haven't asked me to dance. A girl could take it personally."

A tattooed beauty I would swear to Christ was Marcela Pruett. I blinked. Still there. I'd made that mistake before, but not from eight inches. A flush of heat that embarrassed me. I found no words. Dumb grin. *Keep the groove, hide shock.* Yes, it was her. Long clear face and long sweet body and long fingers, unadorned. Green mardi gras beads, a white tank top and black Capri jeans. Keeping the beat, I turned to see if my shredded shirt friend was still there. Affirmative. We did an ass grind. Marcela's voice in my ear.

"I've been watching you."

Fuck. How could she have this effect. I was blushing like a school kid. Caught, yes, but also. "People been looking for you."

Instant pout. She leaned close. "Don't be a buzzkill."

My body responded to her voice in ways I didn't care to think about. *Okay. Change gears.*

Shouting over the music. "You a fan?"

"I come here a lot. I know the bouncer."

"You know a lot of people."

"I'm a pretty girl." A smile fully reawakened my hard-on. Her lips tickling my ear. "So how come you didn't say hi?"

I leaned back to read her face. What kind of game was she playing? I had prospects elsewhere. Tried to think of a snappy comeback. Nothing. Drymouth. A simple, endless groove. Fuck it. I found her ear, close enough to speak soft. "How come you didn't?"

Her hand on the back of my neck. Throaty laugh. This time face to face, an inch away, mischievous grin. Just when I thought she wasn't going to say anything, "Thought you were with someone." Before I had a chance to laugh, she kissed me, soft full lips. I kissed her back. She tasted of ginger and tequila, two of my favorite things. And it was done. She flashed that grin and spun. I blinked. The beat in my chest. She was gone and so was my moment.

Faux blonde had found another groove. I was spoiled for it anyway. I'd love to say it was awakened maturity, but it was something else. Marcela's taste in my mouth. I quit dancing, killed a beer to kill an ugly voice in my head, and pretended to be preoccupied being impatient for Residual Funkitude.

My phone made its text message beep. I checked the screen:

let's get out of here.

meet me outside in 5? M.

How the fuck did she know my phone number? I told myself there were two possibilities: I was being played, or Marcela was hammered *and* I was being played. I also knew I'd be outside in five minutes to find out. I staged a brief internal debate. *–Don't be* *an idiot, Nick. – Shut the fuck up.* I waited through one song, then waited a couple minutes more – I've never liked appearing eager – before I let the doors spit me onto the sidewalk. A few smokers out there, but no Marcela.

Two young hipsters – white shirt and vest for one, jaunty fedora for the other – in heated discussion by a fire hydrant.

I walked up and down the block, checked the back parking lot. Nothing. Walked back. Wondered if my fragile ego could wait another minute. Shoved aside questions about what I was waiting for and leaned against the brick. The hipsters were still at it.

"There are bands you like on first listen, and there are bands–"

"They're ass."

"Give them another shot."

"Ass, ass, ass."

I moved to the other side of the door to ensure I didn't chime in unwanted or snort laughter. I pretended to be occupied with my phone, outlasted the hipsters, and had just resolved to never again open my damaged heart to young womanhood when the door opened and Marcela sauntered out.

She flashed that smile. "You have a car?"

"Down the block." She waited for me to lead the way, but I didn't. I had battles raging inside. I slouched against the wall. It pulsed from the beat downstairs. "How you feel about the Decemberists?"

She cocked her head in my direction. Like most things, it worked for her. "They're OK. Why?"

"Making conversation." Stalling for time. I wasn't sure where this was going. Wasn't sure I wanted to go there. I shook my head. "Activist. Hottie. Party girl. I can't make it add up."

171

She laughed. "Why do you need to?"

I didn't know how to answer.

She leaned against the wall beside me, helped absorb the beat. "You're odd," she said.

That made me like her.

She looked into the distance like she thought that was what you were supposed to do in this kind of awkward moment. "At first I thought *who's the old guy hanging around.* I mean, it was kind of intriguing and kind of creepy both. But then, I don't know, you fit. I liked you." Again with the smile that would rubberize any straight guy's knees.

I stabilized my rubber knees.

"Sometimes a girl gets tired of choosing between fun and substance," she said.

The wall pulsed behind us. She deserved better than a forty-two-year-old's lust. I felt old. Sober. I still had her taste in my mouth. I ran my tongue around inside it. "Nice piece on true cost economics."

I got the cocked head and a guarded smile.

"The blog." The door opened and closed. A blast of music and a specimen of youthful humanity escaped.

"Thanks," she said. Wary, but still willing.

"It made me feel hopeful. I don't feel that way often."

"Sad." Her neck looked my way. Her neck was exquisite.

We stood side by side against the wall.

"You know," she said, "I could use your help."

"For real?"

"For real." The sexy smile softened by a slight furrow in her brow. She shrugged. "Bo trusts you."

172

I tried not to register how sad that made me just then. "Talk to me."

"Not here. The car?"

We walked in the direction of the Dart. Close, but not touching. An odd intimacy. It felt innocent. I didn't examine it.

A taxi whooshed by.

We crossed a side street. A cell phone sounded. Hers. She stopped in the crosswalk to answer. "What? Where are you?" Urgent. Angry. Her eyes on me, then not. "Just up the block. I see your tail lights." She ended the call. Made a point of not looking at me. "I gotta go." Frustration in her voice, and something else.

I felt an almost parental concern. It made me wobbly. "I can drop you."

A car backed down the street toward us, fast and not entirely straight. It looked like Adam's Honda.

She cocked an eyebrow. "My ride." Her face looked young. Confused. Vulnerable. "Can I call you?"

The car fishtailed to a stop and the door flew open. A hyper-intense Adam in the driver's seat. He either didn't notice me or didn't care to acknowledge. "Hurry up," he said. Angry. Marcela hesitated. Marcela looked at him. At me.

The whole thing felt off. I reached for her. "I'll drive you. Don't–"

Adam: "*Let's go.*"

She got in and the car sped away, momentum pulling the door shut. I watched tail lights fade. Exhaust fumes hung in the night air around me.

I tried to understand what had happened. Tried to decide if she was in danger or if I was just an old guy on the side of the road.

Pulled out my phone, found Marcela's text and hit reply.

are you okay?

do you want out of there?

I waited stupidly on the sidewalk, fifteen, twenty minutes. Nothing. Dialed her number, got generic voice mail: *the Verizon customer you have dialed is not available.* Walked back to the club without answers. Without a clue. Flashed my hand stamp and downed a couple quick beers. Pretended to be preoccupied with Residual Funkitude, whose collective talents had been exhausted in choosing their name.

My phone rang. I checked the screen. Number restricted. "Yeah?" My pulse quickened.

"Hey, it's Lin."

"Hey." Disoriented. Ashamed. Weary.

"Where are you? It's loud."

"Club. You?"

"Hospital. Tough night. Was hoping you'd meet me for a drink. But if you're–"

"Sure. Where?"

"Anywhere." Even with the noise, something in her voice.

"What's going on?"

"Evan Tillman died tonight."

10

There wasn't much in the way of cocktails around the hospital, so Lin and I ended up in the bar at the Holiday Inn off Route 128. She was there when I walked in unsteady and overstimulated. Lin's news hadn't registered as real. The bar didn't help. Soft lights. Veneer. Vinyl banquettes. '70s tunes. Lin slumped on the green vinyl. Her work bag lay where it had fallen.

I parked alongside her. "Bad night."

"I broke down. Couldn't finish rounds." A storm brewed behind her eyes. "Kind of a code among doctors not to let a patient's death affect you."

"Lin, you know the family. Christ, you have a son that age. How could it *not* get to you."

"That's not the point."

"It's exactly the point. It's called being human."

Todd Rundgren on the speakers. She drank a gimlet. I got the same. We sat at right angles at a small table, fingers interlaced. We owned the place. The bartender, fortyish, weariness that bespoke a second job.

Lin in profile, hair shadowing her face. "I had to get out of there."

"Tell me."

It took her a minute. "Evan's body. I froze. Couldn't do a thing." She took a sip. "It was like watching Bo die."

I didn't want to think about Bo. "How'd he go?"

She shook her head. Even her hair looked tired. "His system just failed. Not enough resources to keep fighting."

I felt a wave of despair. Hard enough figuring out who the hell you were and how to make a life. I watched Lin try to hold it all in.

"You need to cry, woman."

That got a laugh. "Anyone ever tell you your bedside manner needs work?" she said.

"Don't use the word bed. It gets me excited." The banter felt empty.

We sat and sipped. Both a little raw. I was grateful to focus on something other than the events at the club. The Moody Blues took over from Todd Rundgren.

Lin at half-mast in the banquette. "If they play Air Supply, we're out of here."

"Deal."

Lush strings.

"Look, I'm bad at asking," she said. "I need a shoulder."

I opened my arms and she leaned into them, deeper than I'd expected. It was one strange night. I held her as she wept into my shoulder in the dark. Tears wet the neck of my shirt. I rubbed her back. She burrowed in closer. I dug it. I wished something resembling a prayer: *do not, even a little, get a woody.* The prayer worked. It felt good to be someone's friend. It went on that way.

I wondered how long this had been in coming. We endured England Dan and John Ford Coley. America. Paul Simon launched into "Slip Slidin' Away." Lin's sobs died down. She nuzzled into my neck. Breathed, quiet. A minute later, her voice. "Nick?"

"Yeah?"

"Come home with me."

Languid percussion. My turn to freeze. Sure, I was needy, but I could still taste ginger and tequila, I didn't trust my impulses, and I had years of experience knowing I wasn't what Lin wanted. So I kept my mouth shut and waited for the awkward to pass. It didn't. It sat down next to us and ordered a drink. I felt tension climb back up her body.

"Sorry," she said. "That wasn't fair."

I had nothing.

She didn't move right away, and the awkward didn't disappear. We just got past it. Two drinks past it. Neither of us in a hurry. She pulled herself together, and back into her seat. I pulled myself away from lustful fantasies of teenage girls and somehow it became my turn to crack.

California life post-divorce has never been my favorite topic. But there I was spilling about my marital heartbreak. Cocooned in our banquette, still close but safely separated, I found myself saying, "Once you come out of something like that, you wonder how you could ever let it happen. And you know you could easily have spent your whole life there. Just let it go, one day slides into the next. Career direction way off the radar. I wasn't going to manage anyone other than Terry. And I couldn't conceive of anything that felt worth doing."

My pragmatic friend was puzzled. She stirred her gimlet. Her eyes red. Both our voices soft. "You could have gone back into journalism. Did you try?"

"Nope."

A look.

"Partly pride. Partly depression. Mostly I didn't want to just fall back on what I knew."

"Yeah. Wouldn't want that."

"I felt like I was done with it. To go with the obvious just to have something to do feels empty. Pathetic. I mean, if you're not going to be engaged, why do it?"

"So what *did* you do?"

Ouch. Most of the time I managed to ignore the utter lack of meaning in my life. A fair bit of work I didn't get proper credit for. Some of that work involved avoiding moments like this. But the law of equivalent vulnerability demanded an answer, and I was afraid to be alone. "I don't know. Days drifted by. It happens in California. There's no change of seasons to alert you that you're pissing your life away. You wake up one morning and you're five years older."

"You didn't do *anything* all that time?"

Right. I wanted to crawl under the table. And while the alcohol helped fuzz the sound system, it didn't entirely blot out Ambrosia.

"I read a lot. Got to know a guy who ran a vintage clothes shop in Ventura. Got to be I'd hang there in the afternoons. Got to be he'd ask me to watch the counter. Got to be he'd give me some cash the end of each week. At some point I got tired of driving to Ventura every day. Managed a used CD shop in Santa Monica." A

178

shrug. "Then one day I get a phone call. My dad's dying. Seemed like time for a new chapter."

I felt exposed. Close and distant at the same time. Not sure where we stood. I'd said more than I wanted to. "Sorry," I said. "Just what you need – a monologue on Nick's lost years."

"Get over it," she said. "It's called friendship."

We closed the place. Agreed to attend Evan's service – a memorial had been scheduled for two nights later – and I left feeling better for being with her.

On the table in front of me I had my father's bills divided into three stacks: those with a source and charges I understood; those I suspected contained duplicate charges; and those whose nature I didn't understand at all. The picture depressed me: the height of the stacks, the sheer volume of envelopes and papers. A bill stuck to my elbow as I reviewed the duplicates; someone had dialed up the hazy-hot-humid.

I'd woken with the taste of Marcela Pruett in my mouth. Felt tingly and alive for maybe 15 seconds before the sketchball waves rolled in with a light foam of worry. I checked my phone for messages. Nothing. I told myself not to get caught up in the drama of teen relationships – the shifting sides of a love triangle. Reminded myself it had been a complicated evening, and in such moments my imagination played tricks. Wanting to be needed and being needed were not the same. Time to lose myself in something. Dealing with my father's finances felt oddly attractive.

I scanned the front page of the Globe, then tallied debt totals for each stack while I watched the morning news. Angry sun streamed in through streaked kitchen windows. I hated acknowledging my father was destitute and I could not help him. Would not be responsible for him. I stared at the stacks. Reviewed the numbers again, as if they might change.

Had trouble shaking Marcela. *Can we talk? Bo trusts you.* Right. Bo. *Hey, kid. Your girlfriend's back and boy does she taste good.* Some friend. Some role model.

On the television, Natalie Noone launched into strike news.

"Union leaders have denounced the move to bring in replacement janitors as unethical and counter-productive."

Wait, I thought. *What did I really do? Kiss her back. Once. Whatever else is there is just lonely guy fantasy. Pathetic, but not despicable.* I sat with that to see if I could swallow it.

On the TV, Natalie said, "Our Esperanza Baca spoke with Delfi's Diane Evans earlier this morning."

Why didn't Bo tell me she was back? Fuck it. Later. I picked up my phone again. Thumbed to recent messages. Hit reply.

i didn't like your exit.

call me. text me.

you OK?

Diane Evans' coiffed head appeared on the TV, a microphone held before her by a disembodied, manicured hand.

"Nothing in our position has changed," she said. "There is an offer out to the union. It is our best and only offer. When it's ignored, we must assume that those who have left their jobs are no longer interested in them."

"Are you threatening to make the replacement workers permanent?" asked off-camera Esperanza.

"We will continue work to secure our interests and address staffing needs as we see fit."

Back to Natalie. "Leaders from the group Boston Area Faith in Action have threatened to boycott Endicott, FirstBoston, and State Street Trust if the cleaning companies don't agree to negotiations. Boston Mayor Norm Reeves again urged both parties to avoid hard-line stances and reach a solution to get janitors back to work."

Amen, Mr. Mayor. Natalie turned her attention to international matters and I turned to Channel Seven, where Chris Tillman spoke with a microphone in his face.

"...for the union to align with radical groups is a grave concern. These groups engage in and incite violence. Already there have been extreme acts and scare tactics that the union disavows."

Fantastic. Perfect. Put a microphone in front of a grieving father. He'll be calm and reasoned. Fucking Seven News. I needed to refocus. Muted sound. Time to suck it up and call the Brookline Council on Aging. Their consultant was scheduled to be in that morning, and I'd let this drift too long. When I called him, I found out why.

Hector Escutia told me there were resources available. "That's the good news." Hmm. "Many seniors find themselves in this position." Hector sounded eighty himself. A mensch. I liked him.

"What's the bad news?"

"We'll get to that."

I explained how we had two problems: the stroke with the resulting medical bills Dad couldn't afford to pay; and the housing crisis. Hector listened. His breath rasped on the other end of the phone.

"You've got two choices," he said. "Either he goes home or to a permanent placement – a nursing home or assisted living."

"He can't go home. Half the time he doesn't know who or where he is." Besides, if he went home, I couldn't leave. I stood at the precipice of the exact nightmare I'd sworn to avoid.

"Is there anyone – a family member – that could provide in-home care? Anyone local he could move in with?"

Fuck me. I shook my head. "No. That's not who he is. Besides, it's just me, and I'm only in the area for a short time, to help him get on his feet." I cursed Thomas, myself, anyone connected to health care in this country.

"What about friends?"

"You don't know my father."

That got me awkward silence from Hector and a sour cocktail in my stomach, anger and guilt.

"Assisted living places take a limited number of Medicaid patients," Hector said. "But there's always a wait list. So you're looking at a nursing home. You'll have to be ready to part with his assets."

"*What assets?*" I stopped. Lowered my voice. "Remember, I called about medical bills he can't pay." I took a deep breath. "He's got about three grand in the bank. That's it. Once that's gone, he won't even have money for burial."

Again, a pause from Hector. His raspy breath. "That's the bad news. He'll have to cover a portion of the bills. Pay something toward the nursing home."

"How?"

"Are his children prepared to cover those costs, plus burial?"

Shame was a flood and there was no rescue craft. "I told you, I am his children, and I'm in the same boat he is." Headache. A four-Advil day, and still morning. "One crisis at a time. What happens when he can't pay the bills?"

"Worst case, they boot him. Best case, it's like bankruptcy. You work your butt off to figure out a plan with the various creditors."

I wanted a drink. Or a bus ticket to a distant land.

Hector brought me back. "But let's not get ahead of ourselves." He laid out the strategy. First, determine what Medicare would and should pay. Hector could help with that. Second, call the hospital: they have a patient liaison that reviews cases of inability to pay and will sometimes excuse and often reduce the bill. Third, figure out what we could afford to pay immediately out of savings and apply that toward the largest balances. Fourth, based on Dad's Social Security, determine what we could pay monthly toward the bills and how we'd divide it. Hector could also help with this. Finally, write letters to all creditors, explaining the situation and proposing the payment plan. Meantime, Hector would put together a list of nursing homes that took Medicaid.

"There'll be a dip in quality," he said. "That's just reality."

Reality sucks. I fought the vertigo vision of my own future. Made an appointment to see Hector the following Tuesday and hung up.

Evan Tillman wasn't destined to have the spotlight. Shit happens and the world moves on. I sulked at the *Globe*. Auto insurance rates were going up. Cleaning companies and the janitors' union accused each other of bad faith. The attorney general of the United States had been subpoenaed to testify in an ethics investigation.

What did it matter that a kid was dead. I thumbed through pages resentfully until a story in the regional section caught my eye. *Car Lot Vandalized / Police Target Eco-Terrorist 'Campaign.'* "In Hanover last night, vandals painted environmental tags and slogans on nine SUVs at Davison Cadillac." Blah blah blah. "Many of the vehicles also had scratched body paint and slashed tires." Blah blah blah "according to Hanover Police, vandals painted slogans such as 'planet polluter,' 'gas hog,' and "downsize, dawg" on the vandalized cars.

Fuck.

"Police throughout the region are coordinating efforts to fight what they described as an eco-terrorist campaign where environmentalist slogans have been painted on SUVs."

You little shit. Don't go cowboy. One man's art project is another man's eco-terrorist campaign. I needed to talk to Bo. Dialed him. Hung up. Paced the den. Redialed and left a message, using my serious voice. Emailed him a link to the *Globe* story, subject line *WTF!!!* Checked messages. A note from my teen pal – a link to the SLAM website's blog. The headline: *Janitors' Accident Was No Accident.* Among a lot of incoherent ranting about capitalist oppression, the blog suggested the dead janitors were victims of a strike-related contract killing. Excellent. Bo's remorse button was on mute. Perfect.

I had to do something to channel anger and worry. So I did what I did in the old days. I wrote. What I wrote sounded and felt like a column, a good one even. I set it aside for a couple hours and revisited it. Made some tweaks, but still felt the same. Emailed it to Eric before I lost my nerve.

The next day I waited for a call from Bo that never came, left him another message, bought a shirt appropriate for a memorial service, and spent an hour on the phone with Eric haggling over edits to "a solid draft." Eric's hyper-caffeinated attention left no sentence untouched – some things never changed. He told me I could expect to see it in print within the week. I swallowed hard and tuned that part out.

St. Francis Parish was packed. Half-hour before the memorial service and they were already funneling people into the overflow room. I got lucky and wedged into a solo spot toward the back. We were officially into a heat wave – Channel Seven said so. So did my shirt collar.

Old-fashioned big, the sanctuary felt more cathedral than church, with ornate pillars and a full-on vaulted ceiling. The varsity version of what I'd grown up with. At St. John's in Brookline, it had been all cultural. You went because you were supposed to. That's never been my style. So I walked away after high school. The party line is I'm tough and cynical – religion is for kids, invalids, and the fatally ill. The truth is I've always felt the pull, I just can't find a way in to an experience that's genuine. The infinite ceiling at St. Francis gave me vertigo. I looked around for folks I knew. Saw Lin, almost waved. A few familiar faces I couldn't name. I watched Chris Tillman oversee things from the front – make sure the Gregorys found a place, greet family members and friends, including Seth Gutman – all in the shadow of his son's casket. I tried to imagine what he must be feeling. How he could keep going. I failed.

Just before things started, Bo walked in with his slouchy friend Ben and a couple teens I didn't recognize. I was surprised to see him – I didn't know he knew Evan. They settled on the opposite side. I resisted the reflex to scoot right over, but only just, and only because the organ had started to play.

Music from the high school chorus, including one song written for Evan and another that, I found out later, featured a botched note in his honor, muffed in exactly the way he always did it. Tributes. Laments to lost potential. Tillman gutted out a poem. A heartfelt homage from Evan's youth minister – the same magnet youth group Bo attended. That explained Bo's presence. Then the priest, a bald, birdlike man who looked at least ninety and whose voice suggested to me there are people who really do know God, spoke of the challenge to the living. "We cannot let the worst in human nature sour us and blind us to the best," he said. "Instead, we must act in ways to make grace tangible."

A *kyrie*. An old hymn whose tune I recognized from my own childhood. Gut-wrenching. Voices reached up through all that space. Palpable yearning. I could see it on faces. On Bo, eyes closed in what I guessed was prayer. I could almost feel that yearning met. Almost believe it. So I went with the *kyrie* as far as it would take me and basked in the reflected warmth of those who got taken further. And then it ended, and people were filing out.

I found myself standing in the back of the church. Bo stood with his friends, Ben and a teary-eyed girl named Kara amid a group of teens. Ben did his best to hide in plain sight, tucked behind Bo's shoulder. Kara had the full punk look – spiked hair, safety pins, thick mascara, zipper-laden leather jacket – but not the attitude. Or maybe it was just how she dealt with tragedy. She introduced herself before I could get to Bo.

"How did you know Evan?" she asked. Her green eyes so young behind the makeup.

We stood behind the back pew, just off the aisle. A steady stream of mourners brushed past. Whispers and murmurings. The soft scuffle of feet on the tile floor.

Bo nodded hey. I nodded back.

"I didn't actually. I'm a – an acquaintance of the family." I felt stupid saying it. A voyeur. A parasite. A face caught my eye. Goth girl on her way out. What was I doing there – anywhere.

"Oh," Kara said. Under the leather she wore a black t-shirt and a gray checked skirt.

Out of the corner of my eye I saw a camera crew – Fox News – documenting the departing mourners. I uttered a silent prayer that no one would try to interview Tillman. That he might find at least some measure of grace. I scanned faces, wondering who might know something about how Evan died. Or why.

"Well," Kara said, "it's cool that you came. I mean I went to school with him and all. He seemed okay. He was just this kid in my English class and now he's dead. You know what I mean?"

I did, but I needed to talk to Bo.

Lin and Seth made their way over to us, hesitant in the way parents are when approaching teens. Kara introduced herself to Seth. Lin and I hugged, a real one, and she went past me to Bo. Seth and I exchanged greetings while Kara told him of her connection to Evan.

The service had shaken Seth. I'd never seen him rattled. "No one," he said, "I don't care who they are or what they've done – no one should ever have to bury their child."

Bo stood with his friends and his mother; he and Lin had an arm around each other's shoulder. I tried in vain to read his face. When he broke away, I snagged him.

"We need to talk."

In public. I was supposed to know better.

Bo drew back. "We will."

Lin looked over at us.

I lowered my voice. "Your art project. The wrong people are paying attention."

He winced. "Chill the fuck out, Nick. Not now."

Lin caught my eye, then Kara said something to her.

I had hold of Bo's arm. "I'm officially worried."

He shook me off. "I'll make a note of it."

A silence that went on too long. Then Ben and Kara were back beside him, and Bo was saying, "This is a little freaky. We're gonna go hang."

And he hugged his mom and kind of waved to the rest of us, and Ben followed him to the door, and Kara said to us, "It sounds strange and all, but I'm really glad to meet you." And the adults watched the teens head out the door into a world that already had more claim on them than we did.

Eric Grunow lived up to his word. He'd told me he'd turn the column quickly. Two days after the funeral, there it was. I snagged a copy to read with my breakfast.

The View From Here / Nick Young
"Be on the Side of Making Things Better"
It's quite a summer in Boston, which feels like hardly the same Hub I left 10 years ago. The city is on the national stage, thanks in part to a high-profile labor strike and a well-

188

organized interfaith group that has drawn considerable attention to that strike. But we've also become a hub of anti-globalist activism, led by a loud and angry group of mostly young people clamoring for substantive change to American corporate capitalism.

I understand the anger. I feel it myself. Anger at a government that panders to corporate interests, pillages the environment, and ignores the growing gulf between rich and poor.

I've always been a firm believer in liberal pluralism. Shaped by the nonviolent civil rights work of Martin Luther King and Charles K. Steele, I've believed that you have the conversation – you persist in the conversation – and eventually things change.

But I know a young activist who's challenging all that. Who looks at the dominance of global corporations, their disdain of accountability, and wonders whether the only way to get their attention is to cost them money. My young friend doesn't see destruction of property as a crime. He sees it as a necessary political tool. Direct action as the only effective resistance. Because institutions have learned to co-opt protest. Happy to see anger turn into talk. Or newspaper columns.

My young friend looks at me and says, "Milquetoast. Ineffectual. Unwilling to take a stand."

I wonder if he's right.

This isn't the first time I've been put in my place by a warrior for social justice.

Years ago, I was in Birmingham, Alabama to interview a man who'd been a leader in the civil rights movement, who'd stared down bombs and attack dogs and death threats, and remained peacefully committed to the cause. After the interview he introduced me to a voting rights activist from Selma. I agreed to interview the woman, too, even though I thought her work was unnecessary – outdated.

She told me she had spent the morning at the Selma courthouse disputing a city council election. Her candidate, the black candidate, had lost by fourteen votes. And a locked ballot box had been discovered under a bench in the City Hall basement. The box contained uncounted votes from a black precinct. "Now you can call that coincidence," she said. "Or you can call it something else."

Here was a woman who had been on the national stage as a child, who had marched from Selma to Montgomery at the age of 11, and who, in her fifties, was still fighting racism one city council election at a time.

Once she finished upbraiding me for my white-media-liberal arrogance, we had a good talk over lunch. She spent an hour telling me how to work effectively for change. The last thing she said to me before I left was this: "Be on the side of making things better."

I still think of her. Her words – her actions – have helped shape my core beliefs. How you don't fight injustice with violence. You don't fight it with hate. You fight it with persistence. Getting up every day and doing what you can. Believing things will get better despite what you see. You fight it by refusing to accept the status quo or the alleged truths that underlie it; and by believing that, in the end, truth is stronger than the lies and the liars.

Things seem different now. The lies more pervasive. The truth less clear, more slippery. It's tempting for me to think the challenge to live her words is impossible today.

Except there are activists in Boston right now who claim they're doing just that. Working for change around a different set of issues. Bending and sometimes breaking the law to do it. And I can say that it's different. Their cause less righteous. The historical moment less conclusive. But I can't dismiss them so easily.

Because the moment – whatever moment you live in – is always complicated. Clear vision always obscured by a fog of stances and positions, comforts and fears, conflicting desires and competing interests. The challenge is – has always been – to see through the fog and move toward something solid.

My young friend has me wondering what it means to work for change today. What it really means, where we live, to be on the side of making things better. I know it means more than lip service – more than writing this column. But I still hope and believe it means other than violence. And I'm determined – newly resolved – to find that ground and fight there.

I didn't hate it. A lot of it felt strong even, like a real column by a real journalist.

On the table beside my coffee, my phone made its text beep. I stopped patting myself on the back long enough to check the screen. Marcela Pruett.

i'm ok. no need to worry.

teen drama is all. M.

I don't know why I didn't believe her.

11

I was "stirring" and "thought-provoking." I was "another aging liberal invoking the imagined nirvana of the late sixties." I was "a welcome voice of perspective and context" and "a hand-wringing wanker." To my knowledge, I'd never been called a wanker before. I felt whole for the first time. And that was just the email. Some familiar voices left phone messages.

My old beat reporter pal Dave Doyle: "You've crossed to the dark side, but at least you're good at it. Congrats."

Chris Tillman: "A good read, Nick. Are you officially abandoning objectivity?"

Whatever. I was a hit. Eric loved the column. ("Nice job, Nick. You owe me copy Friday.") His enthusiasm took root in me and I enjoyed it, guardedly. Which helped push aside vague worries I couldn't confirm or refute about Bo and Marcela. Twenty, thirty emails from people apparently as bereft of a useful life as I was. All kinds of messages from all kinds of people. Nothing from the one person I wanted to hear from most. I did have a voice mail from his mother.

"What's up with my son, Nick?" Lin's voice said. "Call me."

Shit. *I wish I knew.* Between the funeral and the column, she was bound to be speculating. I'd call her later. I put away my computer, erased the voice mails. Re-read my column over a bowl of cereal. Rode that momentum to an hour or so of productivity on my strike piece for AJ, then to the Brookline Council on Aging where Hector took it all away. Every drop.

I brought the bag of bills with me. Copies of my dad's bank statements. Hector worked the calculator and came up with a total much closer to the higher end of my estimate than the lower. He made a little clicking noise when he breathed and hummed some half-tune to himself while he punched numbers. A couple times while he worked he stopped, rubbed his face, took a deep rasping breath. He wore big glasses that made his eyes frog-like.

Maybe he'd thought I was joking about how there was no hidden money. Exaggerating. I felt like I was in the principal's office, called in for failing to do my homework.

He stared at the calculator for a while, then looked up and not quite at me. He said we needed to set the wheels in motion ASAP to ask the hospital for relief from *some* of the bills. His emphasis scared me. He made an appointment for us with the patient liaison for the following week. He estimated what Medicaid's contribution should be and assigned me a list of letters to write. "First task," he said. "You've got to keep two thousand minimum toward burial. Set up a bank account in your name. Take it out as cash and stuff it under the mattress. Whatever you need to do. Then write letters. Then," he handed me an index card with the names, addresses, and phone numbers of nursing homes. "Visit these five places and let me know what you think. Top three preferences. I'll work the admissions angle. Then, set some money aside yourself. Get a second job. Something."

No way I could address that one.

Hector did nothing to make me feel judged. He even guarded his tone. That made it worse. Anyway, I left his office and drove to Brentwood Home to see my father. Made it as far as the parking lot, where I sat in the Dart sweating, awash in futility. I couldn't make my body get out of the car. Stared at the windows, painfully aware of my father's state – ailing, alone, and destitute. How much of my life I'd spent striving to disassociate from him; how nothing in my own circumstance suggested a different future. Perfect conditions for a session with wild-card Thomas. I gave myself a choice: go in and see him, or return Lin's call and tiptoe around the topic of her son's "peaceful" activism.

The View, opened to my debut column, lay on the bed in my father's room. In classic fashion, I decided not to mention it. In classic fashion, he didn't either. But then, he also mistook me for his brother.

"Paul, I'm glad you came. This place gets sad." No disputing that. Some days it felt like the waiting room to the abyss. Outdoors was oppressive, too. Deep into a July heat wave. Dead air. Crazy humidity. You'd gladly pay cash for air conditioning. Willingly go to a Barbra Streisand movie.

"I'm Nick, Dad. Your son."

"I know that."

"How you feeling today?"

He shrank from my words as if from an injection.

195

I sat in the green chair across from him, fatigued already at the thought of playing out whatever dance we did, one more time.

"We got a situation, Dad. We gotta talk."

"What are you on about now?"

"Time's up. You can't stay here. We're going to have to find another place. And that means figuring out the bills."

He stared forward. "Old news," he said.

"Dad. Listen to me. It's real now. Official." I felt leathery. As if I'd aged 20 years in the last two days. "They sent a letter. 26 days, you're out."

"I know that." Disdain. "They talked to me." Chewing something invisible, those ruined teeth.

"They did?" That made no sense to me. "So what's your plan?"

"The fuck you think? I'll go home."

Excellent.

Thomas watched the window, his eyes glassy. "I was thinking about your mother, her beef stew. You remember her beef stew?"

I took his hands. He recoiled, but I held on. "Dad. Stay with me on this. It's important."

"Let go of me."

"Listen. You can't take care of yourself. It's not an option."

"What if I had someone to stay with me?" Those deep-set eyes locked on me.

Fucker. I bit back my impulse response and let his words hang there. Years of anger. Disappointment. Guilt – this human husk before me was in name my father; stunning how quickly the strong can decay – in the six years since I'd seen him last he'd gone to shit, and I'd stayed away, not wanting – not caring – to know. A horrific future played out in my head, haunted by guilt, by an impossible desire for a Hollywood ending, a healing that would never happen. I marveled at my father's ability to twist the knife, lucid or not. Muscle memory. That honed hardness of his. I turned a valve somewhere inside me; stemmed a flow. Steeled my voice. "You can't afford it."

All the years of all the failures twinkled like ornaments.

His gaze receded 'til those eyes seemed far away. I had no idea who or what he saw. Never had. Never would. I sagged. The effort to anchor him in time and space. The various strategies to muster a son's active concern. We were at the end of it.

"You remember Dad's stories about the humpback porter?" he said. "The boxer? Nick asks about him. Kid loves the boxing stories."

Clouds. The forecast said thunderstorms were possible. They'd been possible for days.

"Yeah," I said. "I remember hearing about him. Club fighter, right?"

My father nodded. "He fought some tough men. George 'the Marine' Leblanc. 'Mysterious' Charlie Smith. Paul and I would save the clippings." He took a breath, listened as if his own words reached him on a kind of tape delay. Stared out the window. "Think it'll rain?"

I shrugged. My head a dull ache.

"Paper says rain."

My eyes flicked to the bed. "You read the paper today?" Some masochistic impulse. Poking at a scab. "Which one?"

"That throwaway. What's it called?"

"*The View?*"

"Yeah, that's the one. No wonder it's free. Nothing in it. A waste of good ink."

Duty and restlessness drove me to three nursing homes. Gave me a way to tell myself I was responsible while keeping the valve inside turned off. None of the places were awful. You could call them companionable, familiar: the mingled smells of cheap disinfectant and dying flesh; the sullen aide endlessly mopping the same spot of faded linoleum. But my dogged perseverance allowed me to believe I was doing right by a father who didn't deserve it; that would get me through the day even as the smell of decay festered in my nostrils.

I considered a visit to a fourth place, but even heroes have their limits. I considered driving to the beach for a clam roll – my ultimate comfort food. Instead my phone rang. Lin. I couldn't make myself answer. I hated myself for ducking her, but I couldn't talk to her until I talked to Bo. I wouldn't rat him out and damage our friendship – or worry Lin – over something that might just be my suspicion. I waited out Lin's message and dialed Bo. No answer. Stabbed the end call button. This fucking generation and their fucking indifference to return calls. Dialed him back and left a message. "Not cool, Bo. This is not a game and you're not winning. Call me back." Clicked back to texts. Marcela's *i'm ok, don't worry.* Punched in a reply: *why don't I believe you.* It didn't satisfy me. I needed to hit someone. I headed for Newton police headquarters.

A young female officer sat at a high desk centered on a wide hallway, sandy hair pulled back in a ponytail.

"I'm Nick Young, reporter for *The View*. Who's the investigating officer for the Tillman case?" All chipper, as if what's the forecast today.

She eyeballed me, head to toe. Los Lobos t-shirt. Shorts. Flip-flops. Whatever. It was four million degrees outside. "Reporter? For who?"

"*The View*." I said it the way you might say *Time* magazine. She suppressed a smirk.

"That would be Detective Hill."

Two men walked along the hall behind her, one older than me, one younger. The older one looking harried.

"Would he be in?"

She turned her head. "Dennis, are you in?"

The older cop in the hall looked at some papers in his hand, said, "Who wants to know?"

"Reporter." She paused for emphasis. "*The View*."

Something in the papers he didn't like. "Shit." He grabbed the other cop by the shirtsleeve, they started back the way they'd come, toward a row of offices along the far wall. "No," he said on his way past, right arm extended straight out, like a football halfback straight-arming would-be tacklers. "I'm not in." He pointed in the direction of the offices, called out, "Halverson."

The desk officer went back to doing nothing and half a minute later the fresh-faced press officer in his crisp uniform stood at my side. "How can I help you, Mr. Young?" He remained the kid who delighted in denying people access.

I put on the perma-grin and introduced him to my professional capacity.

"You're interested in the Tillman case," he said.

"I'm doing a column on it." I had quickly discovered that advantage. You could always say you were working on a column, and it could always be sort of true.

Halverson led me to his small, sparse office. "What can I tell you?" he said. "The investigation is ongoing."

"You know any more than a possibly suspicious black Lexus that might have been in the neighborhood?"

"There are a number of leads, all of which are being investigated. None of them are ready to be made public."

"A month of digging and that's what you've got. Must be frustrating." I was testing Halverson's extensive goodwill. At least I had that.

His phone rang and he grabbed it. A couple of quick "yeses" into the receiver and done. "Excuse me," he said. "I'll be back."

I waited a respectful ten seconds and meandered down the hallway in the direction I'd seen Detective Hill disappear. At the end of the short hallway I found a small kitchen – refrigerator, coffee pot. At the coffee pot I found Detective Hill. I walked up next to him. He glanced over at me. Poured coffee into a mug. Then pulled a second mug down from a shelf, poured coffee into that, slid it across the counter to me.

"You're a tricky one." He had a high forehead and tired gray eyes. A ring of dark hair and a thinning stripe on top. A fervent gum chewer.

"I've had practice." I hoisted the mug. "Thanks. Quitting smoking?"

"It's that obvious?" He shrugged. "So what, you think I'm going to tell you more than he would?"

"Probably not. I'm just naturally prickly. When I'm told I can't be somewhere that's where I want to be."

"Occupational hazard?"

"Guess so." I sipped the coffee. Black. I didn't want to break the moment by asking for milk. "Know what I'm curious about?"

"Nope."

"I'm curious about how a crime committed in broad daylight can remain such a puzzle. I don't mean that as a knock against you, or the department. I just don't understand. I mean it's now a robbery and a homicide, right?"

He let me puzzle on that a minute while he chewed his gum. "I know how you got to be so good at what you do," he said. "It's your people skills."

Halverson had appeared in the doorway, leaning against the frame. He didn't look happy.

"It's okay, Scott. I got this."

Halverson lingered long enough to let his stare bore through my chest, then stalked off.

Detective Hill crossed his arms. "It happens that way sometimes. More often than you might expect. If there's no witnesses, no prints, you depend a lot on luck. A piece of information falls out. You push and push at every seam you can find and some of the time, sooner or later, something gives. But sometimes it doesn't."

"So you've got nothing."

He worked his gum. "I didn't say that."

"You've got something more than the Lexus?"

"I didn't say that either."

"You got an owner for the Lexus?"

"That would help, wouldn't it?"

"You're not helping."

He grinned. "Not my job."

My turn to shrug. "So can I come back, do this again some time?"

He snapped his gum. "You can try."

Back in the car, a quick check of phone messages yielded three: first, my scream queen ex-wife. *Don't tell anyone I said it, but this is kinda fun. Any work is good work, right Nick? It keeps me busy until someone offers me Lady MacBeth. Just checking in. Everything's good here as long as I remember sleep is overrated.* The second was my new boss Eric Grunow wanting to know if he could buy me a celebratory drink. Duh. The third took me a minute to place. *Mr. Young? Larry Sparks here. Need to ask you about something. Wondered if you'd call me today.*

Marcela's grandfather. The ex-police chief. Holy fuck. What did he want? What had she told him? My mind raced to lurid fictions of our midnight rendezvous, her dramatic exit. I considered leaving the state. Reconstructive surgery. Locking myself in my father's den.

Instead, I sweat through my shirt and drove to Sparks' house. I've never been one to choose my battles wisely. Found him weeding a flower bed – marigolds, irises, gladiolas – in the front yard. Heat so stifling it was hard to breathe.

He was surprised to see me. That made two of us.

"I appreciate this," he said. "You didn't have to come all the way out." He worked on his knees in an old pair of chinos.

"I was in the neighborhood." *And figured if I'm facing a morals charge, I'd rather find out now.*

He stood. Offered me his hand. "If you don't mind a little dirt."

I took it. Focused all my energy on not trembling. "What can I do for you?"

He wiped sweat from his brow. "Get you a cold drink?"

Or any other last request? "No. Thanks."

Sparks watched his feet, clad in old tennis shoes. "I'm a little worried about Marcela." A shot of terror with a twist of remorse. He looked in my direction. "I've got a couple calls into your young friend. She hasn't checked in. I wondered if you knew anything."

Terror got specific. Did I know anything? *I know your granddaughter's hot. I know she was in town. I know she got into a car with an angry teen and sped off and didn't look happy about it.* I pictured Marcela on an extended party jag. Pictured her mutilated body in a dumpster. *Stop. Breathe.* "What is it has you concerned?" I asked. Indirect. Probe for info without exposing myself. "You don't strike me as a worrier."

"I don't think of myself as one." He brushed dirt off the knees of his pants. "Just a feeling. Sounds ridiculous, I know. Old guy gone soft."

I didn't like that the ex-police chief was worried. I didn't like that I couldn't speak directly –*something's up and I have no idea what.* I couldn't reassure him, and I couldn't give him anything without opening a can of worms. Sparks was a stand-up guy. I felt bad. But I didn't know what I knew or what ramifications it had.

"I haven't heard anything," I said. "Bo's not big on returning my calls right now either." I did some quick self-editing. "He's going through something – teen angst – guess I'm not sympathetic enough."

"Hmm." Sparks narrowed his eyes and his mouth got small. "You haven't heard from her?"

My balls rose to my stomach. I told myself he was testing theories, the way cops do, to see how they sound.

I tried to read his face. I pasted on a grin and hoped it didn't look as fake as it felt. "Why would I hear?"

Sparks shrugged. "You spend time with Bo and his crowd. You never know."

Casual, Nick. Calm. Redirect. My balls slowly drifted south. "You try the police?"

He smiled. Shook his head. "I don't think it's that kind of gone." He picked up a trowel off the front step. "I know," he said. "We've been here before and I should tell myself what I told Bo. Nothing to worry about. She'll be back. She's a high school graduate. An independent spirit. I shouldn't have troubled you."

Jovial, Nick. "I'll see what I can find out from Bo."

"Thanks," he said. "And I'll try to re-establish some self-discipline."

My breathing re-established, we shook hands again, and I started to go, then thought to ask him. "You know a detective named Dennis Hill?"

"I do." Guardedness crept into his voice. "Good man."

"Any idea how I can get him to talk to me about a case?"

Sparks looked at me a long time. I watched his face become a mask - not cold, but hard. "I'm old. Hearing's bad. Thought I heard you ask me how to get an angle on a cop. Good day, son."

I felt his eyes follow me to my car, where I rolled down the windows and placed another call to the number that might be Marcela. *The Verizon customer you have reached is not available at this time.* I know, I know.

I killed the afternoon checking email, poring over online news reports and blogs, and trying not to wait for my phone to ring. Went for a long late run around the reservoir – sweat a couple gallons in the humidity then got dolled up in my best un-tucked shirt to meet Eric. The Tip-Top Lounge, a basement-level bar in Cleveland Circle, was apparently a reporters' hangout. I had no idea such places still existed. But I pushed through the door into a welcome blast of cold air and a dark indistinct room that felt like home. I arrived a few minutes early. I parked myself at the bar, ordered a draft, and let the air cool my skin. The bartender had slicked-back silver hair and an Irish nose. Mounted TVs around the room carried the four local newscasts. A well-worn wood bar and a half-dozen booths. A couple of the bar stools were taken, two of the booths stuffed with early drinkers.

I spent a few minutes second-guessing my strategy with Sparks – it couldn't be a good idea to lie to a cop, even an ex-cop – and eavesdropping on booth conversations, one of which featured the intense self-critique of reporters. I located the TV that showed Channel Five and Camille Oliver. Clothed in crimson. I nodded approval; I've always found it a sexy color. Twenty minutes later the Tip-Top was near full. I nursed the back half of my beer and listened to Dr. Barry commiserate about lack of relief in sight for the heat wave slamming the city when my phone buzzed on the bar. A text from Eric – *shit. lost track of time. re-working tomorrow's main feature. gotta reschedule. sorry.* No worries. I'd spent half an hour in air conditioning. I lingered over my last sips, pushed my way off the stool and headed for the door. A familiar voice I couldn't quite place stopped me.

"Nick Young? No fucking way."

My old colleague Lenny Russell walked toward me, hand extended. I couldn't tell anymore what to be surprised by.

"What are you doing here, Nick? I heard you moved west years ago."

"And I heard you were in New York running a *View* knockoff."

"I got bored." Lenny was tall, wiry, ageless, restless, and always impossibly clean-shaven. "Besides, I've got Boston in my blood."

Lenny was a veteran – and a lightning rod – of the Boston newspaper scene. Stints at both the *Herald* and *Globe*. He'd been one of the founding columnists for the *Weekly*, left early in my tenure there to found *The News*, sparking maybe the most intense rivalry – and some of the best journalism – the city had known. Then he became the guy who knew how to tap into new markets for print journalism, sometimes arguably at the price of editorial integrity. Lenny had founded *The View*. He liked the spotlight, and some charged he was willing to invent the news when the available quantity didn't suit his taste. Despite journalistic differences, I found him irresistible.

"What brought you back, Nick?"

"It's short-term. Family stuff. While I'm here, I'm doing the column for Eric, and a piece for AJ on the strike."

Lenny laughed. "What's your take on it?"

"Janitors have a good shot if they don't get undone by simpatico activists."

A young woman came up beside him. Twenty-something, limp blond hair, rectangular glasses and a permanent smirk. Lenny made to introduce us. "Nick used to be a reporter. Old school. Nick Young, TC Haldi." She smiled. I smiled. I recognized the name from a post I'd read that afternoon.

"*Buzz*, right?" *Buzz* was a good local politics blog, her post a variation of the theory I'd heard from Bo and SLAM about the deaths of the two janitors. The gist of it was a report, confirmed through "unnamed Endicott sources," that Chris Tillman and Andrew Sarkis from Pollard had hired a labor relations consultant and that at the BAFA rally the night of the accident, several people had identified two union busters with long track records as muscle-for-hire.

"Right." She looked like she had other places she wanted to be. I expected people to feel that way around me.

"What are you doing now, Lenny?"

"*Buzz*. We work together."

Haldi interjected. "Kind of. He's the boss."

"Interesting post today," I told her. "That theory's been going around town. Too bad about the unnamed sources, though." I turned to Lenny, jocular. "You have actual info on this, or you guys just making headlines?"

Lenny wore his unruffled smile. "Talk to her," he said. "Her story. Her sources."

She wasn't smiling. "Fuck you, old school. Find your own sources." She turned to Lenny. "We gotta go." To me, "I have muck to rake and he's my ride."

My stock rose still further the next morning when email brought me a link to a column in the *Herald*, conservative blowhard Tim Dunn. I scanned the tirade, found my name. "...all we need is yahoos like Nick Young validating radical viewpoints in the local press. Who is this guy and where did he come from?" Fantastic. *Walk proud, Nick.*

Thursday was the traffic blockade, where my hunch got confirmed: this was no longer strictly a janitors' event. Traffic Blockade II had multiple agendas and the intensity had ratcheted up along with the humidity. A crowd of thousands again clogged the Back Bay on cue at 5:00, blocking the Dartmouth Street-Huntington Avenue-Mass Pike artery. I meandered the stretch of Dartmouth in front of the Westin Hotel, sweating into my madras shirt and assessing the crowd.

Still a healthy contingent of purple t-shirt people, with a sturdy supply of Justice for Janitors banners and a steady hum of conversations in Spanish, but the anti-globalist crowd, among others, had ramped up its presence. Young, edgy. Palpable restlessness and disillusionment. A short, solid woman in a red bandanna worked the crowd up past the Westin, toward Stuart Street. *What do we want? Justice. When do we want it? Now.* A boy with a striped Oxford shirt and a mohawk passed out flyers titled "Where's the Media on the WTO?" Vegetarian bodies jostling. Agitation. A woman's voice from somewhere behind me, "a celebration of food that is culturally diverse and healthy." Signs. "Dump Global Capitalism," "Just Say No to WTO," "We Are

Winning." A chubby cop in an orange traffic safety vest, like an out-of-place crossing guard, stiff on the sidewalk, arms at his sides, fingers fidgeting.

My phone. Eric. "There's a traffic blockade, Back Bay."

"I know. I'm there."

"Good. You know it's not the only party in town?"

"What do you mean?"

"Demonstrators chained to entrances again at Endicott, First, et cetera."

"A lot?"

"More than last time. How is it there?"

"Big party. Tense, and just getting going."

"Send me pix."

A line of young people in black t-shirts and fatigue pants snaked through the crowd, looking and sounding militaristic. A boy with a mop of black curls and an early attempt at facial hair tried to spark a chant of "take the streets." A line of black-clad cops on Dartmouth, in front of the library, wide stances. More signs: "Capitalism Is the Real Enemy," "Take it All Down," "Teamsters for Justice."

A trio of janitors beside me – two men and a woman, purple t-shirts and jeans – discussed things in Spanish. An edge in their voices.

Where was Bo? What was he doing?

The approaching streets already a loud parking lot. Gridlock. Horns. Shouted curses. Police lights reflected in the windows of Neiman-Marcus. Cops stuck in gridlock, too. A chant building, bouncing around me.

Hey hey, ho ho

Corporate greed has got to go

Angry car horns like punctuation. Sirens. My whole body clammy. A handful of conventioners watched the show from the bar at Turner Fisheries.

My phone rang again. AJ.

"My dog has developed a taste for sugar cookies. Should I blame you?"

That got a smile. "Not guilty. I don't buy cookies. But I'm in the middle of the janitors thing. Can we talk later?"

"Done. Be safe."

The crowd seemed younger than that of the previous week. Muscled torsos, tight t-shirts, bandannas holding off sweat, like an Outward Bound crew gone urban. I felt hemmed in. Pockets of BAFA recruits kept it responsible-looking, but even there, a wider agenda started to show. More signs: "House People Not Profits," "Housing Is a Human Right."

Police presence. A line of uniformed cops ringed the outer perimeter of the blockade area. Another group in full riot gear – black vests, black boots, helmets and face shields, batons – marched in formation down Huntington, four abreast. This time no one dispersed just because the police had arrived.

There was a festive element. A beach ball floated through the crowd, arms rising to keep it aloft. I made my way up Dartmouth toward St. James, slowly worming my way between bodies. Hoping somewhere in the midst of this chaos I'd find Bo. A banner, red and black paint on a white bed sheet: "Resist Corporate Rule." Another with the SLAM fist stenciled on it.

A line of riot squad cops formed a barrier across Dartmouth at St. James. Behind them, a line of gridlocked cars, then two lanes of perpendicular gridlock on Dartmouth. Overheated drivers who had gotten out of vehicles shouted at the mess from beyond the cops.

Protesters pressed from the near side. A chant began, got loud fast.

This is what democracy looks like.

This is what democracy looks like.

Someone had a cowbell. I was close enough I could see spit fly from the lips of one of the chanters onto a cop's face shield. Blue police lights bounced off store windows – Kinko's, Berkley's. The street felt cramped. Claustrophobic. Stifling. I inched toward the sidewalk. Nowhere to go.

This is what democracy looks like.

This is what democracy looks like.

Again, my phone. Eric's turn. "Quite a day. Enterprising hackers have redirected some Endicott funds to their favorite causes."

This had to be coordinated. "Know who?"

"Seattle10. SLAM. Both. Unclear."

"Eric, it's crazy loud here. I gotta go."

"Get fresh stuff from Tillman, the union. And Tweet. Buzz already has tweets, a full post, pix. I need you on this, Nick."

"Can't talk. Too loud. Gotta go." I wasn't about to tell him I didn't know how to Tweet. Didn't even have a smart phone. Hell, I congratulated myself for bringing a notebook.

Shouts. Car horns louder. Cacophony. A fist fight in front of Kinko's. From what I could see, mostly shoving. A few punches.

Commotion at the Copley Plaza, a half dozen people with signs – "Carnival Against Capitalism," "Strangle Greed" – gathered on the red carpet outside the lobby. The doorman looked for help.

The press of bodies. Wedged against someone's damp shirt. A woman's voice on a bullhorn: *You have the right to be here. These are public streets.* I had my arms, elbows in constant motion, gently but firmly asserting breathing space. I took a couple pictures. From over where the fight was, a sidewalk newspaper box tumbled. Papers spilled into the street.

This is what democracy looks like.

Car horns. A cop's voice? *Move back. Stay back.* The cowbell. You couldn't see the cops' faces. Everyone moving. Jostling. In waves. One cop nudging back demonstrators with a forearm.

This is what democracy looks like.

I had a text. Eric. *If no tweet, text me stuff. FYI: protesters jamming Berkley's, too. Keep your eyes open.* A window appeared over Eric's message. *Lin calling. Answer. Ignore.* I pressed ignore.

Another newspaper box toppled. The crash of metal. The sound tensed me. Then shouts. The cop who'd been nudging had knocked someone off balance. Down. No room to fall. The domino effect took out a half-dozen bodies, rippled. We all bounced off each other. Wobbled. Batons came up as the surge moved back toward the cops. I took a picture.

Clear the streets loud from behind them.

A police helicopter overhead. We were being pushed back. I almost lost my footing. Propped up by a woman behind me, who gently pushed me back toward the line of cops. Bodies fell. The police line broken now. Individual officers advancing. Another line of riot squadders appeared from somewhere. I caught an elbow in the head, a baton in the back before I realized the cop was there. His baton push carried me into a woman in front of me, who nearly lost her feet, careened into a teen in front of her. "What the *fuck*, man?" The teen looked like a football guy, a kid spoiling to make something happen, but he turned and saw the woman then me then the cop, moving slowly steadily, a rip tide. A man's urgent voice over a bullhorn: *This is a peaceful protest. This is a peaceful protest.* Somewhere out there, a thousand drivers honked a thousand car horns. Now two police helicopters circled overhead, strobing all sound.

I let the officer's baton and my own momentum carry me to the sidewalk. A buzz of voices behind me. Shouts. A woman's scream. Two cops elbowed past, dragging a woman by an arm, the back of her shirt. Shouting. *Fuck you, pigs.* Other calls. *Assholes.* Almost a plea – *nonviolence. Nonviolence.*

We Are Winning emerged in red spray paint on Berkley's front window. Another wave pushed onto the sidewalk and I wormed into it to stay close to the curb. A baton caught me in the gut – a cop shoving by with a bearded youth in tow, plastic zip cuffs, grinning.

The bullhorn, somewhere close.

This is a nonviolent protest.

His words had no effect. He was thirty feet from me and I could scarcely hear him.

Things happened fast. Demonstrators who'd moved beyond the police line tagged a limo and an SUV parked on Dartmouth with cans of spray paint. Clusters of people fighting to get closer, others to get away. Someone else had the bullhorn, started a chant, call and response.

No justice, no peace. No justice, no peace.

Riot squad cops, sunlight bouncing off helmets and shields. Scrambling bodies. More fell. I stepped over one, tried to offer a hand up, got shoved along. My gut ached. My lower back. The scuffle by the newspaper boxes in front of Berkley's had grown. A group of people – some of the Outward Bound-ish crew? – rocked an SUV, trying to roll it. Among them, an angry t-shirt that looked familiar. A sandy-haired teen. A group of cops used batons freely to fight toward that. I followed close in their wake, craning for a better look. I caught something – an elbow, a baton – in the thigh. Then spray paint on a police car at the corner of St. James and a crowd around one of the patrol cars, rocking it side to side. Helicopters circling. I'd lost sight of the sandy-haired teen.

"Shit." I was bumped, jostled, carried around. Elbowed in the head. Trying to keep my arms at my sides. My eyes alert. Where was Bo, what was he doing.

The patrol car tipped. Angry shouts of triumph. A collective gasp. More scurrying bodies. Newspaper boxes toppled. Flames shot up from one, then a second. Smoke from the other side of the street, and then more. Tear gas. A crash. Someone had thrown a newspaper box through the windshield of an SUV. Still, in the distance, a cacophony of car horns. Panicked eyes. I pulled the bottom of my shirt up over the lower half of my face. My eyes burned. People pushed past, leaving, or trying to. Everyone looked the same: a blur. Piercing sirens. Riot squad cops grabbing arms, restraining. I bounced hard into the side of a police van.

Disoriented. Looking for a way out. Fuzzy vision. Bodies shoved to the ground, arms held behind backs. Another crash. Berkley's plate glass window gone. More cops than not around me. *Go the other way? No choice. Go where you're carried.* Broken glass underfoot. I caught a baton in the ear. My head rang. Vision blurred, burning. A stricken-looking man in a coffee-splattered shirt emerged from Berkley's and slid down the sidewalk. Momentum carried me past the police van, where cops loaded a steady stream of protesters. I sensed an opening, kept moving up Dartmouth. Broke clear of crowd, into traffic. Drivers stunned mostly into silence. I stumbled to the sidewalk, aching and scared shitless. Sat on the steps of the bank trying to blink my eyes clear. Shirt stuck to my back. Made my way to the men's room at the Back Bay T station where I washed my face – rinsed out my eyes – four, five times until I could see again. Sat myself in a stall – five minutes, ten – until I could stop shaking. My head pounding. Aches everywhere. A part of me said *get back out there. Find Bo. Get pictures.* I don't think so. *Get the hell out of Dodge.* I hopped the Orange Line because it was handy. Leaned back in my seat. Head spinning. Assessed my aches. Very sore head. The worst was my back. Kidney. Could they have ruptured something. The fuck was I doing, anyway? Never mind that now. Dialed Bo. Surprise – no answer. Texted my pictures to Eric.

I started to consider the whole thing in terms of the news coverage. The union would catch hell, and from what I could see, didn't deserve it. They'd been glommed onto, and were now going to suffer for the sins of their supporters, most of whom made more than seven dollars an hour. I knew I should call Tillman, Sarkis,

Juliana. I didn't have it in me. Not even close. My arms trembled all the way home.

I didn't see Lin sitting on the front steps until I got to them. I had a pretty good idea what effect my not calling was having on her. But I needed to talk to Bo. I felt I was protecting him, and that I was uniquely qualified to do so. It's one thing to hold onto that justification through silence, distance. It's another to try when a worried mother is face to face with you.

"Don't do this, Nick. If we're friends. If we ever were. Don't do this to me."

I'd stopped a few feet short of where she sat hugging her knees on the step. My kidneys throbbed.

I pressed my lips together. Stared at the sidewalk.

In the shadows that hid her own shadows, Lin looked young and small.

"It's not like that," I said.

"What is it like?"

In the shadows, I could see the shape of her face, but not the features. I didn't move closer.

"I don't know what to say."

"You have no right." The kind of quiet that only a summer night can be. "Loyalty. Friendship. Great. I get it." She ran a hand through her hair. "But he's my son."

Sticky. Not even a hint of a breeze. I didn't disagree with her position. I thought a minute longer. "I don't know that he's in trouble," I said. "I don't *know* of anything you should worry about."

She stood. Closed the distance between us. Her watchfulness

had rescued me more than once when I was a stupid, reckless teen. Had forged a good life for she and Bo. But it wasn't the only way. Not always the best way.

She stared me down. She looked as weary as I felt. "You're splitting hairs over my son's safety and well-being. I want you to know how malicious and fucked-up that looks from where I sit."

"I need you to trust me, Lin."

She shook her head. The muscles in her neck strained. I swore she was holding back the urge to punch me. "I trust your motives. I don't trust your judgment." She must have seen how much that stung; her face softened a little. "You look like hell."

"I was a spectator at a riot."

"Ice," she said, and left me to slither into the house, tend my wounds, and find out how fucked our city was.

It doesn't make me a prophet to say I was right. The incident led the eleven o'clock news. Even made the national headline reel on CNN – "In Boston today, an eruption of labor and activist violence" with video footage of demonstrators rolling the police car, quick cut to spray-painted SUVs to smashed Berkley's, to demonstrators chained to Endicott entrance, to the State Street logo, to a protest sign I hadn't seen before – "Our City Is not Livable" – and then on to dropping Federal Reserve rates.

Locally, of course, it dominated the news. I held ice to my head and watched every second. Convinced I would live. From a safe distance, it seemed surreal. Chaos. I was struck by the volume of signs. Spotted purple balloons. Close-ups of police dragging cuffed demonstrators past cameras. A dumpster tipped on its side, contents on fire. Then footage of the aftermath. A push broom sweeping up glass. Yellow police tape around Berkley's. A tow truck righting the tipped patrol car.

My phone rang. A local number. I answered it.

"Nick Young?"

"Yeah?"

"Tom Webster, NewsRadio 59. We noticed that Tim Dunn referenced you in his *Herald* column Tuesday, and wanted to get your take on today's events, and in particular on Chris Tillman's comments tonight."

Fuck me. I was old school. I did *not* like the idea of being part of the story. On my TV, images of jammed Berkley's stores. I had no idea what Tillman had said. Maybe if I were a real journalist, I would have. *Leave me alone. I want to go to bed.* I made a slightly more gracious but no more informative response to the radio guy and ended the call.

On the TV, blow-dried blowhard Alvin Fraser did a studio commentary against a background montage of picket lines, snarled traffic, garbage-clogged lobbies and anarchists. And I listened. More fool me.

"A labor dispute is one thing, but when that escalates into violence and property destruction, it becomes something else. Radical fringe groups have attached themselves to this strike. The janitors – and their union – simply aren't doing enough to stop that."

Alvin Fraser, voice of balance and reason. Switched to Seven News and a red-faced Chris Tillman with a microphone in his face. "Let me be clear about this. We are not in negotiation. We have not been in negotiation. We will not be in negotiation. As for these appalling events, let's call it what it is – domestic terrorism."

12

Five-AM-and-change. Lin's voice on the phone. "Nick, it's your dad. He's had another stroke."

Clawing toward wakefulness. An alarm sounded quiet deep inside me, grew louder as it moved toward the surface. "It's bad, isn't it." My back and thigh ached, my ear throbbed, and I had a police baton headache that smacked me as soon as I sat up.

"It's not good. He was admitted at three-thirty this morning." She didn't sound like Lin. "A nurse heard him fall and called an ambulance."

I imagined my father awake at three, wondering why it was dark, walking to the windows to open the blinds, puzzled when that didn't let light in. Unable to fathom a solution, walking back toward bed, or his chair, feeling a punch in the sternum that knocked him to his knees, to the floor. Did he think he was his own father, in the ring against George "the Mechanic" LeBlanc. Did he know what was happening? Or was this one of many instances in which his body betrayed him at random and increasingly frequent moments.

"He's in emergency now. They're trying to stabilize him."

I don't care who you are – how noble or good-hearted. Nobody responds to dark news with pure emotional focus. We're all tainted; we hear the facts through and alongside some distraction or other that's too self-centered to explain. Me, I had a tape playing in my head of certain shining sentences I'd written the night before – hell, a few hours before – in a draft column for Eric. The column addressed how a number of interest groups – Seattle10, SLAM, even BAFA – had attached themselves to the janitors' cause and were using the occasion of the strike to advance their own agendas.

"Nick? You there?"

"Yeah."

I rubbed at my face as though that would help me wake up. As though it would focus me. "Just a little thrown."

The tape played in my head. *Because these events are all in the news, there is a temptation to connect the threads, conflate the causes. Don't. Neither the janitors nor the union are responsible for the acts of those who attach themselves like barnacles.*

"You need to prepare yourself." The detached, deliver-bad-news doctor voice. "There will be damage. The body can't take this type of hit repeatedly."

The charges of domestic terrorism that Endicott VP Chris Tillman leveled at the union this week are patently ridiculous. Irresponsible.

Lin's voice. "You want to hope for a quick return to consciousness, clear lungs –"

The tape stopped. "What do you mean, consciousness?"

"He was unconscious when they brought him in. He hasn't come around. It's impossible to know when – if – he'll wake up."

"Here we go again." The thought came out my mouth.

Silence on Lin's end. I could feel her disapproval. Only then did it occur to me I was surprised to hear from her. And not. Lin, always responsible.

"Good of you to call," I said. "Considering."

Again, a silence. "I almost didn't. You don't make it easy."

No arguing with that. "So what happens next?"

"They monitor him closely for the next couple hours and hope his heart stabilizes. If it does, they keep pumping fluids into him and we hope he wakes up."

I've always been a person of delayed emotional responses. It can make me seem colder than I actually am. I wondered whether Eric had read my draft. I thought about breakfast. I thought about how I was going to make things right with Lin. I thought about how I would trade my failing father for a phone call from Bo.

"I should get in there."

"Up to you." Cold was what I heard in Lin's voice. "I've told Dr. Chang, the attending, I'd like to stay informed. I gave her your number. Didn't know if you'd go in." A soft hum on the phone line. Someone being paged.

Cold. I thought of cold salmon, slices of lox, with capers, an onion bagel. Slabs of sushi arranged on a thin wood plank. I thought of pushing myself off that plank, ineffective and unreliable. "Lin, about Bo –"

"I have things to do. I'll call when I know more." Dead air.

I stood dumb with the phone in my hand. Stood in darkness in my father's den in my boxers and worn t-shirt. Mostly awake and wondering when I would feel my father's situation. Whether I would. A sense of duty – and only that – beckoned me toward the hospital. I swallowed ibuprofen. Shaved. Wiped blood from my neck. Got dressed. Sweat into my shirt. Grabbed my keys. Willed myself toward the door. Didn't work. My body a boulder. Thomas' slow fade so much more than I had bargained for. Tossed the keys on the counter. Checked email. Yes, a note from Eric.

Professor:

This is shit. Step away from the lectern and give me journalism. Where issues touch people. Make me feel something. Do us both a favor: throw that draft away and start clean. Get it to me yesterday.

Asshole. He'd crossed out or deleted all but three or four sentences. Whatever. I'd deal with him later. Breakfast. Grabbed a bowl, dumped in some cereal, sniffed and poured milk. Turned on the Early Bird news, Channel Five. Bright Eyes greeted me with a smile and the fact that, according to the latest figures, economic indicators were down for the fifth consecutive month.

"A fire in Natick destroyed 20 sport utility vehicles last night." Burned-out husks of Hummers floated behind his head. "Fire crews worked for more than an hour to put out the fire that threatened the life of at least one employee." Cut to footage of oversized vehicles tagged with slogans. "Police suspect eco-activists of setting the blaze at Craig's Auto World." My appetite vanished. Bright Eyes' voiceover: "Beyond the fire, more than a dozen Hummers and Chevy Tahoe SUVs were vandalized with spray-painted environmentalist slogans. Middlesex County District Attorney Michael Duff was at the scene."

I grabbed my phone. Hit the first digits of Bo's cell. Stopped.

Channel Five cut to the DA. He was solid and square. I thought I recognized him as a former boxer, a one-time area big shot. He looked like a guy you didn't want to cross. "A witness has provided descriptions of suspects. We expect to move quickly to make arrests." Back to Bright Eyes: "There were no reports of injuries, but damages were estimated at a half million dollars."

A hint of pink light from outside. I killed the TV sound and dialed Bo. No surprise. Straight to voice mail. Texted him.

tell me youre not doing what i think youre doing
call me while i can still help

I paced, my sore thigh complaining. I cursed Bo, Thomas, the cops, and the corporate capitalist system. The hospital would have to wait. I grabbed my keys and headed for Bo's house.

Sun battled clouds for dominance in the early morning sky. A false promise of breeze. I drove with the window cranked, the radio off – too many things I didn't want to hear – and my mind reeling. Told myself I had no hard evidence Bo had been in Natick. For all I knew he'd been home, out listening to music, stealing street signs, or any of a hundred other innocent summer activities. I ran a light at Cypress and flipped off an enraged citizen who took issue. Toyed with going back and giving said citizen a forearm shiver for emphasis. *Lady, you have no idea all the shit I'm juggling. I am so far beyond my skill level.* Congratulated myself for my restraint. Focused on driving. Two blown stop signs later I pulled up at the house, strode purposefully up the flagstone path and had my finger on the doorbell before my conflicting agendas occurred to me. *Talk to Bo. Avoid Lin.* Fuck. The doorbell donged my doom. I imagined Lin answering, disheveled, teary-eyed. *No, he's not here. He's in jail, Nick. Thanks to you.* I couldn't talk to her. The bell echoed, but the door stayed shut. *Get out.* I made my legs move, hurried back down the flagstone walk, and got the hell out of there.

I drove to Natick to see the scene for myself, as if the air of the place would reveal answers. Route 9 was a parking lot. The day began to bake and I crawled through Newton, hoping traffic would ease once the commuters split off at 128. It didn't. I passed the time listening to NPR and worrying about Bo. Thomas. Marcela.

Craig's Auto World inhabited a relatively sedate stretch of Route 9, just east of the retail insanity at the Framingham line. The main lot had been mostly cleared. Twin Chevy Suburbans with vandalized windows and spray-painted hoods – "gas guzzler" and "polluting pig" – were the lone vehicles left facing the street.

A core crew of sales people huddled near the showroom window where an unfortunate promotion announced "Summer Sizzlers" in giant letters. Beside the showroom lurked the charred husk of a warehouse building cordoned off with yellow tape. Two cops leaned against a Natick police cruiser parked across from the wasted building. Overhead, little red-white-and-blue triangular flags strung between light poles. I wandered the lot trying to look inconspicuous. I wasn't alone. A harried-looking guy with a dark crew-cut and a goatee, striped tie, white shirt sleeves rolled up, broke away from the huddle and met me on my way toward the warehouse.

"Morning." His voice hoarse. "I help you with something?"

I dug a business card from my pants pocket. "Nick Young. Reporter."

"Ted Hauser. You're a little late for the circus. We're trying to get back to business."

A trio of dark-haired men in coveralls were relocating cars from the back of the lot, slowly filling the roadside gap.

"I understand. I don't want to take your time."

He wiped at his brow with a handkerchief. "So what can I do for you?"

I didn't have a good answer. I wanted to comb the grounds for physical proof that Bo hadn't been there. Tangible evidence that showed he was all bluster, that all he'd been doing for the past week had been working at the day care. Going to clubs.

"I'm doing a column on anti-globalist activists, the possible connection between them and –"

"Bastards," he said. "People can take whatever political belief they want. I don't give a shit. Really. But have a little respect for property."

I considered trying out Bo's logic on him, but thought better of it. "Any idea why someone would target your dealership?"

He stared at me as if waiting for a translation. *Okay, stupid question.* "The hell should I know. They like Natick, maybe? It's close to the Denny's?"

"So what happens with the damaged vehicles?"

"We got insurance, like anyone else." He was losing patience, and I was floundering to find some purpose for my presence.

"Can I see them?"

He squinted at me. "Why?"

I want to see if I recognize the paint job. "Like I said, I'm doing a column on the activists, there's suspicion they might be responsible

for this, and it will help me be accurate if I can see what they did."
I shrugged. "Maybe I recognize their work."

"Play detective, huh?"

"If I can help, sure."

He led me behind the showroom to a back lot now filled with vandalized SUVs. We walked between two Hummers with spray-painted sides. Red-and-white concentric circles. Targets.

I turned to face them and he stood beside me. I nodded at the Hummer. "You drive one of these?"

He shook his head. "I got a Blazer I like just fine." Arms folded. "You don't approve."

I smiled. "I guess I don't."

"Free country," he said. "Supply and demand."

I walked the lot and examined the other cars. A couple Tahoes, one tagged across the front windshield with "I love pollution" and one with "Fat lazy Americans." Maybe it was my imagination, but I recognized the handwriting. My head hummed; my ear ached.

The pavement radiated heat. Hauser's voice beside me. "I don't figure it's my job to tell anybody what to think. What to drive."

I ran my hand along the Tahoe's hood. Touched the painted windshield. "I get that," I said. "I tend to agree. But somewhere we gotta have principles, right? Something we stand on?"

He played with his tie knot. "What do you drive?"

I grinned. "Seventy-two Dart." I had a car that transcended politics. That would win over any car guy.

He grinned, too. "No shit?"

"No shit." We both appreciated that for a minute, and I played my advantage. "Okay if I wander through the warehouse?"

Behind us, a garage bay door groaned open and a hydraulic wrench whined.

"I suppose."

We went out front and crossed the main lot. I tried to imagine Bo there in the midst of the carnage. To read his face. Delight or fear? Passion or doubt? I couldn't see close enough. I could only see him running across the lot, spray can in hand, acting on his beliefs.

The two Natick cops watched us with mild curiosity. We ducked under the police tape and into the burned-out building. Spent a minute absorbing the aura. Charred husks of a half-dozen vehicles. Blackened concrete walls. Sections of roof gone. The overpowering smell. It all made me sad, and a little sick.

"Shit."

Hauser, hands on hips beside me. "Uh huh."

Yes, a columnist casts a wide net, but this place only revealed to me the stench of destruction. I wanted to get out of there, and I wanted to take it all in. What some people do for the cause.

"Hey, there were no injuries, right?"

Hauser had put a handkerchief over his mouth and nose. He took it away. "That's right. Thank god."

"But did I hear something about a witness? You know anything about that?"

"Crazy thing, that." He pulled his tie away from his shirt, then let it fall back. "Night watchman. He admits he's asleep in the warehouse. A little nap, while this is going on. Gets woken up. Kid in a ski mask telling him he needs to leave the building."

"Kid?"

"Young person, I don't know. Anyway, two of these guys zip cuff him and escort him out before they torch the building. So I guess they have some moral values."

I understood his confusion.

The South End is one of Boston's finest neighborhoods. Block after block of brick townhouses, brick sidewalks, and miniature manicured gardens. I parked in front of one and headed for New Horizons Day Care. By now it was regular morning. Regular people were up and about their business. By my standards, I'd already had a full day. I walked the shaded brick around to Tremont. New Horizons was a street-level storefront in a retail-condo complex. Fronted with a big plate glass window that showed me no one was home. Memory or accumulated local knowledge led me around the corner to a small playground on West Canton.

Hidden behind sunglasses, I approached, scanning for Bo and trying to look inconspicuous. A dozen children shrieked and frolicked. Three cheery young adults in sunshine-yellow shirts supervised it all. I saw Bo before he saw me. Under the shade of a beech tree near the wrought iron fence that lined the property. Arms folded, watching a group of kids dig and shout in a sandbox.

I got next to him, the sandbox in sunshine ten feet away. "Where were you last night?"

His eyes showed as caught, but only for a flash. He leaned toward me. Said in a soft voice, "Fuck you."

"What kind of shit are you in?"

A notch more urgent, but still soft. "Fuck you."

228

My thigh ached. My kidney didn't. "Take a break. We're going to talk."

"No we're not." He extended his hands in a "look around" gesture. Toddlers scurried past us, riding swings, bouncing balls, racing each other up a wide rope ladder.

I grabbed his clammy arm and reached for reserves of patience unfamiliar to me. "Do you talk to your boss or do I?"

He shook loose. I watched the muscles ripple in his forearm. He gave me his hardest teen glare. I was impervious.

"Fine. Whatever."

I hovered in the shade of the beech tree and watched Bo talk to a pony-tailed woman with a clipboard. It was a sweet playground, an oasis in a crowded city block. Swings, corkscrew slide, climbing structure, sandbox, all ringed by raised landscape beds full of flowers and ground cover. I watched Bo consider taking off, then walk back to me.

A curly-haired boy squealed as he reached the top of the rope ladder a second sooner than three other scrambling tots.

"What?" Bo demanded.

"Where were you last night?"

A flash of something that could have been anger as easily as guardedness. "Can you cut to it? What are we talking about?"

"Craig's Auto World. Natick. Couple dozen tagged SUVs. Warehouse fire. Lead story on the local news."

"So?"

"So were you there? So what kind of trouble are you in? So how do I help you?" Bo kept an eye on his charges, which amounted to avoiding my gaze. "And what do I tell your mother?"

"My *mother*? Screw you. I'm outta here." He turned but I grabbed his arm again, tighter. Squeezed the bicep.

"Fuckhead. Were you *there*?"

"Will you stop? You can't talk that way here."

I didn't give a shit about my language.

"Yeah," he said. His voice low. Conspiratorial, despite the playground din. "It was my idea. Planned the whole thing over coffee one morning."

A sand-covered boy with a plastic shovel eyed us like he was gauging what he could get away with.

Deep breath. Another. "Bo, I'm your friend. I'm worried about you. The cops are serious about this. I'm trying to keep you from fucking over your life. Just talk to me."

"What do you tell my *mother*?"

Fucking teens. "Yes. She's my friend too and she knows something's up and that's not the point. Talk to me."

"I know what I'm doing. Everything's fine. That's what you can tell my *mother*."

A wave of laughter from behind us.

Fucking *goddamn* teens. "Forget your mother for a minute. This is me."

"Why are you so panicky? I'm fine. Stuff is fine." Not looking at me. Hands stuffed in cargo shorts pockets.

A boy grabbed at the chain of a swing each time it passed, pissing off the girl who wouldn't give it up.

"Shit is escalating, Bo. Day of Chaos. Arson. Fucking eco-terrorism. Those are words getting kicked around on the news."

He raised his eyebrows. Made a show of twisting his mouth into a scowl. "Media bullshit. It's action."

"Tell me you weren't there. Tell me you're smarter than that."

"I wasn't there. I'm smarter than that."

I wanted to smack him. I wanted to crawl away and nap. "Ding. Round one goes to the kid. Nicely done. Round two over coffee. Let's go."

"I'm at work."

"I'm not letting you go until we figure some things out." I dug out my cell. I couldn't sink any lower. "Or I *will* call your mother."

He talked to the pony-tailed woman again and we exited in silence. I headed up the shaded block on alert, half expecting Bo to run. I steered us toward Killian's, a coffee and sandwich shop on Tremont. I tried to read his face. Failed.

We ducked into the place and I pointed him to a chair. "What do you want? I'm buying."

Sullen. Stubborn. "Nothing."

Half-dozen customers at veneer tables. A counter woman idly watching TV news. An oscillating fan blew on the counter. Overhead speakers played the Traveling Wilburys, which made my jaw clench. I got a coffee and sat across from Bo. Tossed my phone on the table, a reminder of the stakes. Felt like a cop on a cop show. Only without the snappy dialogue.

I smelled home fries and wanted them. "Let's start over."

Bo sat slouched in the chair. His long legs surrounded the table. His eyes scanned the room. One leg bouncing on the ball of his foot. He helped himself to my coffee. "You still don't get it, Nick. Every day you sit and do nothing, the system is crushing people."

There wasn't enough coffee in the place – in the world – to make me get into that. "No," I said. Home fries. Bacon. "Don't even try that." I took my coffee back.

"What?"

"Just talk to me. Outline it. Help me understand." He reached for my coffee again. I slapped his hand away. "What kind of trouble are you in? What kind of trouble is Marcela in?"

His face shut down. "Marcela? What about Marcela?"

My head hurt. "Her grandfather's worried about her, she's gone, she's not gone, what the fuck, Bo?"

"What do you know about Marcela?"

"She asked me for help. I run into her in a club one night, she wants to talk to me, then poof, she's gone."

Bo leaned forward across the table. "In a *club*?" His face flushed. "What's going on here, Nick? Are you fucking her?"

I may have reddened. I held my head in my hands. Part frustration, part shame. "No." If I was telling the truth, why did it feel like I was lying? "I'm not fucking her, Bo."

The leg bounced. His face red. Fists on his thighs. "You're middle-aged. She was my girlfriend. What kind of pervert are you?"

He pushed up from his chair. Started for the door.

"Bo!" My voice stopped him. I had a second, maybe two. I softened my voice. "I *am* your friend. Whatever you need. Just talk to me."

He stood with that. Half turned to me, half to the door. It took all I had to let the silence stand. He sat back down.

"You're not fucking her?"

"I swear to you I'm not fucking her."

Bo looked tired. His hair had had only the briefest encounter with a brush. "She's gone," he said. "Vanished."

"Really? We're going to do this again?" It was like being with my father, except Thomas had an excuse. "I *saw* her. Talked to her."

He looked like he'd swallowed something sour. "She was back. She's gone again. I'm worried."

"You make a huge fucking deal about her being gone, you don't bother to tell me she's back, and now you're yanking my chain again. You going to tell me what's up?"

"Nothing's up."

My turn to stand. "I'm done, Bo. I can't." Started to walk away, and meant it. I lacked the skills. The endurance.

"Wait." He drained my coffee. I let it ride.

"What?"

"You sure you want to know?"

I sat down. A waitress refilled my cup. Steam rose from it.

Bo scanned for someplace to look that wasn't at me. He fingered my cup, then left it alone. "She didn't kill him."

My mouth went dry. "What? Who?"

His voice barely audible. "She didn't kill him."

The coffee ate a hole in my stomach. I tried to convince myself we weren't talking about Evan Tillman. That Bo wasn't implying some knowledge of that murder, or Marcela Pruett as implicated.

He shrugged. There was no sound, anywhere, beyond our voices. "Okay," I said. "She didn't kill him."

"That's what she told me. I believe her."

Reorienting to follow him. "But she was involved?"

"Yeah."

233

I felt ancient. I had to ask, and I dreaded the answer. "Were you?"

"No." No hesitation or equivocation. I believed him. I wanted to.

"How involved was she? Who else was involved?" Suddenly the place just smelled greasy, and I felt cold. "No. Wait. Don't tell me." My mind worked to process it all. I thought about Lin. I walked a line – what I was willing to know and still withhold. "Do you know who else was involved? Yes or no."

He thought about it. I didn't like that. "No."

"Okay. Good." Trying to focus. "Involved how?"

"I don't know. That's all she'd tell me. But I think she knows something and I think it scares her."

"Her grandfather was a cop."

"That's what I mean."

"And you weren't involved."

"I just told you."

"Who else? What about Adam?"

"I told you. I don't know. Adam was with me that day, at the food pantry."

Our communal coffee sat untouched. "Look at me, Bo."

He did.

"Are you okay? No bravado. For real."

His face showed a mix of fear and fatigue that brought out the Bo I'd first known, a three-year-old in a Superman cape. "I don't know."

Dylan came on the sound system. *Forever Young*. Sentimental horseshit. I took a deep breath. "So what do we do?"

"How should I know? You're the adult."

Think. "We need to track down Marcela."

234

"Brilliant. Thanks. Sure glad you're on my team." Bo looked at me: his look said, *come on*, grownup, *what now?*

I stared into the face of my own teen insouciance. It did nothing to improve my mood. "I need some space. I gotta think." My thigh ached. I felt weary. Claustrophobic. I headed for the door. Called over my shoulder. "I'll call you. And you fucking well better answer."

Down the sidewalk. Reeling. Trying to parse fact from speculation. To focus and be tactical. Demanding answers wouldn't get them from any self-respecting teen. I had to decide did I trust Bo, at the core. And if I did, I needed to keep him close – try to protect him from himself, and out of jail.

Fuck. Walked back to Killian's, pushed open the door and almost floored Bo on his way out.

"Okay, listen. Whatever it is, I'm in. I'll help. But you need to promise me two things."

We stood in the doorway, blocking the entrance and violating personal space.

"What?"

"I will keep this from your mother if you step back for now – no illegal activity. And," I searched for the right words, "if you see or hear from Marcela, you both track me down immediately. Oh, and you answer your phone when I call you."

He looked at me like he was weighing my offer. "Technically, that's three things."

I had to work to let that one go. This adult thing didn't come easy. "Deal?"

"Okay."

I needed somewhere I could think. Needed to walk off some frustration. Anger. Get grounded. *Who pushed the "upend world" button?* Ended up at the branch library in a study carrel with some air conditioning and the door very much closed. The day felt endless and it was not yet noon.

On a damp notebook page which caught condensation from the iced coffee I'd smuggled in, I sketched out a thought trail that connected – or tried to – Evan Tillman's murder, Marcela Pruett's absence, anti-globalization protests, anti-capitalist violence, and a 17-year-old's mercurial moods. I sat at that too-quiet particle board table determined to separate out what I knew from what I feared. I knew no other way to determine how urgent I needed to be.

What I knew: Bo was guilty of vandalism against property in at least one case, probably more. The cops were already all over the eco-terrorist activism against SUVs, and would be only more so. Bo was connected to both Seattle10 and SLAM, and would be in the system because he had been arrested in a peaceful demonstration against Endicott scabs. *Gulp. Okay.* What else did I know? Two janitors were dead under circumstances that more and more people found suspicious. And, oh yeah, Marcela Pruett was withholding evidence in the Evan Tillman murder and running very scared.

What I suspected and/or feared: Evan Tillman was not killed by grown-up hoods in a break-in, and Marcela was an accessory to murder, or worse. Bo had rolled and burned cars in the whole Day of Chaos hoo-hah. He had committed at least one felony

236

at at least one car dealership, and might himself be withholding evidence from a murder investigation. The janitors' deaths were not accidental, and were somehow tied to all this. *Fuck.*

I stared at my lists. Tore the sheet of paper in half to separate them. Swapped the halves back and forth. Peeled one off the heel of my hand when it stuck. Outside my study carrel, the collected wisdom of western civilization waited silently to be tapped. I made myself focus on what I knew. Bad, yes, but not the end of the world.

What would a real adult do? No idea. All I could think to do was try to gather info, then decide what to do with it. Like a good ex-journalist, I worked the phone.

Called AJ, had a stilted conversation because only after he answered did I realize I couldn't ask him anything directly. Called Teresa, hoping she could tell me what to do. Got voice mail and hung up. What good is an ex-wife if you can't lean on her when you need her?

An incoming call. Eric. I let it go. *Not now.*

Started to dial the Newton cops, but a text from Eric busted in.

Intrepid Reporter:

1. J's have cancelled noon rally. Find out what's going on.

2. Where's my column?

3. Answer your fucking phone

Whatever. Not now.

Dialed the Newton cops again, asked for Detective Hill. Got put on hold. Hung up. What would I ask him? *Got any leads involving nubile teenage girls?*

Not terribly fucking productive. I scratched lines on the paper. Sipped my iced coffee. Studied the page with my thought trail on it. Tried to find angles. Answers. Nothing. For all I knew, Bo was right now being cuffed by police, Marcela Pruett's dead body decaying in a dumpster somewhere. *Stop. Focus.*

What were my options? To tell Lin or not to tell Lin. Despite a wheelbarrow of guilt, I'd already committed on that one and nothing on my lists made me think otherwise. I couldn't say I supported the laws I knew Bo had broken. All I wanted was to keep him out of trouble. Which for now meant keep him from getting caught. I could give that much to Bo. I owed that much to Lin. So what was my priority? Learn what I could about the state of the Natick investigation. Right. And how could I get a line on that? I smiled for the first time that day. Even said it out loud. "Lenny Russell." My old muckraking journalist pal.

Dialed him. Got him.

"Lenny, Nick Young. You still have contacts in the Middlesex DA's office?"

"Yeah. Why?"

"I need a favor. Extract anything you want in return." He laughed. "Any developments in the Natick car dealership attack I need to know. Any info about suspects. Descriptions. Any sniff that arrests are near. Can you do that?"

"Sure. I ask why?"

"Nope."

"OK, no worries."

My phone beeped. Call waiting. A number I didn't recognize. I thanked Lenny, said goodbye and answered.

"Mr. Young, this is Dr. Chang at Newton-Wellesley Hospital."

Fuck.

238

"Your father is in intensive care. His condition is serious, but stable."

"That's good news, right?"

"There has been damage. He hasn't regained consciousness, and it's too soon to tell when – or if – he will."

"I understand." I tried to pull myself back to Thomas, to his circumstances.

"We just hope that now his body is through the shock, in the next 24 hours he'll start to bounce back."

"I appreciate the information. Thanks for the call."

Well, nursing home visits were one thing I could scratch off my to-do list for the next couple of days. I waited to feel something about my father's condition. I didn't have time. A text from Eric:

J's rescheduled.

4:00 @ old west. be there.

I set the phone down. Smart move by the union. No doubt an attempt to step away from the activists and still get press coverage. Outside my door, a stooped librarian shelved books from a metal cart. My study carrel started to feel claustrophobic.

The thing about living isolated is you can get used to it, almost forget there are other people, or such things as relationships. It's when your life actually touches others you can feel most alone.

I couldn't do much more at the moment, and I had to get out of the library. I walked back to the Dart. Wall of heat. Dead air. Drove out of the city, all the windows open to blow the bad juju away, news radio playing loud. I drove past the hospital. Couldn't make myself turn in. Turned onto Beacon Street and drove through Waban, Newton Highlands. I learned things from the news. People in the world were still poking at each other. Item one: "Governor Anthony Garrett today cancelled the state's custodial contract with Delfi after the Service Workers Union International threatened to expand its strike to four state buildings." I waited for an irate sound bite from Chris Tillman, to no avail. I decided to go to the four o'clock rally at Old West. Item two: Mayor Reeves, bless his magnanimous heart, tired of merely encouraging the two sides to come to the table, figured out a way to pressure them by announcing an offer to mediate talks. Come to the table and stay until an agreement gets hammered out. Nice. I could picture it: Reeves, a fiery old-school pol, reveled in rolling up his sleeves and getting dirty; doling out favors and holding grudges for slights both perceived and real; an ego taller than the Hancock Tower and a two-year-old's temper. A reasoned mediator he was not. Should be fascinating.

I drove the afternoon away. The wind through the Dart blew my thoughts away and I got to Old West with only one interruption: a reassuring callback from Lenny.

"What I know so far on Natick: they're not as close as Duffy would like you to think. They're pretty sure about SLAM/Seattle10. Duh. And young people. Vague descriptions from the witness."

That was something. I had no strategy, but I had time.

Outside Old West, vendors hawked burritos, sausage-and-pepper sandwiches, and ice cream from chrome carts. No ancillary causes. Inside, no fans. Almost exclusively janitors and reporters. The rescheduling strategy had worked. I elbowed my way through to the crabby clutch of reporters in the side aisle in time to hear Juliana address the troops.

"This has become a war of angry words, and actions that serve no one's best interests," she told the crowd. She'd gotten her hair cut. Blunt, not layered. It looked good. "No one here is a terrorist. No one here wants to overthrow the government, or capitalism. No one here is against business or profit. All we want is what we deserve – a fair wage for a day's work, and the chance to work full-time with full benefits. It's all anyone wants, a job that earns you enough to feed your family."

The crowd cheered Juliana. The smell of fried peppers drifted in through open windows. The distant sound of jackhammers. My thigh ached a little less, my head a little more.

Juliana: "We have placed calls to Pollard, Endicott, Delfi, each with the same message. Let's accept the mayor's offer. Sit down together and craft a solution that's fair to both sides." More cheers. She waited until they subsided. "We believe an agreement is possible if we work tirelessly toward a solution."

I couldn't imagine the rhetoric escalating much further. Tillman had set the bar pretty high. And, according to the buzz around me, he was still playing hardball. Vocally unhappy with the city's "soft" response to recent activism, he apparently had an op-ed piece in the morning's *Globe* blasting the mayor and police force. And while he didn't repeat his domestic terrorism charge, he did make it clear he was among a group calling for Federal prosecutions under the Patriot Act.

Juliana finished and Sam took the podium to cover logistics. Blow-dried Alvin Fraser appeared behind me, his ubiquitous cameraman in tow. When Sam finished, Juliana came our way. I made room for her to pass, but she stopped in front of me.

"I enjoyed your column, Nick. Thanks for your perspective."

I blushed. Grinned like a dumbass. I wasn't used to compliments, especially from attractive women. Opened my mouth in an effort to restore my dignity. "I appreciate what you said up there. And how you said it. The protests and activism do raise important questions, but the janitors deserve center stage."

"Will I get to read that in your next column?"

Before I could think of a snappy comeback, Alvin Fraser had pushed past me. He caught me with an elbow in my sore kidney and caught Juliana for an interview. I winced and hoped I'd sweat on him.

I threw Eric a bone – texted him a paragraph quote for the website and promised him 3-4 grafs on the rally. Needed to stay occupied, so I headed back to the house and played journalist before Eric could scream at me again about the column. He wanted real people, I'd give them to him.

By sunset, I had spoken to Eduardo's widow, dug up some telling statistics, and turned Chris Tillman further into the face of the wealthy establishment in a redrafted column I grudgingly acknowledged as a vast improvement. I painted a picture of Eduardo, his wife, three kids, three jobs, and lack of health insurance. I described their apartment and quoted the widow. I allowed myself one crusading sentence – *The people and organizations that benefit from their labor bear a responsibility to provide fair compensation for that work.* I offered up Chris Tillman and his $1.6 million Newton home as a contrast. And I sent it off to Eric before I could reconsider.

I'd hardly had a chance to fear idleness before my phone rang. Bo.

"You okay?"

"Yeah. Good." Voices in the background. "A few of us are heading out to hear some music. Thought maybe you could come."

That sounded perfect. A bit of release, and the certainty that Bo was, for the moment, safe. I made plans to meet up with them at ten. Rode a wave of professionalism and worked on my strike piece for AJ. Showered and ate leftover pasta cold from the fridge.

Hot, sticky night. The kind you picture city kids bursting open fire hydrants to cool off. Where people sit out on fire escapes and front steps hoping for a breeze. The kind of night that makes you think deep summer is all there is, all there ever has been or ever will be.

We headed down Lansdowne Street. Fenway dark and quiet with the Sox in Chicago. Me and Bo and five of his friends, including Adam and Ben and a few I hadn't met. It was good to see him, to be with him, even though he seemed distracted.

"Who's the band?" I asked him.

"I forget. Friend got us on the comp list."

We crossed the bridge on Charlesgate West, then cut down Ipswich. Walking in the road. A line of parked cars on one side. The steady hum of the Turnpike behind us. The occasional cab a block over on Commonwealth. I'd fallen into step with Adam and Ben, who carried a backpack. Adam talked politics to Ben. I tuned him out, slowed my steps and fell back, content to watch the kids three car lengths in front of me. These teens always purposeful, even in their stride. They came up on a Lexus SUV. Black. Glossy in the streetlight.

"Gas hog," a girl named Bonnie called. "Planet polluter."

No breeze at all.

Another girl, magenta-haired, shrugged off a backpack. The teens clustered loosely around the SUV. Fuck. I knew where this was headed. I looked at Bo, anger rising. Looked around at the condos that lined the street. Lights in windows. Down the block, a woman with a golden retriever, the dog squatting at the edge of the sidewalk.

Two cans of spray paint emerged. Bonnie had one. A boy named Tim the other. The metallic clack of the little ball when you shake it. Laughing.

I tensed up.

"Small," Bonnie said to Tim. "Leave me room."

I had a sour taste in my mouth. I looked at Bo. Thought about leaving. About calling him out. Told myself I should wait. That this wasn't something he planned. I retreated to the sidewalk and watched as Tim painted "Hour of reckoning" on the hood, and Bonnie decided to work the back windshield. I kept an eye on the woman and her dog. She bent to pick up a pile.

"Bo," I said. I looked around the quiet street.

He avoided my eyes.

I heard Bonnie laugh. I studied Bo, trying to gauge a reaction. He circled the vehicle, not participating but not backing off.

"Come on," I said. "We should get going." I was pissed at being implicated; at Bo being part of this. I feared getting caught. Ben laughed. I watched the woman and her dog cut off onto Ipswich. Listened for cars. Told myself Bo didn't know this was coming. It was spontaneous.

"Check it out," Bonnie said. Everyone clustered to the rear of the car.

"Cool," said Matt. "That'll be a nice surprise. A fine way to end his night."

"Save the planet" in white paint on the rear windshield.

I stood next to Ben, the only one not involved. Lobbied. "We should go. We're going to miss the show."

Ben gave me a puzzled look. "What show?"

"The band. The club. We should head over."

"We're not going to a club."

Tim grabbed the paint cans and went to the driver's door.

I watched the teens, playful as if in the midst of a school prank. I circled the vehicle. Personalized license plate: TLLMN2. A terrible knowledge fired in my brain. I finished my loop around the SUV on the driver's side, where Adam had painted red and white concentric circles. A target.

I backed away. Slow steps. Registering how I'd been played. The last thing I saw before I turned around was Bo, standing on the sidewalk, inscrutable in the shadows.

13

Blue carpet. Pine chairs upholstered in rust-colored vinyl. A nondescript coffee table strewn with dated issues of celebrity mags. The same soulless decorator must outfit all waiting areas.

I sat at Newton-Wellesley Hospital waiting to see my father. Waiting for Bo to find Marcela or take down global capitalism. Waiting to discern what I wanted to be when I grew up – for some sage to show me where and how to re-start my life. Waiting to hear what I'd tell Lin when she finally pinned me down.

The doctor was in with Thomas. I fancied myself a busy man, so I paced the waiting area. My column appeared in the morning's *View* and I didn't hate it; I did rework a flawed sentence in my head while I paced. Asked for information three times in five minutes. The ongoing effort not to feel – there were moments I stumbled on awareness of the toll it took. An aide sat at the nurse's station, tired hair pulled into a ponytail.

"The doctor's with him. That's all I can tell you."

A woman in her sixties, cream-colored blouse, jeans, perm,

waited too. Reading *Time*. Patient and calm, or good at faking it. I snuck glances, searching for some sign she was on the brink with me.

A nurse strolled by with a pregnant teen. I knew something of her circumstance. I too had been fucked over by a young man. But I had at least one big advantage on her – I could deal with it later.

I paced to the end of the drab room, reversed direction and nearly walked into Lin. Shoulders drooping. Doctor coat disheveled.

I considered what I might tell her. Came up empty. Went into a clinch. "Your son can be a real pain in the ass."

"Really. I had no idea."

I hugged her – tried to. She resisted just enough to make it awkward. Shadows under her eyes.

"You look beat," I said.

"My natural state. You're not helping."

I had nothing for that. She had wrinkles. Crow's feet. So did I. Somehow we'd become middle-aged humans too weary to take on big challenges. I wanted to smooth her face. "You feel like you belong in your life?"

She looked puzzled. "What?"

"You know. When you comb your hair, brush your teeth, you see yourself in the mirror, do you think, yeah, this is me, this is my life?"

Her eyes searched my face for some kind of clue.

"Me, I wonder how I got here." I wanted to sit with my friend and puzzle out life, as if it all lay ahead. I should still be twenty-five, deciding how to apply my vast potential to make a better world. "So much road behind us."

Lin's gaze slid past my shoulder. I felt exposed. Stupid.

"Never mind," I said. A phone rang down the hall. "We had a long talk, Bo and I."

"That's supposed to make me feel better?" She tucked stray hair behind her ear. Checked her watch. "How's your Dad?"

I nodded toward the nurse's station. "I'm told the doctor's in with him." My tone may have been snarky.

"Wait here."

She pushed through double doors into the treatment area.

My companion in waiting grabbed a different old issue of *Time*.

Fifteen lengths of the room later, Lin was back. She led me in to see my father. Pulled back the curtain. The worn figure on the bed was a pale shadow of Thomas Young, tubes in his nose and mouth, arms thin as chicken's legs. I couldn't detect breathing. The thought flashed that he'd kicked. Then I registered the slow, feeble rise and fall of his chest. And the heart monitors behind his bed, which ticked off the triumphs of his most steadfast muscle with slow, steady beeps. Each one a reassurance. Each one inviting the question would it be the last. His face twisted in a freeze-frame of discomfort.

Lin: "Take a few minutes. I'll call with an update when I can."

I nodded thanks. Touched his hand with the tips of my fingers. Cool, papery. How strange it felt. How rare physical contact had been between us. I sat on the edge of his bed – two, three minutes that felt like days. The room smelled of decay. Death. We all die alone, sure, but this? *I don't know how to help you, old man. We all lie in the bed we make. Just hope to hell there's mercy somewhere.* Felt myself tearing up, fully aware it was not over my father as

248

much as in premonition of my own future. The possibility I was looking in a mirror at someday.

The hand my fingers rested on was punchless. The human shell on the bed had been – even a couple weeks earlier – the belligerent Thomas Young, jabbing at the world, at his only son – *you always did think you were too damn good for the rest of us* –maybe not with vintage power, but plenty strong.

I had to get out. I took my hand away, pushed gently up from the bed, and high-tailed it down the hall, past the nurse's station, past the permed woman who waited still with a patience I'd never have. Out the sluggish automatic doors to an airless afternoon, the sky heavy with rain that wouldn't come. Reached the safety of the Dart.

I needed to breathe. Buy myself some space. I decided I'd head downtown and play journalist – check in on the city's high-profile labor negotiation. A forced sit-down between two of the city's most powerful companies and its largest union, brokered on the mayor's reputation. It promised to be a heavyweight bout; the power elite gathered to slug away at each other for as long as it took might be enough of a distraction.

Turned on to Washington Street and turned on the radio. Top of the hour, NPR. *The president's latest appeals court nominee faces the Senate Judiciary Committee again today. Opponents vow to block her based on her views on immigration. Now, with more on the hour's top story, here's NPR correspondent Emily Boully. "The activist group Seattle10 has claimed responsibility for the shutdown of three major brokerage websites this afternoon, a shutdown that has already cost millions of dollars in lost revenues and shaken financial markets across the country."* I had to pull over to listen. I wasn't a great multi-tasker under the best of circumstances. From what I could gather, State Street and Polk Financial and another brokerage house had all had their websites hacked – total shutdown.

Cars buzzed past. I wanted everyone to slow down. I'd pulled over in front of what used to be a junior high school but was now senior housing. A pair of public tennis courts beside it. On one, two athletic women in white went about their summer afternoon, enjoying lives I could not fathom. I listened to Emily Boully tell me Seattle10 had not only claimed responsibility, they'd announced this as the first major salvo in a campaign to shut down global capitalism. Law enforcement had no solid information, just a suspected link to the Boston chapter – the strongest chapter – of the radical group. Because in what law enforcement is viewing as a related incident, Endicott announced discovery of nearly $800,000 in unauthorized wire transfers from company bank accounts.

I wanted to know where Bo was. I wanted confirmation that his computer skills were merely average. I told myself that was panic talking. I needed perspective. A long run. I got back on the road and headed for the house. On the way, my phone rang. I glanced at the number and pressed answer.

"Here's one for you, Nick."

Lenny Russell always dove right in, as if all life were one continuous conversation subject to occasional interruptions.

"Talk to me, Lenny."

"So I'm on the phone with the governor's office, my staff contact, trying to get some dirt on the Senate's back-room sellout of the health care bill, and he tells me he can't give me anything about that, but what he can give me is some juicy news about the janitors. How maybe those two dead janitors weren't an accident. These rumored union busters in fact had an assignment to intimidate, the assignment traces to Tillman and Andrew Sarkis from Pollard, and Sarkis is pissed at them for fucking it up. And nervous the story will leak. He's looking to deal – he'll give his guys up quietly if Pollard gets the state custodial contract back."

"Holy shit." Sometimes reality was too dark even for me: *My thugs killed some guys instead of just scaring the shit out of them, so I'll rat them out for a fat government contract.*

"Thought you'd like that."

You think you've got no innocence left to lose, then something comes along and rips raw another layer. "I've heard the rumor around town, but no substance. What are they gonna do?"

"You kidding? No way they touch that. It ever comes out, Governor Garrett's fucked. Nick, I gotta go. Big news day, huh?"

Indeed. This was starting to feel like ancient history.

Reversing my usual running route, I headed south, zigzagged the side streets between Kendall and Cypress. Running seemed like a good idea. Fast enough to prevent thought seemed better. My body wouldn't cooperate. My thigh ached, and I was on day three of a police baton headache. At the corner of Hart, I waited out a spurt of traffic, already winded. Across the intersection, in the shade at the edge of Robinson Playground, stood a familiar figure. I flashed on the kid whose face I'd messed up, but it wasn't him.

It was Bo.

251

I let the cars pass and crossed the street.

"Nice legs," he said. Hands stuffed in the pockets of cargo shorts. T-shirt and sneakers.

"How'd you find me?"

He shrugged.

I walked in a small circle on the sidewalk, keeping Bo in my peripheral vision.

He didn't look good. Tousled hair. Sleepy eyes. He squinted at me. "I need to talk to you."

"What, you have another felony you want to involve me in?"

"Whatever. This is me apologizing, OK? Bad form. Not funny. Whatever you need to hear. Now can we talk?"

I nodded. My legs already stiffening. "Run with me."

I started, and he fell into step beside me. My quads felt like cement. "You okay?"

"Yeah. It's not me."

"Marcela?" I turned us up Cypress. "You talk to her?"

"No." His running effortless. Painless. He set the pace without trying to. "You going to let me talk?"

"Go."

A breeze stirred the air. We tackled the hill that brought us behind Jamaica Pond.

"All I know is something about that day freaked her out, and it did even more once Evan died." His eyes focused somewhere other than me. "That's all I know."

I was confused for a second. "Bullshit." I sucked wind. Full sentences were an effort. "You've already told me more than that. That she was involved."

"Not *involved* involved, Nick. Not like that."

My side hurt. My chest burned. "Like what, then?"

"Jesus, Nick. You're going all CSI on me."

"You wanted to talk. Talk."

Bo's eyes bounced to my face, then away again. We started around the path that circled the pond. "She knows someone who was there and she hasn't said anything to the police or anyone." The words came out in a rush. "She's afraid to. 'Cause this person didn't do it, but she's afraid it would look that way. That if that person's politically active, you know, and there's no one else to pin it on. How it would look." I swore he had picked up the pace. "Plus her granddad being police chief and all."

A chill ran down my back. "Tell me this *person* isn't you."

"It isn't." His breath even. "For real."

We ran through a patch of shade. I tried to ground myself in the physical effort of keeping up with him. "Wait," I said. "You talked to her?"

"No. I told you."

"So this is shit you were holding out on me."

He left that alone.

My head hurt. Every step. "It doesn't make sense. The fact that Sparks was police chief, she'd have every reason to talk to him." We passed the boathouse. A group of dogs played in the grass, their owners huddled in dog park *bonhomie*. "If she knows her friend is innocent, he'd help her. Help them both."

Sailboats on the water. A hint of breeze.

"We need to go see Sparks. Tell him this."

"No way. Call a cop with hey, your granddaughter's involved in a murder?" He blew out a breath. "Are you crazy?"

253

We reached the duck feeding area. Reluctant mallards scattered before us as middle-aged Nick, hurting and winded, relied on pure orneriness to keep up with the teen track star. Bo's story didn't sit right with me.

"You're lying."

He stared ahead. Lengthened his stride. A small boy tossed bread to the ducks while his parents watched.

"I think she might have been the one to find Evan." The words burst out in a puff of breath. "She and maybe some others. And I think she – they – may have just left because the police would think they did it, and I think she's feeling really guilty about that, like if they'd stuck around and called the cops or an ambulance they could have maybe saved his life. And the longer it goes, the more scared she is to tell." He channeled nervous energy into his track star legs. He almost looked at me.

"You *think* she might have been the one, or you *know* she was?"

"I think."

My knees complained with every step, but I wasn't about to slow down. "I'm going to run your head through a meat grinder if you don't start telling me the truth."

"That *is* the truth. She didn't tell me exactly how she was involved. She doesn't like to talk about it. But that's kinda what it adds up to."

There was another beat coming. I could feel it. I just hoped I'd survive long enough to hear it.

"I know she was at Tillman's house sometime that day. I know her grandfather owns that Lexus. I know she used to drive it all the time, and then she didn't."

There it was. Marcela was tied to the only real clue in the Tillman murder. And so, indirectly, was the ex-police chief. "You tell me this *now?*"

"We've got to find her," he said. An air of desperation. A hint of pleading.

The pond path turned us into the woods. High cover of maples and oaks.

"Fucking well right." Was she in hiding, or in danger? A couple walked hand in hand through dappled shade. For some people, it was a normal summer day. "Anything else you care to share? Kidnapping? Treason?"

"You baiting me?"

I wasn't. I was picking at him. It's what I do when I'm in way over my head.

"Now I understand why the owner of the black Lexus was never found. Why that lead died."

Detective Hill stood next to the coffee pot in the cop station kitchen, perusing notices on a bulletin board. He looked at me, back at the notices. "It's Nick, isn't it?"

"That's right."

"I'm glad to see our security is airtight. Boosts confidence in the department." He didn't offer me a chair. No problem. I wouldn't have taken one.

I wasn't entirely sure what I was doing there, other than the Newton Police were my favorite punching bag and I had this crazy idea I could trick a veteran cop into divulging information that would help me help my favorite teens.

"I used my invisibility cloak," I bantered.

The front desk had been unattended, and I'd tried Hill's office before finding him in the kitchen. On the way over, I'd called Lin – straight to voice mail – and the hospital, where one operator insisted there was no such patient – *are you sure* – *we have no record of any Thomas Young* – and I started to play out the idea that he had died, but I couldn't deal with that, so I hung up, called back, and heard from someone competent, on first request, there was no change in his condition – *critical care unit, stable*.

"Coffee?" Hill was not so much muscular as solid, a rock not easily moved.

"No thanks." The walls carried java traces, both odor and grounds. The counter needed cleaning. The room was almost cool. "So that Lexus near the Tillman house the day of the robbery. It's registered to Larry Sparks."

Hill gave up on the bulletin board and turned his attention to me, and his coffee. "Very good, Matlock."

"And the fact that the police department stays silent on that doesn't look good to a journalist."

Hill laughed out loud. Sipped his coffee. "You sure you don't want some?"

I shook my head. I was wired enough. "Bad for you."

"Better than smoking." It has been my impression that people who wear ties almost invariably wear them too short or too long. Hill wore his too short.

"So?"

"The intrepid reporter. His question hangs in the air, pregnant with implications." He sipped his coffee. Someone paged Halverson, the kid-faced press officer. "That's an interesting perspective. Here's another. Retired chief of police driving around town. His travels take him within a few blocks of where a robbery takes place. The Lexus traces to Sparks, and we lose our best – only – early lead."

"I don't buy it." Fuck protocol. I knew some things. "Let's try a different version. One where Sparks wasn't driving the car."

Hill folded his arms across his too-short tie. "You mean stolen?"

"I mean someone else driving."

No reaction. "Like who?"

"Like his granddaughter."

We both sat with that. An alarm went off in me to shut up, but I ignored it. I needed information. Hill was as inscrutable as fucking Buddha, and that ate at me. So I kept talking.

"Let's say she was there that afternoon. Found the Tillman kid. Got scared and left."

Hill didn't flinch. Didn't blink. His coffee cooled beside him. Fucking cops.

"Let's say she gets more scared after it's in the news – the Lexus and all." My words came out as the thoughts formed. I let them, fascinated to hear what I'd come up with. "She talks to her grandfather. He knows what to do. He brings her here and she tells you off the record what she knows – how she found the body – and you grill her and that's all there is. Bad timing by the ex-chief's granddaughter. So you bury it. Because there's nothing to be gained by making that public. Because cops need to stick together."

Tell me I'm full of shit. Tell me I'm right and there's nothing more in it.

Detective Hill picked up his cup. He thought about saying

something. Didn't. Set the cup down again. His face showed me nothing. "That's a good story." He smiled. "Got some intrigue." He sipped coffee. "You're a cop, you hear all kinds of stories. Before long, none of them surprise you. You sift them for the keepers is all."

I tried to affect a whimsical grin, but my patience was thin. "So how much of that is true?"

He laughed. "That's good. Assume your premise. Push for confirmation." He unfolded his arms, put his hands in his pockets. "I told you, it's a good story. I appreciate a good story in the middle of a long day."

My patience ran out. "No. We're not going to do it that way. I have a column due tomorrow. How about you tell me what's what. Confirm or deny. Or I go with the info about that Lexus belonging to Sparks."

It was an asshole move, but it was the only one I had.

Hill smiled again. A less friendly smile. He shrugged. "Do what you gotta do."

I waited for him to crack. It didn't happen.

I had only one other place I could go.

I found Sparks tending tomatoes in his back yard. He had a swimming pool-size garden carved out of the back lawn. I'd tried the front door, even banged on a window. He was tying plant shoots to wooden stakes. He more or less faced me and let me walk over while he finished with one.

Wisps of clouds in a high, brutal sky.

Halfway across the lawn my cell rang. I answered.

"Nick, bad news." Lin's doctor voice. "They've had to defibrillate.

His vitals spiked and he flatlined. They've drained fluid and re-established heartbeat, but –"

Deep inside a trap door opened. I turned my back to Sparks, as if for privacy. "He's alive?"

"He's alive. But you need to make some choices."

Not now. Not in Sparks' garden. I looked over my shoulder. The ex-chief watched me.

"I gotta call you back."

A beat. "Did you hear what I told you?"

What could I say? "Five minutes, I swear."

I killed the call, stowed the guilt, and made my way across to Sparks, who hunkered over his tomatoes in khaki shorts and a red t-shirt stained with sweat.

"I grew up in western New York, near Niagara Falls," he said. No greeting. "Best tomatoes I've ever tasted. Incredible flavor. My nephew – he runs a farm stand out there – teases me it's all the toxins in the soil. Love Canal. Erie Chemical. But it goes back before that."

The plants stood waist high. I stood across a row of tomatoes from him. There were other vegetables. Zucchini, peppers, lettuce. He took a twist tie from the pocket of his t-shirt and went to work on another tomato shoot. Inside I was racing, but I couldn't show it. I didn't know what he knew, or how much of what rattled around in my head was even true. Tomato talk didn't give me any insight, or a graceful opening.

"I've been growing tomatoes for years, trying to reproduce western New York flavor. I've hauled water from there. Carted in soil. A dozen types of seeds."

This riff wasn't working for me. I needed to ask direct questions, get direct answers. I needed to make choices. What choices? How long did I have? *Stop. Focus.*

"Chief Sparks, I got a question."

"Hang on, son. I'm not finished," he said. He had a penetrating gaze. Hard blue eyes under thick white eyebrows. You could see where he was a great cop. "I've raised some fine tomatoes. Some almost as good. But there's something beautiful about the fact a thing can be unique, not reproducible."

"Chief Sparks."

He rescued a drooping branch, heavy with fruit, and brought it up next to a stake. Looped a twist tie. "I thought you might come by." He wiped his hands on his gardening shorts. "Dennis Hill just called."

Fuck. He'd have his guard up. But if Hill called to warn him, some of my speculation must be true. Right?

Sparks surveyed his tomato rows. Seemed satisfied.

My phone rang. "Shit." Loud in the garden. "Sorry," I told Sparks. Turned my back to him a second time. "Lin, what's up?"

"I'm hearing about body blows at the strike talks." A man's voice. Eric. "Tell me you're there."

"I'd be lying."

"Get your ass over there."

"Can't do it. Get someone else."

"That's not–"

"Eric, I can't. I gotta go."

I ended the call. Turned back to Sparks.

"Busy man," he said.

260

"Not usually." *Push it aside. Be smart.*

I could feel him taking my measure. "You wanted to talk about my granddaughter and my Lexus," Sparks said. "You've got a theory."

I watched a bee explore the tomatoes. I didn't want to play games. Didn't want to jab and dance. But I had no idea how to proceed. "I understand she's not allowed to drive it anymore."

"The car was a privilege. She lost that privilege." Sparks' eyes neither left my face nor wavered. "Why don't you say what's on your mind?"

Good idea. Deep breath. "Yours was the car seen near the Tillman house the day of the robbery."

"We both know that," he said. "So what's on your mind?"

Too much. I struggled to stay with this, and only this. Was Sparks ally or adversary? Didn't matter. "Marcela drove the car. She was at the house that day." I watched his face, attuned for any giveaway. "I think she found the body. Got scared and left."

The bee lighted on a swollen tomato near Sparks' hip. I squinted to read his expression. Nothing. Just stood in the dirt of his garden.

"That's a jump." He examined his palms. "I'm guessing you've got more to make."

You bet I did. "I suspect you don't always like the people your granddaughter spends time with. I think she made a bad call. It was an awkward spot and you kept her out of trouble. You got her to tell the police what she knew, and you used your influence to keep her out. Keep your name out. Something like that."

He finished with his palms. Looked at me. He and Hill must have had the same inscrutability training. "You're telling. What exactly did you want to ask?"

261

"I'm asking if it's true. I'm asking if that's as far as it goes." My gut said my theory wasn't wrong, but how much of that was because I liked the story. It fit my world view.

Those blue eyes from under deep brows. I could feel him thinking.

I'd had enough of cops and their reserve. "She was *at the house* that day. Isn't that a big fucking coincidence?"

Nothing.

"She just *happened* to be in the neighborhood, the door just *happened* to be open?"

The bee left the tomato and hovered around Sparks' shoulder. He swatted it away without ever looking at it. "That boy's death is a tragedy, no question. And Marcela can make some boneheaded decisions. Like all of us. She was at the house earlier that day. They were friends from school. No one was home. She didn't tell me until after it came out about the car, but she did tell me."

"And you believed her? What do we know about teenagers? They lie. They do stupid, destructive things and they lie." There had to be better answers. "What are you hiding? What are you afraid of? Did she break in? Did she kill him?"

"Calm down, son."

"I'm trying to get to the truth about a murder. I'm trying to help Marcela."

He toed the dirt. He had spindly legs for a cop. "I appreciate your concern. But I find the intensity of your interest in my granddaughter unusual, and a little unnerving."

I absorbed the sting. We stood there, face to face. Me with

my not-good-enough answers, him with his not-good-enough tomatoes.

"One piece of advice," he said. "If you want to get to the truth, be vigilant about the difference between what you know and what you think you know." He went back to his tomatoes.

Class dismissed.

I maneuvered the Dart out of Sparks' neighborhood and onto another quiet side street. Pulled over. Punched the steering wheel. I knew nothing more of substance than I had when I'd left Bo. Just burned precious time. And I had nowhere else to turn right then. I took a series of deep breaths and dialed Lin. Thick oak trees provided a canopy of shade under which to hear my oldest friend deliver bad news.

"There's damage to the brain. For sure. Reduced activity from being without oxygen."

She stopped there. Giving me time to absorb. There was more.

"He won't come back, Nick. It's the machines keeping him going. You have to decide if that's what you want."

Two months earlier, I'd have been relieved to hear those words. Happy, even. But a lot had happened in two months. I wasn't sure what the tangle of emotion in my throat was, but it wasn't relief. I thanked Lin. Told her I needed to think. Hung up and turned off the phone.

I'd spent a lot of years in this town. Driving these roads, looking for mischief, for a sense of direction or just a way out. Once I left, I never thought I'd be back. It's a good thing we don't know when we're young how complicated life will get. Decisions. Choices.

How roads close off. How others lead you back to places you don't want to be. Middle-aged and alone. A once-respected journalist directionless in his father's house.

I drove Route 20 west. Route 2. Gardner. Grafton. I liked being behind the wheel of the Dart. Tried to savor it. The summer day. The open road.

Turned on the radio, looking for news. Had to resort to AM, WHDH. "Mayor Reeves is pushing compromise, insisting the parties either agree or counter by tomorrow night, or he will remove himself from the process."

Enough. I drove out 114, back country roads, numb and wanting to stay that way, until the day faded and darkness came on. I stopped for a burger. Found Route 30 and headed east, not knowing where I was going until I was mostly there. A swimming hole we used to visit on wandering high school nights. Okay, a private swim club in Weston. But it was a pretty pond and a quiet spot to think. I found my way there down a gravel road still closed off only by a rusted chain that hung across the road and looped over a metal hook to latch. Or unlatch. So I sat in the grass by that pond as night fell. The first stars. And I tried to feel something. Tried to focus on my father. Hard to do because of Bo, because of Marcela, because of all the ways I was pointed toward the same bitter end as Thomas. Conventional wisdom would be to honor his wishes, but of course he hadn't made those known. So it was left to me to decide what he'd want. As if I'd ever had a clue.

I leaned back on my elbows in the grass and watched the stars emerge. We all die alone, yes, but how alone. How empty. We had to have some influence over that. Some measure of choice. What would it be like for me to start here, start now? I had no idea. Be awake, for one. Eyes open. Alive to each day. Hope like hell that added up to something over time. Grass tickled my forearms and a half-moon shimmered on the water. I thought about my father's generosity with his car my senior year in high school. How he'd give me the keys, no questions asked, so I could discover places like this one. That was something. I felt all the years between then and now. I felt a catch in my throat. An old yearning for connection that had never, would never, come. In the end, it came down to what I'd want for him. What I'd want if I was in his shoes.

Easy.

Conventional wisdom said you went to the hospital to say goodbye. But what was that about? Some romantic desire to bridge distance and heal wounds and find closure to protect against future pain, guilt, doubt. The whole idea that you could neatly wrap up a drama, an episode, a life.

I laid on that grass at that swimming hole he'd helped me discover and I told him goodbye. There were even a few tears, but they were for me as much as for him: for what Thomas and I were never able to find. Then I got lonely. A lot lonely. Found myself thinking about Terry and me. Bad idea. About promises I'd made to myself as a young man and how I'd broken them. That I'd never succumb to the force of inertia. That I would not quit. As I walked back to the car I called Terry to see if she wanted to have a drink, but I got voice mail, and I wasn't up for that. So I got in the car and drove back to the city.

Took Route 2 to 16 to Memorial Drive and right past the BU bridge exit. My arms wouldn't make the turn toward the house; instead I hugged the river, took comfort in the lights of Boston and let the night air blow my thoughts around. Inertia was a killer. I didn't know anyone who'd found a way back from it. Pulled over at the MIT boathouse. Stared at the skyline. I'd always liked the view from there. A major American city clustered on a small, rolling hill. That view felt as close to home as anything I had.

14

I got back to my father's house by 11. Passed out on my fancy futon by 11:05. Fitful sleep punctuated by peculiar dreams: burying animal carcasses in a moonlit field with Bo; arriving late with my father to a cooking class, the two of us called up front to demonstrate whatever technique had been presented. An ache in my throat. Repeatedly, I woke up believing I'd seen and heard a dripping faucet. After my fourth trip to the kitchen sink to check the phantom leak, I managed a few dreamless hours.

Woke after 10 to bright sun, trash trucks and the all-too-real prospect of death logistics. Thus began the first day of the rest of my life.

I dragged my ass out of bed. Snagged my gym shorts off the floor. Started coffee and turned on my cell.

Two messages. First, Eric. *You might just be a columnist. You see all those responses? Even some psychos are adopting you. Congrats. And tell me you're on Tillman. What a circus.* I wondered what inflammatory comments Chris had made now. I didn't wonder long, because the next message was from him.

"Nick, I need to meet. Give a call as soon as you can."

I'd forgotten completely about the strike talks. Figured there must be a development. Dialed him back. Got an answer, but the voice that answered wasn't him.

"I'm looking for Chris Tillman."

A strange pause. "What do you want with him?"

What the fuck. "Who is this?"

"Meyers. Waltham police. Who's this?"

The den felt stuffy as hell. "I'm a journalist. Nick Young. Chris had information for me. Wanted to meet."

A hand over the receiver. A murmured voice. Then: "Okay, Nick Young. Don't you watch the news? Tillman's at Mass General. Hit-and-run last night. His car forced off the road."

A picture in my head, Tillman's SUV, a red-and-white target painted on the driver's side.

"He okay? He gonna be okay?"

"Stable, I hear. You want more, call the hospital."

I poured coffee and sipped it. I had a touch of vertigo. I swear the floor tilted toward me for a second.

Once I got my bearings, I dialed Bo. Call it paranoia. No go. Straight to voice mail.

Threw the phone on the table. Fired up the laptop. Browser opened to Boston.com. I didn't have to look far.

Endicott Chief Operating Officer Chris Tillman is recovering today after his car slid down an embankment and struck a barrier late last night in Waltham.

Fuck.

Tillman has charged that two unidentified assailants forced his car off an isolated stretch of Trapelo Road in Waltham. Tillman was hospitalized with minor injuries.

Fantastic. Either Tillman was understandably paranoid or the lunatic fringe had taken over the world. I finished my coffee and poured another. As long as the situation wasn't critical, a guy might as well feed his ego.

Launched my column on the Metro site and scrolled through the eighty-nine responses. More favorable than not. *A compassionate characterization of the issues.* A couple that accused me of crass manipulation in using a dead janitor to make a point. And one that was a note from a sort-of friend.

Hey, Nick. Adam here (Bo's friend). Nice eulogy to Eduardo. But soft. Change NEVER comes from compromise. Only from revolution. And a revolutionary has no friends, no interests, no identity outside relentless destruction of the existing order. By any means. That's not just me. That's history. Check it out: Sergey Nechayev, dude who helped take down Tsarist Russia – and inspired the Black Panthers.

I didn't like anything about that. A revolutionary would push a car off Trapelo Road. But revolutionary could also be just a posture for a teen vandal. Attacking Tillman did nothing to advance the cause. Adam was a smart kid. I needed to step away from drama and gather information. I showered, shaved, and headed for Mass General. The Dart got me there in record time. A powerful engine on mid-morning roads.

Got to the information desk where I asked a pimply-faced kid in a blue blazer where I might find Chris Tillman at about the same moment as I heard Tillman's voice behind me.

I spun to see an entourage in motion through the lobby – a half-dozen suits with a polo-shirted Tillman strutting in the lead. Apart from a black eye and a large bump on his forehead, he was back to being a captain of industry.

"Chris!"

He turned at my voice. Stopped when he recognized me. His entourage stopped with him. We crossed toward each other.

"Chris. I'm glad you're okay."

I got a cold stare from the lead suit under expensively cut blond hair. He imposed his substantial torso between Tillman and me. "Can I help you with something?" It wasn't a sincere question.

Tillman touched the guy's arm. "It's okay, Michael. I know Nick. I'll be out in a minute."

Michael hesitated, then took his expensive hair and his minions out the automatic doors.

"What happened?" I asked Tillman.

"Someone paints a target on my car, then I get hit. Coincidence?" He glanced at the Blackberry in his hand. The back of the hand had a strip of adhesive tape where an IV must have been. "I thought the car had pulled out to pass me, then it squeezed me off toward an embankment." He didn't sound rattled. "Someone's misguided idea of tit-for-tat."

"You can't think the janitors–"

No expression. "I don't know what to think."

"Chris, this has gotten way out of hand. It's a labor negotiation."

"Negotiations are over if I have anything to say." The Blackberry beeped. "I'm on my way to have that conversation now. We'll have an announcement today at 4." He checked the screen.

"Got your phone back? I talked to your new assistant this morning."

He shrugged. "What can I do for you, Nick?"

"I got a message. You wanted to meet."

He laughed. Winced. "Sore ribs. Right. A lot has changed since yesterday." The PA system above our heads paged Dr Rebecca Harris. "I was heading out of the grand labor talks – Mayor Reeves' follies. I heard a reporter buzzing about that damn union busters *theory*. One place reports it – unnamed source – suddenly people are talking as if it's real." His Blackberry beeped again. He talked faster. "I liked your column – persuasive, well-done for one-sided reporting." He let that land. An orderly squeaked past with an old woman in a wheelchair. "A while back you said you wanted to be balanced and responsible. I wanted to challenge you to act on it." Dark eyes on me. "Debunk that union buster crap."

How could anyone be hopeful about the world when people kept fucking it up?

"Can't do it, Chris. I've got confirmation of that *crap*."

Tillman's eyes went small. "Not possible. From where?"

I shrugged. Listened to his Blackberry beep – the captain of industry soundtrack. Tillman should know: it's Boston, information is like water, it seeps out in every direction.

He tried to mask anger. It almost worked. "So what are you going to do with what you think you know?"

"I haven't decided."

Tight-lipped and bruised, he walked away. I let him, pretty sure I'd scored a point in whatever game we were playing.

Most of the time, when you think about the death of a loved one, you don't think about it as a process you initiate. It's news you hear on the end of a phone line that wakes you up, say, the way Terry got the news of her mother's death, she and I in bed on a Sunday morning, sun slanting through our Silver Lake window, our mattress on the floor in those days because we couldn't afford a frame. We'd been to a party the night before and had reveled in the thought we had nothing to get up for. I was dimly aware of the fact the phone had rung, then gradually aware of the tension of Terry's body, her rigid posture at the edge of the mattress, how she wasn't saying much. How she just sat there, we both did, for much of the morning, absorbing the news. Watching the changing blue of the sky out the small square window whose sill met the floor of our crazy attic apartment. Trying to reconcile how you knew it was true but didn't feel like it could be. Or you're there, a witness, by the bedside, tending to any last desires, savoring the last ounce of life in a loved one, saying goodbye.

Me? I went to the hospital to pull the plug on Thomas. Paperwork. Logistics. *What are his wishes for the body. What arrangements have been made. Sign here please. And here.* A cubicle. A clerical aide. A catch in my throat I couldn't swallow away. A futile wish that my father and I could have gotten past our own shit for even a few minutes and seen each other – once – in some warm human light. Yes, I could have had Lin there with me, but I didn't want her. The truth: I wanted this to be impersonal. A formality. I wanted to treat it as though he were already gone. Dr. Chang stopped by, professional concern on her face. *Would you like a few minutes alone?* But there was nothing to say. Nothing to finish. There it was, from my blind side: the price I paid for all those years of not risking with my father. My throat ached. Dr. Chang seemed

272

surprised when I said no. I forced myself to walk away, stiff with self-reproach. A sense of foreboding. What Thomas and I didn't have was my failing as much as his. What had I done – what would I do – to be any different? To learn from this troubled history?

I went for a walk along the Charles, trying to think about something other than my father's brain being deprived of oxygen at my behest. What, if anything, he was aware of. If he blamed me. I thought about how I should be running rather than walking. I thought about Sparks and Marcela, Bo and Adam. I thought about Seth and Tillman and Lin and thousands of other people who had careers, pursuits that involved them every day, that left them little time for idle speculation on walks along the river. I thought about how much easier it was to not deal. I thought about my father coming home from work looking so often defeated, worn out, and how at age ten-eleven-twelve I had the singular ability to make him laugh. How good it made me feel to affect him, to bring him a moment of joy. I tried to remember when that had eroded. I parked along Soldier's Field Road across from Harvard Stadium, walked past the Cambridge Boat House toward Harvard Square. There were joggers. One of them passed me, then circled back.

"Nick?"

Juliana Reyes, aglow with perspiration.

"I didn't know labor organizers had time for recreational activities." These things come out of my mouth before I can stop them. It's not as though I yearn to be alone.

She kept her legs moving a little. I thought of sparring. "I'm glad I ran into you," she said.

273

I stopped myself from working the pun.

Her feet kicked out behind her at an angle, rather than straight back. I found that attractive. I've also always had a thing for sports bras. I tried not to stare. "You heard about the talks being postponed? About Tillman?"

A single scull glided by behind her. A guy, white hair, balding, worked the oars.

"I did. I was sorry to hear it."

The strike felt far away. I thought about oxygen to the brain. Pictured my father in his basement workshop rearranging tools. Organizing. Mildew and dust in the air. Him reluctantly instructing me on how to help. I had no idea I was intruding.

Juliana was saying something. I was trying to breathe.

"I'm sorry," I said. "Preoccupied."

"We've got hungry janitors who are getting nervous. Sam and I are trying to figure out how to distance ourselves from the radicals with some measure of political integrity," she said.

The guy in the scull disappeared under the Harvard footbridge, gliding his way toward the harbor, steady, persistent. I was willing to bet he was someone's father, the river his workshop.

"We're at a critical juncture, trying to keep the janitors motivated, believing this is a worthwhile and winnable stand. That they won't lose their jobs. It's tough to stand on principle when you don't have a paycheck. And we can't catch a break with everything else that's going on."

Our encounter had something illicit about it. Intimate. Or I was so starved for human contact that any informal encounter with a woman's exposed flesh was an instant turn-on.

"You think they'll come back to the table?"

She brushed hair off her forehead. "I hope so." Her feet stopped running. We were talking now, for real. "We need advocates. I appreciate what you wrote, Nick. And I hope you'll write more. We need your voice."

Her words rattled sour in my stomach. I tried to hear them as appreciation, not agenda.

A trio of teens crossed the footbridge toward us, in heated discussion.

"Maybe we could grab a drink sometime." Her head cocked. Half question, half suggestion.

On the bridge, flowing black hair flanked by two males. Either I was hallucinating or those arguing teens were Bo, Marcela, and Adam.

"Nick?"

"Catch up with you later." I sprinted across the grass, cut a diagonal toward where the bridge met the footpath. Someone had some explaining to do. A tattooed arm. A Dropkick Murphy's t-shirt. The unholy trinity – it *was* them – were coming off the bridge onto the path. I ran harder. Anger and determination. Dodged a cyclist. I was maybe fifty feet away when they saw me coming. Whether it was instinct or something practiced, they scattered, turbocharged, in three directions. I hesitated. Lingered a beat on Marcela, then ran after Bo.

He charged along the river toward Boston. A trained athlete 25 years younger than me. Confident. Not looking back. I took it personally. Zeroed my gaze on his spine. I could almost keep pace as long as we didn't go far.

At a break in traffic, he cut hard left across Memorial Drive. I ducked in behind an SUV that jumped the green, in front of a Honda that started slower. Both drivers worked their horns, but I made it to the sidewalk with a half-spin for effect. Followed Bo down Plymouth Street. He glanced back. I put on a burst to close the gap. Sucking wind, I gained a few paces, but not enough. The heat an attack. I needed an edge. Plymouth cut at an angle toward Mass Ave, and I guessed he was headed that way to lose himself in Harvard Square. I ducked into the wide driveway of a dorm, hoping to find a way through and not be stuck in a dead end. Cunning versus conditioning. I motored along the brick sidewalk that hugged the building, looking for a sharper cut to Mass Ave. Around the corner of the building I got lucky. A tall wrought iron gate stood open. I forced my legs faster and hauled ass through. Bo was ten feet ahead to my left. He felt me there. Looked back. Lost his footing. He tumbled and I was on him.

I planted my knee in his kidney. Pinned his body with mine.

"Fuck! I'm hurt. Get off me."

"No."

His palms were raw and bleeding and he'd ripped up one forearm. Bits of dirt and rock stuck to scraped skin.

"I'm serious, Nick. My knee."

I let up with my forearm against his side and found myself on my back on the sidewalk. Bo on his feet, poised for takeoff. I got my arm around one leg and tripped him up. He went down again hard. I landed on his chest.

"You're done making an ass of me." I pressed my forearm against his sternum for emphasis.

"Ow. Come on, Nick. I fucked up my knee."

"Too bad." We were on a brick sidewalk just outside the square, one of us bloody, both panting for breath. "Tell me and tell me now. What's going on."

Hot sun. I was slick with sweat. The brick burned my skin.

Two students walked past, a he and a she, laden with backpacks, engrossed in conversation. They made an effort not to notice us.

"What do you want to know?"

I pressed him against the sidewalk. "You fucking try my patience. When did Marcela show up?"

"I don't know. She's worried about Adam." Bo squirmed beneath me. His breathing had regulated. Mine hadn't.

"Talk, Bo. Make sense."

"He's lost his shit." Saliva hung at the corner of his mouth. "I mean, we're all working for the same stuff, but what Adam's doing. It's just wrong."

The sweat on my spine went cold. "Be specific."

"Let me up." He winced from the pressure of my arm on his chest, or from other injuries.

"Fine. But you run, I hurt you."

I got off him, still poised to pounce. He sat up. Slid his ass to the granite curbstone, his feet into the street. Examined his hands. Forearm.

I sat next to him. Parched. "You'll live. Keep talking."

"He thinks Tillman is the antichrist. Some evil capitalist overlord." Bo flexed his cut knee. "We gotta stop him."

"It was Adam last night? Tillman's car?"

"He's going to take the guy down, Nick. For real." He wiped dirt

277

off his bloody forearm with the back of his hand.

I struggled to slow my breath. My brain. My shirt stuck to my back. "Who was with him last night?"

"No one. Nobody wants to go there."

"What else?"

"What do you mean?"

I felt like a parent. I had to extract everything bit by bit. "What's this about? Why Tillman?"

"Pirate. Robber baron. Plus, he has this history."

I could feel him holding back. "What else?"

"*What?*"

"What are you not telling me?"

"It wasn't supposed to go like this."

Hot, still air. It made me shiver. "Explain."

"I didn't know until a few minutes ago."

I could feel the hairs on my arm. Gravel in my throat. "Talk."

"*Fine.* I told you Marcela was there that afternoon. At the Tillman house." He stared at the street. "So was Adam."

"Okay." All the days we'd spent. Bo as a child. Telling me things in his own time. His own way. How the world had encroached.

He spoke slowly, sculpting each sentence. "They didn't know Evan was going to be there. Marcela got a key from him a few weeks before. He had a thing for her. She let him think it was mutual. They – Marcela and Adam – went there to take some stuff. You know. Cash. Jewelry."

You hang around long enough, sometimes the answers come to you. There's no guarantee you'll like them. "They went there to rob the place."

"*To send a message.* Tillman's not immune, not protected. Vulnerable, like the rest of us. They didn't expect Evan would be there. Adam didn't like him – none of us did – so they thought they'd mess with him a little. Rattle him and shit. Adam fucked it all up."

I wrapped my arms around myself. "Adam killed him."

"He didn't *kill* him, Nick. He did a stupid thing, and he took it too far. The kid fell."

A noise escaped me. A low, feeble sound. I wanted water. A shower. A clean start.

"*No.*" My hands were fists. "What he did was beat a boy to death. Break his ribs. Puncture a lung. Fracture his skull."

Bo's face got all red. His voice insistent. Afraid. "That's not how it went. Not what they told me. Marcela wouldn't –"

"*They fucking lied to you, Bo.*" I shivered. I couldn't get warm.

My mind spun for strategies. Found none. I took a breath. It stung. "What else you need to tell me?"

He didn't say anything. Hunched over, head between sweaty hands. I heard a sound like sobbing. Watched his body shake. I put a hand on his back.

"You gotta stop him, Nick." The words halting, choked out.

"This is beyond me."

He pulled his face out of his hands. There were tears on it. Mucus hung from his nose. He wiped at it. "*He didn't mean to kill him.*" He swallowed a sob. "Besides, it's nothing worse than what Tillman has done."

"Don't even–"

A child's face, pleading. "I don't mean that."

279

"What, then?"

He took a shaky breath. Another. "Tillman killed a kid when he was our age. Marcela's grandfather covered it up."

"Bullshit."

"Marcela found out a few weeks ago. It's why she took off. Talked to Adam about it. That's when he went batshit."

When I was a teenager, my only problems were girls, grades, and boredom. I thought about the times I got in trouble back then – landing my dad's car teetering on a snow bank a block from home on a drunken escapade; caught shoplifting golf supplies at a sporting goods store. How my father had reacted. Matter of fact, like it was normal shit that happened, a part of growing up. How would he have reacted to a politically committed activist anarchist son? "How deep are you in this, Bo?"

"I told you, I wasn't there that day."

"Not that day. The whole thing." My quads started to hurt. My calves. "Once we open this up, all kinds of shit's going to come out. It's connected, and we're not going to be able to stop it. I need to know where the people I care about stand."

"You're getting dramatic."

"You could go to jail, shithead. And your friend committed murder." I took a breath. Saw Lin in a courtroom watching Bo get sentenced. Saw my oldest friend finding out all I withheld from her. "I want to know how deep you are. Exactly what you've been up to."

I got that pissy teen look. "Can't this *wait*?"

"No." I let my voice shake him. Extended my sore legs. "Tillman, Berkley's, Craig's Auto World. Take your pick."

"I haven't hurt anyone."

I cut him off. "No excuses, no qualifiers. Details. Now."

"Jesus, Nick." Head hunched into his shoulders, he stared into the gutter. "The dumpsters at Endicott. Tillman's car you know about." He thought a minute. "Other SUVs. Some piddly shit."

"Anything else?"

He mumbled something. I had to get him to repeat it.

"The car dealer."

My stomach sank. "Which one?"

"Route 9."

"Fuck." We were into felony territory. "Whatever happened to drinking, getting high, skipping classes?"

"Can we *please* do this later? We gotta find Adam."

"I don't give a shit about Adam. I give a shit about you."

"He's going after Tillman, Nick. *Today.*"

It registered. A gut punch. I had half a voice. "Where?"

"Wherever Tillman is."

Announcement. News conference about the labor talks. "What about Marcela?"

"She's all about stopping Adam."

I helped Bo to his feet. What passed for a breeze came by. It moved the hot air around. "Downtown. Let's go." What had Tillman said? Four o'clock. I checked my phone. Three-twenty-five. We hustled for the Red Line. I considered a cab, but the subway would be faster. Bo's knee had stopped bleeding, but he limped. So did I, from stiff quads.

We waited on the inbound platform. Bo fidgeted. I texted Eric, found out the news conference was at Endicott HQ. Conference room off the lobby. Let Eric believe I was headed to cover it. Tried Tillman's cell. Voice mail. Work phone. Same.

Three thirty-two. A train came. Crawled to South Station. Spit us out the doors at three forty-five. We covered the few blocks to Endicott in three minutes, limps and all. I tried to formulate a plan. It went something like this: find Tillman and tail him, all the while keeping an eye out for Adam and/or Marcela. Rudimentary, but all I had. The Endicott lobby rose two stories high with a marble floor, mod leather chairs that looked like lumps of dough, and a prominent security desk made of the same marble as the floor.

"Eyes peeled," I told Bo. I scanned for Adam. Marcela. No sign. A flow of bike messengers, uniformed couriers, suits. A few fellow journalists. I recognized Danielle Dwyer, Stefan Andros and one of Alvin Fraser's lackeys.

Brad Mighty of the *Herald* spotted me and made his way over. "Here to join the chase?" he asked.

My eyes searched the lobby. "Yeah. Why you out here?"

"Same as you, I'm guessing. Try to catch Tillman on his way in." He looked at Bo. Torn knee. Soiled shirt.

"Tillman's not in there yet?"

"If he was, we would be too."

After that, it all happened pretty fast.

Tillman emerged from a bank of elevators. Crisp blue suit. Andrew Sarkis and Diane Evans behind him. My colleagues converged, firing questions. A News 5 camera appeared from somewhere. Shouted questions. Tillman straight-armed them all.

"No comment. We'll see you inside."

I watched the lobby. So did Bo. A crowd trailed the newsmakers, hindered our view. It occurred to me we should be positioned between Tillman and the conference room, rather than behind him. I grabbed Bo's arm and headed that way. Then the revolving door revolved and delivered Adam. I saw him see Tillman and the media. He stood still, just inside the entrance.

A shouted question. Alvin Fraser. "Chris, what about the car accident, the accusations you made last night?"

A quick glance at Tillman's face. "No accusations. Just observations."

Adam watched him, a half-grin.

Tillman said something else, but I got distracted again as Marcela spun her way through the door, landing next to Adam. She grabbed his arms, immediately in close conversation.

A flurry of animated follow-up from my fellow journalists, who smelled blood in the water. But Tillman moved for the conference room.

I triangulated the distance between us and Tillman, Tillman and Adam. Could Bo and I race across the room, throw a high-low cross-body block to take him down? Was he really even here to act?

Too late. Tillman broke away from the journalists, Adam broke away from Marcela and the two of them moved toward a convergence at the back of the lobby.

It's not so much that things happen in slow motion – that's movie bullshit – but that your brain moves too slowly to register and act on what you're seeing. The speed of light faster than the speed of thought.

I yelled Chris's name loud enough to set off alarms – I sure as hell wanted it to – and ran toward them, Bo at my side.

They met, Adam offering his right hand as if introducing himself, Tillman backing off, looking around to see what the yelling was about. Adam grabbed Tillman's right hand and used that leverage to swing his left hand, which held a hunting knife, into Tillman's stomach. A buzz of voices, TV camera lights. Bodies scattering. Tillman slumped to the floor. Security guards and cops appeared. More journalists spilled out from the conference room. They ringed the crime scene, angling for position, a view of Tillman bleeding on the floor. A flip cam, and another. Flash of still cameras. A guard used one side of his jacket to shield Tillman.

Shouts of *what happened* and *give him room*, and a few journalists stepping back. Adam dropped the knife to the floor like a character from some movie he'd seen – the principled assassin – and tried to shove his way to the door. Two cops grabbed him, threw him to the floor. I dialed 911, then hung up when someone called out that an ambulance was on the way. Danielle Dwyer and Brad Mighty worked their mobiles side by side, furiously filing copy. I tried to catch a glimpse of Tillman, to see how bad, to see was he breathing, and it only then occurred to me to look around for Bo, for Marcela. They'd both vanished.

Two more pairs of police arrived and three security guards. One set of cops delivered Adam and what I guessed was the basic information to another pair while the third pair worked to clear the room.

Tillman laid eyes open, holding his lower abdomen as if he had appendicitis, as if he was merely confused at this strange development. He caught my eye, and then one of the cops had me by the elbow escorting me to the door.

"Show's over." His grip didn't leave room for negotiation.

I backpedaled in the direction of the revolving doors, and he escorted me through, back out into a perfect summer afternoon.

It was only later, as I drove south on 134 through Stoughton trying to get my head clear enough to figure out what to do next – hadn't been able to reach Bo, hadn't heard news of Chris – that my cell phone rang. I'd forgotten I had it with me.

"He's gone, Nick." Lin. The weariest voice I knew. "A few minutes ago." My mind went first to Bo and then to Tillman, before logic took over and I understood the meaning of her words. "I thought you'd want to know."

My mind was covering a lot of ground, not very well. Trying to catch up to something it couldn't grasp. And whatever connected it to my emotions had gone MIA. I wasn't so much numb as I was a malfunctioning pinball machine. *Tilt.* My throat raw.

I thanked her. Told her it was hard for me to talk right then, which it was, especially without saying *by the way do you know that your son is a felon and his friend a murderer, possibly twice over.*

"You okay, Nick?"

"No. But I will be." I didn't know that, but it seemed the thing to say. It hurt to push words out.

I turned on the radio. For solace, or news, I wasn't sure which. Truth was, I had way more going on inside than I could process. What I got was news. *No indication of when or if negotiations will continue in the janitors' strike. Today, a giant step backward as embattled Endicott Chief Operating Officer Chris Tillman was stabbed by an unknown assailant in the lobby of the Endicott building. His attacker was arrested on the scene. No word from police on the identity of Tillman's attacker or on a possible motive. Tillman is in fair condition at Mass General.*

In other news, a young Brookline woman was killed tonight when her car ran into a telephone pole on Hammond Pond Parkway. Police are investigating the cause of the accident, but drunk driving is a possibility.

The Brookline teen, of course, turned out to be Marcela Pruett.

15

Adam Slyvotsky was going to prison. And Marcela Pruett, like my father, was going in the ground. I couldn't do much about those. But there was one young felon whose fate I could influence. In the next few days the media picked over the Tillman attack and speculated on connections – from wild conspiracies to shared affinities – between Seattle10, SLAM, and the janitors' strike. Seattle10 claimed credit for night banking shenanigans in Providence and Worcester. Mayor Reeves condemned the cleaning companies' decision to "indefinitely postpone" the labor talks and, in one of the dramatic news conferences he reveled in, threw his official support to the union. Adam faced a judge at arraignment. Marcela's wake. Thomas' funeral arrangements. It all happened. And I focused on getting Bo out of trouble.

With the police zeroed in on Adam's – and Marcela's – activities, nothing that any involved teen had done was likely to stay in the shadows. And when the journalists get on it, it's only a matter of time before they flush out everything, real or imagined.

Bo would be implicated. It was a question of when and how. Technically he was a felon. Even, it might be argued, part of an eco-terrorist conspiracy. Or, he was a smart kid from a good neighborhood with an impressive record of community service who had fucked up. In short, a prime candidate for mercy: a second chance with a clean slate.

So I went to see Larry Sparks to see how that would play. Took me a couple tries, but I finally caught up with him in his garden on a Tuesday afternoon. He wore the same khaki shorts with a button-down shirt. I carried a spindly cactus in a plastic pot. He followed me with his eyes, squinting against the sun.

"Chief."

"It's Larry. Sparks if you must. I haven't been chief in a long time."

We shook hands.

"What's that you got?" he asked.

I handed it to him. "Cactus."

"What for?" He inspected it as if it might reveal a clue.

I stared at the dirt for a minute. Shrugged. "Condolences," I said. "I'm sorry for your loss."

He made a noise in his throat. Set the cactus on the ground at his feet. Picked a small green pepper off a plant.

"Look at that," he said. "Jalapeño. You can grow 'em pretty well in this climate. Lot of people don't realize that. About the only kind of hot pepper that does worth a damn here, though. For whatever reason."

He handed it to me and I took it. Put it in my shirt pocket. "How you doing?"

He shook his head. Fingered a leaf from the pepper plant. Shooed some gnats away. I'd have to continue to wonder what a guy like him felt, and what he did with it. "What's on your mind? I appreciate the cactus, but that's not what brought you here."

Fair enough. I was sadder than he knew, but we couldn't touch that. We watched the cactus for a minute, but it didn't do anything.

"I heard a story from a teenage friend," I said. "Wanted to run it by you." I told him what Bo had told me about Tillman. I didn't tell the part about Sparks' connection.

His face looked papery. Drained of vigor. "I don't suppose anyone gets a life unclouded by doubt," he said. "There's things that happen to us all – choices, decisions – we answer for, one way or another, the rest of our lives."

Yeah. However long – or short – they might be.

He pulled a pair of drug-store glasses out of his shirt pocket and put them on. "Walk with me," he said. "Let me tell you a story."

We walked to the end of the pepper row, then over a couple rows to the tomatoes. "Looking for late blight," he said. He fingered leaves, thrust his face toward them, studied them through the glasses. "You can be vigilant as you like, the spores will blow over from a neighbor's. Ruin your whole crop."

I wondered if he'd forgotten the story, or was stalling to figure a way to duck it. But he launched in.

"There was a fist fight," he said. "Tillman and another kid, Spencer Hart. They were eighteen, maybe nineteen. Summer between high school and college." He checked leaves. Waved me toward him and showed me how. "We're looking for greasy-looking gray spots."

I bent to the work with him.

We went slow. There was no hurry anymore.

"They were good kids, both of them. Smart. Privileged. No one knows what started it. Doesn't matter. Stupid stuff between boys.

"Whole group of them playing baseball. Cabot Field over there." He waved a hand vaguely westward. "Summer day, probably a lot like this one. Anyway, by all accounts, fight's pretty even, maybe even wearing down, like neither of them can remember why it started in the first place. Then Chris hit Spencer, a roundhouse right. Boy went down, lights out." Sparks' voice like it was all as fresh to him as it was to me. Like it all happened last week. "Everybody waiting for him to get up. Except he didn't. Few minutes go by. He's not moving. Somebody runs to call an ambulance – this is before cell phones, of course. Spencer's still breathing, but they're scared shitless, all of them. Meanwhile, Chris is holding his hand. Turns out he hit Spencer so hard he broke two bones." We finished with one set of plants and moved down the row.

"I knew these kids," he said. "Knew their families." He handled the tomato leaves gently, a precious commodity. "Kyle Clifton. Andy Malone. Tim Speer." I tried to match his care. "Well the ambulance comes and they get Spencer to the hospital, but he'd hemorrhaged. The punch burst a blood vessel in his head, and he died. Everyone's devastated, of course. I was chief at the time. Supervised the investigation myself."

Focus on the plants, I told myself. *Handle with care. Don't distract him. Don't break his rhythm.*

"Talked to each of those kids about it. More than once. A tragedy. No one's more upset than Chris, and it's genuine. I've always had a good bullshit detector." A quick glance my way. His face – those glasses – inches from the plant. "So the third, fourth time I talk to the kids, one of them – Clifton – has new information. After Chris threw the punch and Spencer went down, he looked back over at Chris, a reflex – like what the hell just happened – and saw Chris unclench his right hand, the broken one, and saw a rock fall to the ground."

My work was redundant. Sparks, in the lead, checked every leaf himself. Every plant. No worries. I just wanted to hear where he was headed.

His breath rasped a little. "I ask him does he think it or does he know it. And he tells me it's a memory that kind of unfolds backward in his head – those were the words he used – as he watched Spencer not moving on the ground, as he saw Chris's hand broken and realized the impact of the punch, how hard it must have been to hurt Spencer that badly, to break a hand. And that then he remembered seeing the rock fall from Chris's hand when he unclenched it.

"I ask him again, do you think you saw it or do you know you did, and he says I know I did."

Another plant done, and down the row.

"But I've seen guys bust a hand with a regular punch, and I've known of times when a fluke fist killed someone. And I asked him why he was telling me this now, why he hadn't told me before. He said Chris was his friend and he was scared of what would happen to him."

There are times when the world is so small and familiar. When thirty years can fall away and one group of kids merges with another. Interchangeable.

"Now you could argue it makes all the difference in the world whether or not Chris had been holding that rock," Sparks said. "If he was, you can make a case for murder. If not, it's easier to write off as an accident. Especially back then." He looked at the underside of a leaf. I watched him rub it. "But that's not how I saw it." He looked at me as though weighing me on some set of invisible scales. "I couldn't believe Chris would do that. Didn't want to. I also thought what if he had – and he did have a temper – what then. It wasn't going to bring Spencer back, and he – they both – had such potential. And I thought, do you ruin both their lives over a mistake?"

A sadness hung in the air, more pungent than ripe fruit.

"They were kids. And I decided it was an accident. No criminal action, or intent." He'd stopped inspecting. Looked at me over the drug store glasses. "Did it matter that I knew this kid, knew his family? Absolutely. Some kid off the street, I might not have handled it the same. But I *did* know him." One knee in the dirt, his forearm resting on the other. "No one was much surprised it turned out that way, or wanted it to end different. But then, no one else knew about the rock. Or alleged rock.

"I've never asked Chris. Didn't want to know." He wiped loose dirt from his hands. "These are different – less forgiving – times."

"Do they have to be?"

He went back to the tomato plants.

I hadn't stopped, but I worked slow. Listening. Thinking. "There'd be a record of those conversations. Those interviews. Wouldn't there?"

He didn't answer. He didn't have to. He was the careful kind of cop. A detail guy.

I thought we were done.

"A couple years later, from a young cop, I heard the crab apple story. How Spencer had, back when they were twelve, hit Chris in the ear with a crab apple. They used to have crab apple fights in a field down by the brook, they'd hurl 'em at each other with all they had – it's a wonder there weren't worse incidents. Parents would cut the trees down before they'd allow that today. But the story goes that, during one of those, Spencer caught Chris full on the ear. Caused hearing loss."

Sparks had his forearm on his knee again. Looked straight at me. "Now to believe there'd be a connection between the two incidents, a motivation, is to take a dark view of human nature."

Around us, the sun ripened tomatoes, squash, peppers, and the world ripened children, as it always has. I met his eyes. I don't think I imagined the challenge I saw in them. "That the story you heard?"

"A variation," I said. "Not as nuanced."

"Not as long-winded."

He didn't ask what I thought of it. Didn't rehearse with or for me the decision he'd made, the moral quandary. We finished the last plant in the row.

"Someone we know is in a similar situation," I told him. "Not so drastic, from one perspective. More easily prosecutable, from another."

"What are we talking about here?"

"It's a felony. But a crime against property." I had Bo's word he hadn't torched anything. In my view, that mattered. "And he's a good kid, with a lot of potential, who fucked up." Maybe I didn't need to throw Sparks' words back at him. Maybe he would have been on my side, on Bo's side, anyway. "Seems we've seen enough young people's futures destroyed this summer."

He pushed himself to his feet. "Any chance this boy used to date my granddaughter?"

I let it ride.

He was quiet a minute. "I'm retired, so we're gonna need someone else on our side, but I know people."

I had one more person to win over. Riskier and arguably less necessary, but he'd be in a position to either charge Bo, or be a potentially powerful advocate. Chris was convalescing at Mass General, and he was not in a jovial mood. I arrived as he hung up his cell phone, scowling.

"Nick Young. I have nothing to say for publication."

"I'm not here on business."

Tillman's torso was heavily bandaged under a hospital gown. He looked pale, but stronger than I had expected. Eyes alert. Bed cranked to half-seated. "You've heard our mayor is forcing the issue."

"I have."

"Thank you for not gloating."

I suppressed a smile of satisfaction. "You going to play ball?"

"We'll concede the benefits package and get a contract done. I was wrong to say what I said. But Reeves is short-sighted. He's pushing this because it's good press. Business can't absorb it. Won't. He'll pay come election day, and the pendulum will swing back."

A nurse poked her head in the room, saw me – a visitor – and ducked back out.

"How you feeling?"

"Lucky for me that kid wasn't as strong – or as cool under pressure – as he thought," Tillman said. An IV drip plugged into his left hand. The gray hair at his temples more pronounced than it had been a few weeks before. "Can you believe it? Same kid killed Evan." From far off, the unmistakable odor of hospital food. "What'd I do to him?"

I heard anger in Tillman's voice, and a kind of loss I'd never know.

"It wasn't about that, Chris."

"Anarchist fucks. No values."

From across the hall, I heard the tinny laughter of a TV audience. The sound bounced off linoleum. I glanced over, half expecting to see my father.

"I understand."

He adjusted a pillow behind his head, winced. "You're sympathetic to them."

I stopped myself from answering right away. Considered how honest I wanted to be. What angle of attack would best make my case. "We're not talking about Adam. He's a different animal." I felt a little bad about that, but I also believed it. "I'm impressed by how deeply they care about the world at their age. I admire their idealism. Their willingness to act in commitment to a cause." I stopped there.

"Torching cars is commitment to a cause? Smashing store windows is political action?"

Careful. This isn't about winning a debate. "You look good. All things considered."

He laughed. "Now you're scaring me. What do you want?"

Outside the window, an elm bough rattled in a breeze. A few of its leaves already yellowed. Tree stress.

"You might not believe it, Chris, but in the end I think we're on the same side. Want the same things." Once I said it, I wasn't sure I believed it.

He looked at me. Suspicious. Half-amused.

Time to dive in. "I came to ask you a favor."

"What?"

"One of these kids."

"No."

"Wasn't involved at your house. Or the car accident."

His eyes small. "How dare you."

"One kid, Chris. Involved with the dumpster stuff at your office. Some of the car vandalism. Police are willing."

"Fuck him. Fuck all of them."

I walked to the window. How to play this. What to say. I might be able to swing it without Tillman. I didn't want to take the chance. Outside, another summer afternoon. I'd spent too many of them in hospital rooms. Make a fresh start. Clean.

I walked back toward the bed. "He's a good kid, Chris. He fucked up. Most of us do at that age." I looked right at him. "Remember?"

"What are you getting at?"

"I heard a story. About how you got a second chance. Thought maybe you'd be willing to extend the same consideration to another young man with enormous potential." I told him the story, and where I'd got it.

His eyes watched out the window. I had no idea what it took to build a successful business on any scale, let alone a national stage. How hard you had to make yourself. But I knew something about the fallibility of human nature. I was counting on it.

"Things are different now."

"Yeah," I said. "And not."

He watched out the window. "Exactly what do you figure you can do with this?"

"It's not like that, Chris." *Doesn't have to be.* "I'm asking you, one imperfect human to another." I rubbed the back of my neck. Tried my best to sound innocent. "Must have been scary. Sparks told me about it. The investigation, the interviews. All those years ago – still on record." My head ached. I maintained eye contact. "Where would you be without that second chance?"

He was good. His face showed nothing.

We listened to a wheelchair squeak down the hall. The hospital food smell stronger. I hoped I hadn't misplayed things. Then the tiniest hint of anger: behind his eyes, in the tightness of his mouth. It went away before I could be sure I'd seen it.

"I know this kid?" he asked.

"You've met him."

A tiny smile. A deal-making smile.

"What exactly am I agreeing to?"

I willed my face to show nothing. "Trashing your car. The vandalism that night. It goes away. Unsolved."

The salt-starch aroma of hospital food wafted dangerously close.

He nodded. "OK." He worked his face toward amiable. "Anything else?"

I shook my head. "Smells like your lunch is about here. I don't want to bug you."

Finally, I could tell Lin. Bo was safe. But now that he was out of the woods, it wasn't for me to tell her what he'd been up to. That was his to do – the sole condition of my rescue plan. Bo swallowed hard and did it. I joined him in their living room. I wanted Lin to tee off on Bo and me and be done with it. Instead she leaned forward, elbows on knees, and listened. Tears leaked down her cheeks and she didn't notice. She didn't interrupt her son, not once. Didn't look at me. A couple times she looked poised to say something, then didn't. Just folded in on herself and listened. By the time Bo finished, assuring her that he wouldn't go to jail and that they had me to thank, Lin had receded so deep I wasn't sure who or what looked out at us.

At me, finally.

"And you knew how much?" Her eyes red. Directed at my collarbone. Her voice so soft it hurt my stomach.

We buried the old man on Thursday. St. Michael's in Roslindale. Wind and a steady drizzle ensured the proceedings were dour. We stood on a hill that overlooked the city. Thomas would rest on the down slope of that hill, next to his embattled Mary. We did the standard Catholic service because I had no idea what he might have wanted.

Nurse Joan came, and an orderly from Brentwood I recognized but didn't know. I introduced myself. Thanked them for coming. I wore a suit and a raincoat and a Red Sox cap. The priest didn't know Thomas. We all felt embarrassed. Add for me a healthy dollop of shame. I wished I was better at so many things. But the four of us got wet and did the ritual. The priest was young, maybe thirty. I wondered what led someone to that career at this point in the history of the world.

I felt a jumbled-up sadness, more for Evan Tillman and Marcela Pruett, for Bo and even Adam and all of us who lived in a world where idealism got beaten out of you as a rite of passage, where human relationship and even human life hung on so fragile a thread, with rare do-overs.

Marcela didn't get one.

Bo did. Detective Hill worked out the details with Chief Sparks and I, and of course Bo and Lin. Between Endicott, Craig's Auto World, and a variety of community service projects, he would be a busy boy his senior year. But he wouldn't be in prison. Adam, on the other hand, was raw meat for lawyers. Felony murder, breaking and entering, assault and battery. Adam wasn't the sort to seek – or generate – much sympathy.

We commit this body to the earth, for we are dust and unto dust we shall return, the priest recited. I watched the city under my soggy Sox cap. All that held me here was finished. I thought about whether I could live here. As good as anywhere. Better than most. I wanted Lin, my old friend, beside me. Holding my elbow. Holding an umbrella over us both. Resting her head against my shoulder blade in comfort and solidarity. But we were a long way from that, if we'd ever get there again.

The strike settlement had been announced the day before. Endicott and Delfi agreed to a benefits package for full-time workers and an opt-in for part-timers. There would be no immediate increase in the percentage of workers who went full-time, but a commitment to up that the following year. In some ways they'd merely postponed the real battle, but still it felt like an important win. Hundreds of janitors would keep their jobs. Be a little more able to eke out a living.

Score one for the little guy.

The funeral home people shoveled the first wet dirt into the hole. Fifty yards behind us, a backhoe that would later finish the job. My feet got wet in new shoes.

Teresa sent flowers for the graveside and a bottle of tequila for me. With a short note. *Nicky, I'm sorry about your Dad. Proud that you hung in there with him. Don't drink this alone. Love, T.*

I felt an ache of loneliness as we put the old man in the ground. For what might have been with him, always that. For my own wayward journey. I determined then and there, moist in my raincoat, to not die alone.

I did head back to my father's house alone. With a couple DVDs from the library. Some generic neo-noir and a classic Richard Widmark. Dumped them on the futon and went to the fridge for a beer. Caught my foot on a stray carpet tack. It hurt like hell. What was I doing there. Bare walls. Bad memories. Darkened windows. This wasn't where someone lived. It was the last of what I hadn't been willing to get rid of. I forgot about the beer and started sorting my father's things. Stuffed the contents of dresser drawers into trash bags for Goodwill. Moved furniture and anything else with plausible value into the garage.

Three hours later, I had that beer. I didn't have the appetite for noir. Enough darkness for now. Flipped channels. Caught *Casablanca* and wept my way through it. Cried over Rick and Ilsa. Rick and Sam. Rick and Louis. Anyone who cared about anyone that deep. Had another beer and channeled that yearning into action. Finished a draft of the strike piece and sent it to AJ. Checked listings for one-bedroom apartments in Jamaica Plain. When the first glimmers of daylight snuck through the windows, I went to bed. All that remained in the den were my fancy futon and my father's TV.

Juliana called, wondering about the drink she thought she owed me. We tried the social thing. We shared an affinity for vodka martinis and lefty politics. There wasn't spark, but there was fondness. A start.

"I'm sorry about your Dad," she said. "Were you close?"

If there is such a thing as a rueful smile, then that's what she got. "No. Not very." I'd packed up the house. Looked at two apartments.

We met at the Last Hurrah, the bar in the Parker House. They give you warm nuts and let you watch Boston pass by. Boston was still wet. Day three.

We made a couple stabs at personal life conversation. Neither of us very good at it. She was recently divorced, and she didn't want to go there. It shadowed her face. I redirected with a toast to the union's victory.

"So what do you do when you're not wielding a club against the giants of industry?"

"Back to mundane stuff. Strengthen membership. Recruit.

Advocate with the state on issues important to us." She munched peanuts. "What's next for you?"

Funny thing: the question didn't horrify me. There were traces of a resurrected writing career. AJ would find the gold in my strike piece, slated for the September issue. Eric liked the column and wanted me to continue. I didn't want it for the long haul, but it was good for now.

"I'm going to stick around a while," I told her. "See where this column takes me." I felt self-conscious. Exposed. But she wasn't squirming.

"You like writing it."

"I do."

"What's the next one?"

"Not sure. I've been sitting on one that might be good."

"Tell me."

"It might also be crap, and painful to some people. It would start conversations."

"What's wrong with that?"

I liked that she said that.

I had a draft of something I hadn't shown Eric. Hadn't had the courage to re-read it myself. I'd titled it, semi-sarcastically, "What I Learned from the Teen Anarchists." Applying my rapier wit to recent events, trying to understand how and why we grownups accept so much compromise in the name of maturity. How there was something to be said for principled stands that refused to back down, regardless of the cost. Wondering how to make sense of that. What to do with it.

I told Juliana that last part. Anxious how she'd take it.

She smiled. "Sounds like a worthwhile conversation."

I didn't like that I liked her. Felt new. Felt risky. A sick part of me had wanted Terry to come for the funeral. To suggest we meet in Memphis for a fuck-it-all weekend of debauchery. But of course she didn't. When I talked to her, she was juiced about her new lease on life, horror-movie-tenuous though it was. The flowers and the tequila were a solid act of friendship. Nothing less, nothing more. I reminded myself to be grateful for that. I had a smart, attractive woman drinking with me. Something to build on.

Bo got his wings clipped big-time. Watching adults undertake the delicate process of navigating his freedom left him chastened. Sparks and I pulled strings to make criminal charges go away. Lin helped Bo work out a plan for reparations and community service; it would require a gap year after high school – no way he'd be done after senior year. She set strict boundaries about where he could go, and who with. She also made it clear she didn't trust me – as her friend or as Bo's. I was allowed to see him only after two weeks, and then only if she knew our plans. I swallowed that one and hoped it would serve as penance. When the curfew lifted, Bo and I made a date for music. I was eager to see how he was doing. When I rang the doorbell, Lin answered.

"I've come calling for my young charge."

She left the door open for me and walked away.

I waited stupidly in the hall, then followed her into the living room, where she stood beside a leather chair, a quilt draped over it.

I stood just inside the threshold. "Can I say something?"

She'd taken a week off and it showed. She looked rested. "Go ahead."

"Takes guts to raise a kid who's willing to take a stand. Risk himself for it. Knowing it won't play out neat and safe."

Her face reddened. She held back tears and probably anger. I watched her think about whether to answer me. "It's strange to see my son push values I hold – held – to an extreme," she said. She fingered the quilt, which dated back to her Central America days. "I start questioning do I really believe what I think I do? Wondering to what extent I should be out there with him." She met my eyes, the first time since it all blew up. "We're having some animated conversations about what activism means."

I let her say what she wanted to, and kept my mouth shut. Glad she spoke to me.

That afternoon I'd volunteered at Angell Memorial, the animal hospital. Walked a few dogs. Two brown mutts and a black one. Cleaned up their shit. Showed them some love. Felt better than I had in months. I also re-read my draft column. It had a pain-in-the-ass vibe, but I liked being a pain in the ass. It wouldn't be a bad way to go until I could figure out something else I was good at. Writing it helped me understand something of how the church thing fit for Bo. Something about grace. How it wasn't always clean. How maybe god was implicated, too. In the soup with us by choice. By design.

Bo and I took the T to Cambridge. Tentative. Walked to Skybar to see Schism.

"Am I going to like them?" I asked him.

"Depends," he said. "How old are you tonight?"

We walked Mass Ave past MIT. Adam and Marcela hung in the air between us. He told me about her memorial service. We hadn't talked about her. About whatever had happened between her and me. We walked quiet for a while. Mid-August, and you could feel the change in the air, summer already packing its bags. I got teary. A sense of loss I didn't know what to do with. Marcela. What a waste. I wiped at my cheeks. Almost disappointed to realize it wasn't about the sexy. It was about potential. That word. Lost forever. And not. *Still alive, Nick.* Still alive.

Bo looked gaunt. He needed a few days eating and sleeping. "Guess I'm fucked for senior year."

"Guess so."

He wore his Dropkick Murphys t-shirt. We shared that sense of anticipation you get before live music – you never knew when a great night was going to happen.

"The system still needs to come down," he said. "And I'm still gonna be part of that."

I nodded. "I don't doubt it."

We walked past the unfinished furniture place outside Central Square.

"I'm reading up on nonviolent resistance," he said. "Ideas. Tactics."

"Can we not do this now?"

"I just want you to know all this doesn't change who I am. What I'm working for."

I could see the neon club sign up the block. I hoped I lived long enough to see what world Bo and his peers would bring into being. "I'm not at all sure I'd want it to," I told him. "Even if my opinion mattered."

Acknowledgements

None of this would ever happen without the love and support of friends and family. Barb and Megan, you amaze me.

Headlong would not have crossed the finish line without Michelle Seaton. Coach, you made it a better book and pushed me in all the right ways. Thank you.

Thanks to Virginia Center for the Creative Arts, Sitio Serra de Estrella, Dorland Mountain Arts Colony for residencies and fellowships. And Jan Ramjerdi, David Doyle and Mari Perez-Alers for their generosity with unofficial but equally important residencies (the Tancook Island Home for Wayward Novelists and the round table at Martha's imbue every page).

Fred Dillen, Lisa Borders, Becky Tuch for encouraging and insightful feedback on early drafts. Jenna Blum for crucial moments of humor and equally crucial conversations about plot. Bob Thomas for advice on criminal law. Larry Bean for reality checks on journalism. Josh Hyatt for being you. Dan, Clara, Elena, Will, Ben, Jenny, Nathaniel, Christine for inspiring this.

I can't say enough about Grub Street. A guy couldn't have a better writing community. Unbounded gratitude for the joy, confidence, and camaraderie you bring to my life.

Let's do this again, soon.

RON MacLEAN is author of two previous books of fiction: *Blue Winnetka Skies* and *Why the Long Face?* His work has appeared in *GQ, Fiction International, Narrative,* and elsewhere. He is a recipient of the Frederick Exley Award for Short Fiction and a multiple Pushcart Prize nominee. He is former Executive Director at Grub Street in Boston, where he still teaches.